OUTSIDE
IN

a novel

OUTSIDE
IN

DOUG COOPER

GREENLEAF
BOOK GROUP PRESS

Published by Greenleaf Book Group Press
Austin, Texas
www.gbgpress.com

Distributed by Greenleaf Book Group LLC

For ordering information or special discounts for bulk purchases, please contact Greenleaf Book Group LLC at PO Box 91869, Austin, TX 78709, 512.891.6100.

Design, cover design, and composition by Greenleaf Book Group LLC
Cover image: ©iStockphoto.com/Ron Bergeron

Cataloging-in-Publication data

(Prepared by The Donohue Group, Inc.)
Cooper, Doug, 1970-
    Outside in : a novel / Doug Cooper.—1st ed.
    p. ; cm.
    Issued also as an ebook.
    ISBN: 978-1-62634-004-6
    1. Hedonism—Ohio—Put-in-Bay—Fiction. 2. Teachers—Fiction. 3. Drug abuse—Ohio—Put-in-Bay—Fiction. 4. Identity (Psychology)—Fiction. 5. Responsibility—Fiction. 6. Put-in-Bay (Ohio)—Fiction. I. Title.
PS3603.O664 O98 2013
813/.6   2013933503

Part of the Tree Neutral® program, which offsets the number of trees consumed in the production and printing of this book by taking proactive steps, such as planting trees in direct proportion to the number of trees used: www.treeneutral.com

Printed in the United States of America on acid-free paper

13 14 15 16 17 18   10 9 8 7 6 5 4 3 2 1

First Edition

TreeNeutral®

For all the people who wanted more and went searching for it.

ACKNOWLEDGMENTS

I would like to acknowledge the following people, without whom this book would not have been possible.

My parents, Mary and Jeff Wadsworth; sister, Trisha Eblin; grandparents, Elaine and Leroy Maillard; and all the family on the Wadsworth and Maillard sides. Your love and support have given me the confidence to create and share this story.

My dad, Gene Cooper. Your unwavering belief and sage advice have provided the strength and guidance to trust my instincts and follow my dreams.

The Hubans family—Bill Sr., Cheryl, Billy, and Mike. Over the years you welcomed me as a member of the family and provided a haven of love and laughter.

My longtime friend and accomplished musician, Bob Gatewood (www.bobgatewood.com). Your song "Friends of the Bay" provided inspiration for this story and your friendship has guided my path to becoming an artist.

Singer, songwriter, comedian, and barroom philosopher, Mike "Mad Dog" Adams (www.mikemaddogadams.com). Thank you for allowing your persona to appear in this story and for being so unique that I didn't have to embellish.

My longtime friend and artist, Terence Galvin (GalvinismArtwork). Your influence is woven within these words and pages.

The residents and workers of Put-in-Bay and South Bass Island. Thank you for opening up this special place to me.

My teacher, coach, and friend, Gregg Hedden. Your motivation and inspiration showed me how to not only dream big but also how to put in the work required to achieve my aspirations.

My friends in Norway. Thank you for giving me a home for five years and the perspective to see beyond my American lens.

My editors over the years, who helped bring the manuscript to its current form: Rebecca Heyman (Rebecca Faith Editorial), Laura Garwood Meehan (laurameehan.com), and Jeanne Thornton (www.fictioncircus.com/Jeanne).

My publicist, Tyson Cornell, and his team at Rare Bird Lit (www.rarebirdlit.com). Thank you for your energy and professionalism in tirelessly promoting this book.

The team at Greenleaf Book Group. Thank you for your passion and belief in publishing this book.

All my friends over the years who listened to my ramblings and shared their experiences: Jim Horst, Jason Merhaut, Steve Scalf, Brad Richardson, Hayden Gill, Heather Harvey, Charlie Hilse, Luke Szabo, Sharon Thibodeau, Leslie Lynch, Guy Finkman, John Spearry, Tom Bachleda, Huck Johns, Matt Haynes, Eirik Andersen, Jay and Susan Moore, Chuck Badnarik, Steve Krampf and the rest of the crew at Beau Brummel, Mellanie May, Tammy Zirke, the Alavian family, and many, many, more.

CHAPTER ONE

I NEVER GET USED TO THE FACES—WIDE-EYED AND FULL OF POSSIBILITY—STARING BACK AT ME. All I try to do is weather the uncertainty between when I stop talking and they start acting.

"Any questions?" No hands rise. Just eyes swallowing faces. Are the thoughtful looks eager anticipation or utter confusion? I scan the class one final time. "So everyone knows what to do then? Good. Let's begin."

On my direction, the energy level in the classroom spikes. The achievers battle for control; the slackers resist joining their assigned groups. Most of all, the Mr. Shepherding begins.

"Mr. Shepherd, can I work alone?"

"Mr. Shepherd, so-and-so won't join the group."

"Mr. Shepherd, can I use the bathroom?"

Sometimes I wonder why I even bother with group activities. It's so much easier to just stand in front of the class, teach the lesson, assign the work, and assume everyone understands. But every time as the chaos subsides and the students engage, I watch their heads move toward the center, bodies prop up on their elbows, and butts lift toward the ceiling, knowing more learning is taking place than any lecture I could give.

"Mr. Shepherd! Mr. Shepherd!" Willow's tone pierces the clamor of the activity now in full swing. Immediate silence follows. It's obvious this is not the usual request for attention or attempt to avoid work. All movement ceases except for Team 3 by the windows. Each of the students, except for one—Barry Christenson—rise and drift backward from their conjoined desks.

Barry has been pestering me all period for a hall pass, first to his locker, then to the restroom, and only moments before to the nurse's office. He now slinks in his chair, head back with eyes closed and mouth open, arms languidly at his side.

I rush over. He's not breathing. I enlist the help of the student who called me over. "Willow, go get the nurse."

She just stands and stares, the weight of the moment stretching her face toward the floor.

I motion at the door to break her trance. "Willow, you have to go to the office and get the nurse." I turn to another girl in her group. "Penny, go with her."

Penny grabs Willow's hand and pulls her toward the door.

I open a window. "Everyone just step back and give him some air." I put my fingers on his exposed neck. A faint pulse flutters.

"Come on," I say to another student standing close by. "Let's get him out of that desk." We lift Barry and recline him on the floor. I lower my ear to his mouth. His breath sputters. I drop my ear to his chest, his pulse still fluttering. I pat his cheek. "Barry? Can you hear me?"

His body convulses. I jerk backward. Several students scream. Barry stills. We all wait for another movement. Nothing. I shake him by the shoulders. "Come on, Barry. Fight!"

His eyelids tremble.

I say, "That's it. Don't give up."

The quivering steadies. His eyes pop open.

A collective gasp shutters through the students. I lean over Barry. His eyes penetrate, pleading for help. Tears stream. I cradle his jaw. His gaze deepens, holds, then travels through me. I move my face closer. His stare withers. I shake him again. "No, no, no. Come on."

His body heaves, sucking a deep breath, then nothing. My fingers scour his neck for a pulse. Nothing. I grab his wrist. Nothing. The nurse and a guidance counselor rush in and administer CPR. Nothing. Paramedics arrive and escalate the treatment. Nothing.

All I can do is watch—every thrust, every breath, every injection—pleading to see some reaction. But there's nothing: just a fourteen-year-old body occupying the space life used to fill.

The gray sky reflects across Lake Erie and mirrors my inside. Swells rise and attack the shore. Almost there.

"Just me and the car," I say.

The lady in the ticket booth looks me up and down. "Thirty dollars, please."

I point to the price list. "Isn't it only fifteen?"

"Not for a round trip."

"I'm not coming back—at least not anytime soon."

After twenty-eight years, my ticket to freedom costs only fifteen dollars. Why didn't I leave sooner?

I park the car at the end of the load line and get out. Although only the middle of May, the thick air signals that a humid day is ahead. I stretch and work out some of the kinks from the nine-hour drive from St. Louis. The temperate asphalt soothes my bare feet. I'm not sure why I decided to drive all night. No one is expecting me until tomorrow. But after another argument with my parents about why I was leaving, I couldn't get out of there fast enough. I waved good-bye to the Gateway Arch one final time, made a stop in Effingham, Illinois, to take a piss and refresh my coffee, then powered through to Ohio to make the first boat to South Bass Island.

I walk toward the front of the line. The waves pound the armor stone on the sides of the pier. Passengers gather under the shelter house. Regulars focus on reading materials in their laps; tourists stand and gawk at the ferry plowing toward the mainland. All just waiting for the docking to reanimate them.

Inside a minivan a teenager, half-asleep, stares through me as I pass. I search for a distinctive detail in the face, one that will distinguish it from the faces of the students I am leaving behind.

Don't get me wrong. I never wanted to leave. But what choice did I have? The school district sold me out.

I knew something was up when Principal Raines stopped by my classroom while I was working late grading papers a week after the incident. She put her briefcase on an empty desk chair, removed her coat, folded it in half, and placed it on top. "Grading papers is one part of the job I don't miss," she said.

I looked up from the stack of papers. She never just popped by without a reason. "A necessary evil," I said. I glanced at the clock. "You're here late. What brings you by?"

She hesitated for a moment then got right to the point. "Have you talked to your union rep?"

I got up and walked to the board to erase the notes from the day. "Do I need to?"

She sat in a desk in the back row. "Things are starting to get ugly."

"Starting to? Seems like we began with ugly."

"The parents have lawyered up and are threatening to sue." Her hand tapped on the desk while she talked, the sound of her ring against the surface emphasizing her points.

I put the eraser in the tray and spun around. "For what? It was the mother's oxys that he OD'd on."

"They're claiming negligence," she said. "Saying Barry asked for help several times and you refused."

"Come on. You know that's a bunch of BS. If we gave passes to every student who asked to go to the restroom or the nurse, we'd never get anything done."

She rose from the desk. "Be that as it may, the district thinks it best if you go on administrative leave."

I thought I might've heard her wrong. After all, it was his mother's pills. How could they blame me? I said, "Wait, you're suspending me?"

She tried to soften the impact. "Not a suspension. We're hoping it's a voluntary, paid leave."

I felt the blood drain from my face. Lightheaded, I eased down into my desk chair. "For how long?"

She said, "Until this whole thing is resolved."

"Excuse me for actually trying to teach."

"You know teaching is the last thing we get to do around here." She walked toward me. "I understand this is upsetting. But we think it's best for all parties."

"What if I refuse?"

Her tone became formal. "We hope it doesn't come to that. After what happened, you are entitled to a leave of absence. We would like to see you take that time."

My disbelief gave way to anger. "Like you really care about my well-being. You need a scapegoat and want to blame the young guy."

"I'm sorry you see it that way." She rose and collected her coat and briefcase. "We should probably set up a meeting with your union rep to discuss the options in a more official capacity."

And that was that. After busting my ass for five years, the

school district cut me loose. I was just a pawn in the mitigation of the lawsuit.

———

Maaaahmp. The horn signals the ferry is in its final approach. From his perch high above the deck, the captain uses the waves and wind in conjunction with the engine to rock the boat into position.

The boat is twelve feet from the dock. A deck hand flings a rope toward a large cleat on land. The toss looks as if it'll be long, and a worker on the dock swoops in to collect the errant throw, but the back end of the loop catches the gray metallic hook.

Holding his hands eighteen inches apart above his head, the worker signals the distance from the dock. He brings his hands together as the boat moves closer: ten inches, six inches, three inches, closed. The other crew members fasten the lines and lower the ramp.

A faded maroon Taurus is the first car to drive off. *Ja-jink*— the ramp absorbs the weight of the car and bounces on the dock.

After four cars, twenty people follow on foot. Some appear eager for their tasks on the mainland; others look lucky to escape the island, appearing to have been stranded for days: unshaven, clothes wrinkled, taking one step sideways for every two steps forward.

I return to my car and follow the line. A crewman on the pier straight from the pages of a Lands' End catalog takes my ticket and directs me onto the boat. His name, Robin, is visible on the right breast of his Miller Ferry polo shirt.

Ja-jink. My car echoes the others as I climb the ramp.

A raisin-faced crewman orchestrates the maneuvers on deck. Following his signals, I ease my car forward. He brings my car within inches of the one in front. Lowering his hand, he taps the hood of my car. "Put your car in park. Set your brake, please."

Car by car, I watch the crewman fill the ship to my right and left. He's got some serious skills. The size and number of pieces may change voyage to voyage, but the goal of maximizing the deck space remains the same. During busy times, being able to fit an extra car on the boat is only fifteen dollars for the boat line, but priceless for the patron. It gets the lucky recipient an extra half hour on the island.

Visible in my rearview mirror, the car behind me creeps forward. I wait for a bump, but instead I hear, "Put your car in park. Set your brake, please."

The ferry shifts, accommodating the weight of the next vehicle. The familiar symbol and letters M-I-L-L-E-R L-I-T-E are emblazoned along its side. The delivery trucks have priority, especially the ones delivering beer. If the beer isn't flowing, the cash registers aren't ringing, and as in any tourist area, the quicker the visitors spend their money, the quicker they go home. They may not be respected, but their dollars are always accepted. Locals' hearts may say, "Fuck off," but their faces smile and say, "Thank you, come again."

Two more cars drive on, then a flock of people rounds the building. Barely noticeable except for their excited chatter, the added weight of fifty-some people doesn't rock the boat in the slightest.

I open the door and squeeze through the narrow opening between my car and the next. The ferry is full, but I find some open space along the front of the boat. The three miles of Lake Erie between me and the island now radiate a greenish hue, resembling a rolling pasture. A solitary tower pokes above the tree line on the east side of the island.

"Perry's Monument," Robin says as he coils a rope nearby, his sandy hair flapping across the Ray Bans welded to his tan, angular face. "The third tallest national monument."

"Cool," I say. "I'm moving from the home of the tallest to the third tallest."

"Coming from St. Louis, eh? You know the second tallest?"

"Washington Monument." I extend my hand. "Pleased to meet you, Robin. I'm Brad Shepherd."

Robin appears confused, then tugs on his breast pocket. "Oh, yeah. Sometimes I'll kill myself trying to think how someone knows my name, then I remember it's on my shirt."

"That's happened to me at conferences."

"What do you do?"

"I *was* a teacher. Five years of junior high math. Guess you could say I'm retired."

He shakes his head. "Whoa, I hated math. My teacher was the worst."

I laugh. "My students probably say the same thing."

"Why'd you quit?"

"Cutbacks. They offered a package and asked for volunteers, so I held my hand up. Gotta be more to life than going to work day after day." It's not totally a lie. I could've refused the offer and fought for my job. But even my attorney recommended I take the deal since I wasn't tenured. If I fought and lost, it would be in my permanent employment record. Leaving quietly allowed me to retain the positive recommendations I had earned and at least offered the opportunity for another job. I turn away from Robin, toward the island. "What's the monument for, anyway?"

Robin delivers a speech that sounds well rehearsed. "There was a crucial naval battle fought in the War of 1812 off the shore of South Bass Island, during which Oliver Hazzard Perry left his damaged ship and moved to one of the other boats. From there he defeated the British, sending the famous message to American headquarters: 'We have met the enemy and they are ours—two ships, two brigs, one schooner, one sloop.' The victory secured the north shore for the American forces, and peace between Canada, Great Britain, and the US has ensued ever since."

"I wasn't aware of the history," I say.

"There's more to the island than a hangover, but most never get past the drinks." The ferry horn sounds. "Well, I'd better get ready to dock. Nice to meet you, Brad. I'm sure I'll see you around. South Bass is a small place. Couldn't hide if you wanted to."

"Call me Shep."

The crew moves just as they had on the mainland, but now the positions are reversed. The front of the boat becomes the back, and in order for cars to drive straight off, the captain backs the ferry into the dock. As the boat approaches, Robin launches the rope into the air. Unfortunately he is not as lucky as the crewman on the mainland, and the rope misses the mark.

Five cars go ahead of me. I release the brake and move forward. *Ja-jink.*

Yellow arrows painted on the road direct me: jog right, then up a hill to the main road. Several taxis and a tour train await new arrivals.

Poplar and cottonwood trees line the side of the road and reattach above, forming a canopy that erases the sky for seconds at a time. Tucked between the trees and the occasional cottages are several businesses, including a bicycle and golf cart rental, the island quarry, the airport, and the Skyway Restaurant, which reminds me that I need to eat. The caffeine from my trip is knotting my stomach.

Like flipping the page of a pop-up book, a left turn onto Delaware Avenue transforms the pastoral surroundings into the quaint village of Put-in-Bay.

The Crescent Tavern stands on my left, another golf cart and bicycle rental on my right. The water and docks, sparsely populated with boats, beckon on the other side of the park, which serves as the center of the town square.

A flash of red—fire engine red—snaps my attention back to the left. No mistaking this structure. A round, red building with a white porch and a dome roof: the Round House. Next door is the Park Hotel, a large Victorian-Italian villa with a wraparound porch, similar to many of the buildings I've seen on the street. My new home, at least until I find something more permanent.

The screen door of the hotel rattles as I open it, waking the man sleeping on his hand at the front desk. "Can I check in early?" I say. "I drove all night from St. Louis and could really use a bed about now. My last name is Shepherd."

His yawn transforms to a nod as he checks his register.

I slide my credit card across the desk. "Where can I get something to eat?"

"Snack House next door," he mumbles, minimizing words in his sleepy state, the lines from snoozing on the back of his hand still visible across his cheek.

"People don't spend much time thinking of names for things here: the Depot, the Round House, the Snack House."

"What you see is what you get. The island is imaginative enough. Creativity don't need to be wasted on naming things."

"Sounds perfect. Exactly what I need."

"Well, I can help you find anything else. Just holler." He rubs his eyes and releases another yawn. "Bathroom is down the hall, European style."

All I can do is shake my head and smile at my new life. I'm unemployed and homeless, living in a European-style hotel on an island in Ohio. On the outside it seems so logical while remaining carefree with a hint of crazy. But beneath my outwardly adventuresome spirit, I know that I am lost and that I have been for some time. Worse yet, I don't have a clue as to how to find my way back. Hell, I don't know whether I want to go back, forward, right, or left. So instead, I choose a fixed point in the middle of Lake Erie to sort things out.

The blaring of an electric guitar rips me out of sleep. Where am I? Did I sleep through the day? I check the clock. Three p.m.— time to get moving. I want to surprise Birch and Haley.

Oedipus Birch is my link to this whole new life. His band, Whiplash, played occasionally at a Saint Louis U bar where I used to stop after graduate classes. Teaching junior high for eight hours followed by evening classes and several hours in the pub made for a long day, and an even longer day after, but I needed something to make me feel like a normal twenty-eight-year-old.

The first time I saw Whiplash, Birch and I struck up a conversation during one of their breaks and instantly became friends. His given name of Oedipus made me think that his mother either had quite a sense of humor or that she should've been committed. Either way, the more time I spent with him, the more I realized that the name was only a precursor to the tangled mess that lay within. When you're searching, there's something comforting about being around people who are even more twisted than you are.

When I showed up the night of Barry's death, Birch had heard on the news about it, but he didn't know it was my classroom until I told him. I was beating myself up pretty bad. I couldn't escape the thought that if I had let Barry go to the restroom or the nurse, things might've been different. Birch's response to that was: "Maybe Barry would've died in a stall alone if you had." Birch always has a way of flipping a situation on its head and seeing it from a different perspective. Another reason I love being around him. That night he could tell I needed to forget but didn't know how. He said, "Why don't you take some time off?"

There was no way I would desert my students. I said, "What kind of example would that set? If the students have to be there, I should too. Besides, spring break is only a week away. We can all take some time then."

Almost as if it was his plan all along, he proposed, "Just come down to Key West with me and the band for spring break then."

Of course I had a list of excuses why I couldn't go—no money, no reservation, too much schoolwork—but he had an answer for each one. By the time I left the bar, he had me convinced to work as a roadie, bunk with the band, and take my work with me.

As to be expected, when I told my parents about this plan, my mom accused me of running away and blamed Birch for being a bad influence on me. She never has liked him. Thinks he's a dreamer who needs to grow up and get a real job. It's always easier to reproach the friend than address issues with the person closest to you.

This kind of meddling was exactly why I moved out after my first year of teaching. I would've loved to live rent-free and save money, but most days I was just trying to survive the school day. I'm not going to lie; in that first year it was a difficult transition from the college quads to the corridors of a junior high. I would come home exhausted and frustrated, and all she wanted to do was talk about what had happened. If I did open up about how tough it was, she would get worried that I was planning to quit, and she reminded me how she wished she were lucky enough to have such a good job with full benefits, retirement, and holidays and summers off. Ever since I was a kid, I was never allowed to quit anything. If I started something, I had to see it through to the end.

I know she meant well, but she has this remarkable ability to make every situation relate back to her and make me feel like shit in the process. Just like when I told her and my dad that the suspected cause of Barry's death was an overdose on his mother's pain pills. She went to the sink, picked up a dishcloth, and dried a bowl in the rack that wasn't even wet. She said, "Oh my—I can't imagine how she feels. To know you played a part in your own child's death must be unbearable. You'll understand if you ever have children."

I didn't need to have children to know that what happened was fucked up. But I kept my mouth closed and let the words pass unchallenged. All I said was, "I just wish I could've done more." I felt like I had to remind her that it did have a little something to do with me.

My dad picked up on my jab. He said, "Knowing you, I'm sure you did everything you could've. Now you just have to move forward."

Usually I'm cool with my dad. He's the peacemaker between my mom and me, and he stays pretty neutral. But this set me off. What did he know about the situation? What did he ultimately know about me? He married my mom right out of high school and has been working the same auto mechanic job for twenty-nine years. I said, "How in the hell do you propose I do that with an empty desk glaring back at me every day? I just need to get away from everything for a few days."

"There's no reason to use that tone or language," my mom said. "We're just trying to help."

And there we were in the same spot we always ended up: me pissed off, my mom upset, and my dad trying to fix the situation with clichéd advice. He said, "It's only a week. A few bikinis might be exactly what you need. Just remember who you are."

Gee, Dad, thanks for the words of wisdom. I'll get right on that.

———

A shrub of a lady, much more awake and energetic than the

clerk this morning, asks for my key as I pass the front desk. "You can pick it up on your way back," she says. "That way, you won't lose it."

I smile back, understanding the real reason for the precaution: Management can also keep track of who comes and goes.

I walk outside and down the porch to the Round House. I peer inside through the window on the side door. A red-and-yellow-striped parachute serves as a ceiling, concealing the dome roof. A single globe light hangs in the middle, and a ring of bulbs outlines the perimeter. The bar, which stands four feet high, almost like an altar, circles out from the back wall and around the stage toward the door.

Whiplash is on stage, but last night must've been a rough one. The guys are pale and scruffy and seem eager to breeze through the afternoon set. Haley and two other bartenders work in the three-foot area between the stage and the bar.

I push through the door as the band finishes the song. Why does the music always stop right when you walk in?

A look of surprise washes across Haley's tan, round face. Her sun-streaked rusty ponytail swings back and forth as her eyes flip between the band and the crowd and eventually rest on me. She leaves her post and welcomes me with a hug. Her hugs are like a good handshake, firm and secure but not overpowering. "What a nice surprise. I didn't expect you until tomorrow."

I relish the contact and pull her close. "Couldn't wait to get here, so I left early and drove all night. Came over on the first boat."

Since Key West, it was imagining moments like this that got me through all the crap. Although Haley and I haven't known each other long, we have become quite close. I know about her family, her numerous failed attempts to get a college degree, and her relationship difficulties. She has spent twelve summers on the island and feels a sense of belonging here, where the wind isn't as harsh on her face and the sun doesn't scorch her skin as badly. Haley probably should have been a guy. She dresses like a guy, drinks like a guy, and talks like a guy. A lot of turmoil seems to reside inside her, but she rarely shows it. Her pain remains buried, only revealing itself in swift, caustic strikes.

Nothing romantic has occurred between us, but we've slept in the same bed twice. The first time was the night Birch and the band and I arrived in Key West. We had been on the road for twenty-two hours straight. Anyone who romanticizes life on the road for a band just needs to drive 1400 miles cooped up in a van with three other guys. On the map it looks like such an exciting journey—Nashville, Chattanooga, Atlanta, Orlando, Miami—but you don't have the time or money to stop and enjoy any of it. And if you don't kill each other from the forced captivity, you might die from all the noxious odors that emanate from men subsisting on fast food and gas station delicacies. Understandable why two of the guys flew down. I guess the result is either you end up with a band or a cult. Fortunately Birch and the guys have musical talent.

About the only thing all of us agreed on the last six hours of the trip to Key West was that our first stop should be Sloppy Joe's. When we got there, Haley was working behind the bar. After Birch introduced Haley and me, her idea to get acquainted was to pick up a shaker, fill it with ice, and pour four different liquors into it, all too quickly for me to even recognize what they were. After a few shakes, in front of each of us was a perfectly poured shot.

At that point I was still angry about being squeezed to take a leave of absence and feeling worn from the long drive. I wasn't much of a drinker, so a shot wasn't really my first choice. Not that I was a complete teetotaler. It's just that with teaching, coaching, and going to school, I had to give something up, and partying seemed like the most logical. Birch could tell I was uncomfortable. He said, "No pressure. I'll do yours if you don't want it."

"Nonsense," I said, "I'm on vacation."

If I was going to let go, I had to be willing to do something different. I cheered with the others and drank down the red concoction, which tasted like cough medicine with a sweet aftertaste.

From there, we kept drinking . . . and drinking. It was one of the most drunken nights I could recall, or rather not recall, in a long time. I woke up the next morning one eye at a time, not really sure where I was or how I got there. Still fully clothed, I did the panicked pocket inventory check of phone, keys, wallet. All were there, but I still had no idea where I was. I looked to my right and saw Haley, who was also fully clothed. Together we pieced together the evening, resolving that anything we'd forgotten must not have been worthy of being remembered.

The second time that Haley and I slept in the same bed was my last night in Key West. I was so physically spent from partying that I couldn't endure another night. I didn't want the week to end, but the impact of the drinking and minimal sleep and knowing that my fight with the school district was waiting for me in St. Louis had put me into a foul mood. Fortunately Haley had the evening off and recognized I couldn't be in a bar another night. During the band's first break, she suggested we get a bottle of wine and go back to her place.

The offer sent a wave of instant relief through me. It was exactly what I needed. The rest of the evening Haley and I sat at her place retelling stories from the week, attempting to separate the blur into memorable chunks to prolong my inevitable departure.

Stretched out on the kitchen floor, I rested my head in her lap. She stroked my hair. The coolness of the tile comforted me, as did her gentle petting. I, although sad, was strangely at peace. For the first time in a long while, I felt no pressure to do anything. I wanted to lie on that kitchen floor for the rest of my life. Nothing or no one could've made me leave. Tears pooled up, eventually streaming down my face. I don't know why. It wasn't solely because I was leaving. It was much deeper.

For nearly two hours the words and tears poured out of me. She listened in complete silence. I told her about Barry's death and how it made me feel like a failure as a teacher. I admitted that without teaching, my existence in St. Louis would be hollow. The only other thing I had was graduate school, and I was graduating at the end of the semester. In my admission, I released all the pent-up emotion that had been building since long before that week. My work, my parents, my whole situation. If I no longer had my teaching job, what would I do? Another teaching job? After what happened and how I was being treated, the last place I wanted to be was in a classroom in front of students. But what else could I do?

Haley hadn't said too much up to that point. But after hearing this question, she lifted my head from her lap and peered deep into my misty gaze. "Maybe you're asking the wrong question. Maybe you shouldn't ask what you can do, but what you want to do."

Her words shot to my core, vibrating and sending tremors through my whole body, forcing me to realize something I had been denying all along: I had no fucking clue what the answer was.

As I contemplated her question and my emotional barrage lessened, she leaned down and whispered the epiphany that brought me here: "Fuck St. Louis. Move to Put-in-Bay."

———

I nod toward the ornate display of bottles behind her. "I think this calls for a shot."

She whisks behind the bar and scoops a shaker full of ice. "Why not? My sobriety can wait for another day. Lemon Drop?"

"Whatever. You're the professional." I say, still a novice at the shot game.

Birch exits the stage. On Put-in-Bay, Whiplash is pretty universally regarded as the "island band." There are bands equally as talented, but Whiplash has endured, and that means something. Loyalty is still respected on this island. While it's easy to make friends here, time spent on the island is a valuable commodity, and Birch has put in his time. He says, "Well, if it isn't my favorite Key West roadie." His black curly hair stands six inches high and falls to the middle of his back. Black, crescent-shaped lines extend under his eyes. "When did you get in?"

"From the looks of you," I say, "probably when you were getting to bed."

He pushes down the top of his rising mane. "How are we? Too loud?"

Haley removes a yellow foam earplug. "You're always too loud, Birch." Haley can say whatever she wants to people, and they're never offended by any of it. Her consistently rough exterior and sarcastic tone make everyone think she's always joking because no one could be as bitter as she always seems to be. She swirls the shaker. "Hair of the dog?"

He forms a cross with his fingers. "No way. I'm not ready to get on that bus again. I'll catch up with you later. I need to sneak in a shower during the break."

"Don't be late for the last set, slacker." She removes a piece of paper from her pocket and hands it to me. "You can always work security here, but I gathered some information on other places that are hiring. You got here early, so it shouldn't be too difficult to find work."

Afraid that one shot may lead to five, I glance down at the list that Haley gave me. "Let's continue this reunion later. I gotta find something to keep me out of trouble. First stop, the Boat House."

She says, "I'm off tonight. Let's meet here at eight."

"Deal." I lean across the bar and kiss her on the cheek. "So good to see you."

I exit through the front door onto the porch. The rays of the sun weave down through the leaves and speckle the ground across the street in the park. The sticky air feels like jelly on my skin, but the sight of the water, now a royal blue, refreshes me as if I've been dropped in it.

"Beautiful, huh?" a voice from behind me asks.

I turn around. The man sits on a stool against the wall and stares out at me and at the park behind me. His body is a red pillow wearing the same Round House shirt as Haley with thick, stubby legs that poke through baggy khaki shorts; his head is a tan egg. Wrap-around sunglasses conceal his eyes, and his lack of hair makes it difficult to discern whether he's twenty-five or thirty-five.

"My favorite view in the whole world," he says. "Sometimes I can't believe I get paid for this. First time on the island?"

"Just got in this morning from St. Louis."

"Oh yeah, you're Haley's friend, the teacher. That's my planned profession, too, when I grow up. Cinch Stevens. Nice to meet you. Shep, is it?"

"You got it. Great to meet you. Can't believe I'm finally here. Only problem now is that I have to find a job. Any suggestions?"

"Stop back later. You can get paid to stand here with me. You may not make the big bartending bucks, but there are plenty of other fringe benefits. You could probably even start tonight, if you want."

I extend my palm like a crossing guard. "Slow your roll, turbo. I'm not in that much of a hurry. I just want to find a job; I don't necessarily want to start working today."

"Who said anything about working?" Cinch says. "This is the Round House."

I hop down the steps and head right along the park to the Boat House. It has an open front with sliding glass doors that allow the sights and sounds of the restaurant, which appears to double as a nightclub, to flow into the street and through the park. Suspended canoes and ice boats hang in the rafters and oars, nets, and other nautical paraphernalia cover the walls to round out the theme.

Except for their blue polo shirts with gold sleeves, the workers at the Boat House wear a similar uniform to everyone else I've seen working on the island: gray rag wool socks bunched around ankle-high boots, khaki shorts held up by a brown leather belt, and often sunglasses in situations where they're not entirely appropriate. A stunning waitress with jaw-length blonde hair pushed behind her ears approaches. "Just one for lunch?"

Her crisply defined eyes and mouth contrast with smooth, creamy skin that I'm compelled to touch. Her neck melts into a collarbone and shoulders that I make a conscious effort not to stare at. "No, I'm here about the job."

"Which one?"

"What's available?" I ask. She has the frame of a girl who was probably thin and often overlooked throughout her youth, but now, in her mid-twenties, she's blossomed, retaining her thin frame but swelling in appropriate areas.

The coy smile on her lips reveals she is onto the fact that I'm taking in every detail of her. "Cook or bouncer?" she asks.

I look left, striking a stoic pose. "Which do you think?"

With one eyebrow raised, she scans me up and down. "I'm going with cook."

"Ouch." I laugh, dropping my head forward in feigned shame.

She winks. "I'll get the owner. Would you like a beer while you wait?"

I shake my head. Drink a beer while interviewing? So that's how they do it here. Never heard a guidance counselor recommend that job search tip before.

A man wearing a grease-stained apron emerges from the kitchen and asks if I've ever cooked in a restaurant or worked as a bouncer. I explain that I worked construction in college and spent the past years teaching high school math. I don't reveal that I was a failure at both.

"If you're trusted with kids," he says, "you must be responsible. The rest you'll pick up as you go. I can offer you eight dollars an hour and housing for forty a week to cook during the day and work the door at night. When can you start?"

"Um, well, I just got here this morning, and I have a few other stops to make. How about I let you know tomorrow?"

"No guarantee the job will be here."

I accept the risk and cut through the park on the way to the next place on my list.

Seated cross-legged on a blue and black Navajo blanket under an oak tree in the park, a man in his fifties plays a mandolin. He wears a black baseball hat that reads "Wine, women, and walleye—South Bass Island, Ohio." A beard conceals his tapered face, and scraggly, mostly gray hair extends from under the hat.

The comforting music floats through the air and draws me in. I deposit a few dollars in the tip jar. He nods in appreciation.

I'm envious of the ease with which he lives. Why can't my life be so simple?

—

The other places I stop for interviews go like the first: a five-minute discussion followed by an offer. I return to the hotel with three opportunities, not including the Round House. Since I cashed out my five years of teaching retirement, I'm not in that much of a hurry to start working. Do I want to be a cook-slash-bouncer, a bartender, or a T-shirt salesman?

Questions from earlier circle like buzzards. Am I running away or moving forward? There was no way I could've stayed in St. Louis. My parents would just nag me about getting another job. They never understood why I quit without a fight. They had a hard enough time understanding the week in Key West with Birch's band. Having a master's degree and moving to an island to work some meaningless job for the summer was a complete waste of time in their eyes. We had already had two fights about it when they stopped by the night I was packing up. If I wanted to go away peacefully, maybe litigation with the school district was the better choice.

My mom immediately took out a cigarette when she saw the empty apartment and the small collection of belongings that I planned to take with me. She hadn't smoked in years, so I knew things were not going to go well. I said, "If you want to smoke, you have to go out on the terrace. I don't want the place to smell like smoke and lose my security deposit."

She fumbled with the cigarette trying to put it back in the pack, eventually breaking it. She said, "I still don't understand why you're leaving."

My dad took the pack from her. "It's just for the summer. He'll be back."

I couldn't believe we were talking about it again. Did they really think they could come over and change my mind? The deal was done. It wasn't a matter of if I was going but how long I was staying. I said, "Not sure what I'm going to do at the end of the summer." I close up a box and stretch tape across it. "Maybe I'll stay there or maybe go down to Key West for the winter."

My mom stomped toward the window and stared outside, unwilling to even look at me. "I can't believe you're giving up so easily."

I made the same "What other choice do I have?" argument I had for the past month. "I tried," I said. "I really tried to fit into that world. But how much of myself am I supposed to sacrifice to blend into my surroundings? At some point, I have to mold my environment to reflect who I am."

My dad accused me of being a drama queen. "No one is asking you to be something you're not," he continued. "You've worked hard to get where you are, and we just don't want to see you throw it all away to go live on some island and become a drifter."

I said, "You know the best part about my life? It's that it's *my* life."

I wanted to take these words back the second they came out, but it was too late. Tears began streaming down my mom's face, and my dad contorted his to hide the pain they caused.

My mom wiped her eyes. "We didn't come here to fight. We just wanted to say good-bye and wish you well." She kissed me on the cheek and headed for the door.

My dad didn't say anything, just began to follow her.

"Trust me. I know what I'm doing," I said. "I'm just taking a vacation." It was what I had been telling everyone who challenged my decision or asked questions that I didn't want to answer. On vacation you can be and do whatever you want— exactly what I needed.

"You didn't have to be so mean," my dad said, and my parents left.

A waft of barbecue chicken greets me as I approach the hotel. On the side of the building next to the Round House on the patio in front of the Park Hotel, there's a sixteen-by-four-foot gas grill half full with quarter chickens sizzling and glistening with barbecue sauce, which a sign next to the grill divulges is made with island wine. Patrons sit at round stone tables ravenously tearing meat from bone. The sauce covers their hands and clings to their chins. The picture is more reminiscent of medieval times than a resort destination.

Cinch is there by the Round House. "How'd you make out? Are you employed?"

"I'll decide tomorrow," I say.

"Add another one to the list," he says. "Haley gave me the go-ahead to hire you. Come upstairs and see where you might be living."

"We'll have to do it later. I'm supposed to meet her at eight."

"No one's on time here. Come up and have a beer."

Cinch and I walk behind the Park Hotel to a decaying red wooden building that leans slightly to the right, creating rhomboid rather than rectangular sides.

"People live here?" I say.

"The bands stay below and I stay upstairs. We call it the red barn. There's plenty of room for another."

I close one eye, further examining the geometry of the structure. "Is it, um, safe?"

"A lot of good years left. The red barn is always the last place open on the island. We'll pack fifty people in here some nights. The downside is that there's no privacy."

The ripped screening on the door at the top of the stairs flaps in the wind, calling us. I bound up the steps. The sway in each aging plank offers extra bounce.

Cinch holds the door for me. "If you're a private person, this probably isn't the place for you, but then again neither is the island. There's no hiding here. The truth always comes out. You can make it a short time on bullshit, but if you're going to last, you have to be nice and tell the truth."

Inside, the dominant decorating theme is no theme: mismatched furniture, 1970s efficiency sink, stove and refrigerator unit plastered with stickers and decals, beer signs on the walls, and pallid green carpeting that looks like it hasn't been cleaned in thirty years. Beer bottles and overflowing ashtrays decorate the coffee table. When was the last time coffee was even on that table?

Cinch picks up two Heineken bottles from the floor, spinning them in his palms before sliding them into imaginary holsters at his side. "Actually, this mess is only from last night. That's pretty good for here. Sometimes two weeks pass before we clean after a party."

"At least you drink good beer."

He tosses the bottles in the trash. "Nothing but the best. Got a twelve from the cooler last night at four a.m. Birch and I sat here until six." He reaches behind the couch and pulls out a two-foot Graffix bong.

"Gooood morning," I say.

"I hope this doesn't offend you."

"Not at all. It's your place."

"Well then, don't mind if I do," he says, as if he had ever considered otherwise.

Instant comfort and understanding soak the room. Our banter flows as if scripted. The flame glows, darting in and out of the bowl. A thick cloud emanates from the green skull-shaped base and climbs the clear tube that has yellow and purple stains streaked along its surface from extensive use. Cinch lifts his finger from the carburetor and easily clears the tube. He extends the bong toward me.

"No thanks," I say. "That's not one I do."

He exhales his hit. "More for me, then."

"Hold on," I say. "I'm on vacation, right? It's not like I've never smoked. I just reserve it for special occasions, sort of a ceremonial peace pipe kind of thing."

"Then wrap your lips around this, Tonto."

I mimic Cinch's actions. The skunky smoke tickles my nostrils but scorches my untrained lungs. With each hack Cinch laughs, straining to hold in his hit. I chug half of my beer. "I think one should do it for now," I say. "You going out tonight?"

"Wouldn't miss it. Consider me your personal tour guide to thrills, chills, and spills. Well, maybe not spills, and probably not chills. But plenty of thrills." He sparks another pull off the bong. "Will you grab me another beer on your way out? I had a rough day at the office."

CHAPTER TWO

HALEY EMERGES THROUGH THE RED SATIN CURTAIN THAT COVERS THE DOOR-WAY BEHIND THE BAR. With the exception of the tan RHB baseball cap, she has traded in her Round House gear for civilian attire, permitting her to receive drinks rather than serve them. She spots me perched at the bar and ducks under the opening at the end to belly up next to me.

Whiplash kicks into the Doors' "Roadhouse Blues," and people push to the front like children looking for free candy at a parade. Haley barks an order for four Red Snappers. If mixology were a major, she probably would have breezed through her college curriculum. Her arm wraps around and pulls me close. "This isn't even busy. Wait until the weekends. A lot of people arrive Thursday night to secure dock space and enjoy the island before it gets busy. Unless we're working, most of us don't come in here from Friday to Sunday. But on Sunday night, the island is ours again."

A green fluorescent light flashes by the front door. Cinch

enters, wearing an Australian roughrider hat and twirling a glow stick on a string above his head. Baleful emerald eyes punctuate his priestly face and communicate that I could be in for a night of trouble. The bouncer at the door makes a move for him but, recognizing Cinch, returns instead to talk to the female who has been occupying his attention.

"Christ," Haley says to the bartender. "You better make it five." She turns to me. "Only Cinch can get away with that shit. It's good to be him."

Cinch doesn't question the contents of the shot Haley gives him. He just says, "God bless you," and throws it back like communion.

When Whiplash takes a pause for the cause, Haley suggests we go to the Boat House between sets. Our tribe has grown to eleven. Everyone seems to know one another, but then again, it doesn't matter. Etiquette is not really a priority. Tonight is about feeling good; the more, the merrier.

The walk to the Boat House is a tempering break and a sobering lift. The air is both warm and cool, alternating as it blows. The beacon of the monument flashes in the near distance. I turn my face to the stars.

Cinch says, "Over by the monument, I guarantee you'll see a shooting star every night. It's remarkable how much you can see when you're in the dark in the middle of nowhere."

Nightlife has replaced the diners at the Boat House. On the right a traveling piano bar has been set up where patrons gather while the performer plays. The musician behind the keys acknowledges our arrival with "Copacabana." He's in his late forties and resembles Ronnie Milsap, but he wails with the animation of Meatloaf.

While most of our party sits at the piano, Cinch and I go to the bar. He says, "We need to make a pit stop when we—hey, Astrid!" Cinch rises to greet the hot waitress I met earlier. "Come meet the newest member of the Round House staff." He turns to me. "Right? Come on. You know you want to."

Although I still haven't officially accepted the job offer, I don't refute him. I'm too captivated. Astrid has also changed costumes. Her dangling golden hair is now held back by barrettes that match her cotton sundress, which hangs from her shoulders, cups her breasts, and falls straight to the ground, stopping just past her thighs. I love sundresses. If I were a woman, I would wear nothing else—no underwear and no bra—just the sundress, a piece of free-flowing cotton between the rest of the world and me.

As she approaches, the muscles in her thighs tighten and flex with each step. Her shoes are open-toed sandals made of hemp that strap only around her ankle and around the balls of her feet. The cork sole is four inches thick by the heel and slopes downward to an inch in the front, causing her to lean forward, almost shuffling, when she walks. She says, "You guys seem to be headed for trouble."

"Why?" I ask. "Are you looking for some?"

"It usually finds me." She punctuates the comment with a coy tilt of her head.

Cinch says, "Don't worry, we'll protect you."

"Who'll save me from you two?" she asks.

I return a sportive smile. "Guess you'll have to take your chances."

Cinch tosses some money on the bar, which is the first time I've seen anyone pay for drinks at any of the bars I've been to today. "Want to join us for a pit stop at the red barn?" he asks.

"You boys go do your thing," Astrid replies. "I'll catch up with you later at the Round House."

She leaves. I motion at the piano bar to Haley doing shots with some customers. "What about her?" I ask Cinch.

"She won't even notice we're gone," Cinch says. "She's always popular when she goes out. People attempt to befriend her, hoping she'll come through for them when there's a line halfway down the street to get into the Round House."

On the way out of the bar, he jabs me playfully in the back. "Are you ready to take it up a notch?"

"Bring it on. I'm not afraid," I say. "Time to smoke again?"

Cinch breaks into an exaggerated skip. "Greens were the appetizer. Dinner comes on a plate."

——

In the red barn, Cinch disappears down the hallway and returns with a brown paper bag. Thrusting his hand into the sack, he reveals a white chunk. "La Blanca Dama."

The responsibilities of my former life trigger my answer. "Cocaine? Count me out." Things are moving too fast. Drinking, the pot, and now this? I have to slow down.

"Embrace the Lady. Be the man you always wanted to be." Again leading the ceremony, Cinch retrieves a plate with a plastic hotel key card and a three-inch straw on it from under the couch and crumbles the rock into smaller pieces. Pushing the fragments into a pile, he covers the mound with a twenty-dollar bill, repeatedly scraping the card over it. "This shit is so hard, it flies everywhere if you try to chop it first. This gets it to a pretty fine consistency." He lifts the bill, exposing a flat, off-white pancake.

"Oh, the things you learn. I try to learn at least one new thing a day. I guess the pressure's off for today," I say, still unsure what to do.

He chops the card through the flakes, never lifting his eyes. Saliva forms on the corners of his mouth. His nose runs. He sniffs, pulling back the drops before they fall into the focus of his concentration.

Small talk is all that comes to mind. Anything to hide my fear. I say, "Is it good stuff?"

"Only the best." He separates the gram into four thick rails. "Time to board the train, baby. One for each nostril." He extends the straw toward me. "Guests first."

"What will it do? I mean, what if I have a reaction?"

"Ladies and gentlemen, we have a virgin in our midst. Nose cherry about to be burst. There ain't no line like your first line, my friend. Insert straw, bend down, inhale, and follow the white powder road. Time to stop being Mr. Shepherd. Just be Brad."

I wish it were that easy. The body changes locations much quicker than the mind. I stare at the lines and push back the fear. "No more Mr. Shepherd." Bending down, my hair falls in my face and drags across the plate.

Cinch says, "Pull that mop back. I'll hold it. There's only two times when I'll hold another man's hair: snorting and puking. Hopefully the latter won't happen tonight."

Ssshhhump. I huff the first one down. An ether smell fills my face, but I feel nothing.

Cinch follows, inhaling powerfully. *Ssshhhump.* "Cocaine and alcohol are like hamburgers and French fries," he says. "Pancakes and syrup, turkey and dressing."

I say, "My nose burns a little, but I don't—" My throat swells, and the back of my neck tingles. I'm both energized and relaxed.

Cinch laughs. "And Brad discovered the drip. Don't you love how that medicinal flavor trickles into the back of your throat? Your life will never be the same."

The cocaine erases my alcohol buzz. Thoughts bubble like baking soda added to vinegar and erupt as rambling speech. I say, "I never thought I'd be doing this tonight. I mean, it's my first time. Not like I've never seen it, but I wasn't interested. It's got to be bad for you, right? But it's really not a big deal. I mean, I feel really good, like an intense caffeine buzz. I hope it lasts.

Hey, been meaning to tell you, made a decision about my work dilemma—I'm moving in."

"All righty then." He hands me the tooter. "Let's celebrate."

Ssshhhump.

Ssshhhump.

Cinch slides the plate under the couch. "Just be cool when we go back to the bar. People love the white, but they don't like to admit it. There's a lot of guilt and deception with it. If you have any doubt about people, just ask me."

More concerned with the effect on me than others, I say, "How much was that? I mean, how much should I do? I don't want to overdo it."

Cinch says, "Don't worry. We'll just take it one line at a time."

In the Round House, Whiplash charges into the Clash's "Should I Stay or Should I Go?" and transforms the barroom into a dance floor. Cinch dances wildly. Feeling conspicuous, I trail a modest distance behind. The frenzy intensifies my buzz. My mind accelerates: third, fourth, fifth gear. I look around. The rest of the world tries to keep up.

Cinch bounces to the bar for drinks. Astrid, standing by herself a few feet away, winks at me. "You two were gone for a while. The night is almost over."

I slide over next to her, trying to be nonchalant, but inside, my thoughts shove one another out of the way to get to the front. "But we're just getting started. I mean, the night is young. You should join. That is, if you want to. You know what I mean."

Astrid motions toward Cinch gyrating to the music at the bar. "Hope you know what you're getting yourself into."

"No worries. I'm on vacation," I say, reinforcing my battle cry.

Cinch returns, bringing a cocktail for Astrid as well. "Tonight's going to be one of those nights. I can feel it."

The parachute ceiling billows from the movement. I scan the room. Perched above the crowd in the front and next to the restrooms are two bouncers in lifeguard chairs. I say, "Were those chairs here before? I didn't notice them. But they had to be, right?"

"Yep, but no one was in them," Cinch says. "When it gets busy, it's the only way we can see the whole floor. You'll be up there with a flashlight. Pretty simple: no one's allowed to stand on chairs or tables, and both feet on the floor at all times. We use the flashlight to get people's attention, so we don't have to keep climbing up and down. You'll see some unbelievable shit from there."

Almost on cue, the guy in the chair near us shines his beam on a young lady standing on top of her stool. Since she doesn't respond to the light on her face, he shakes it back and forth and then raises his hand and points to the ground.

"Reminding people of the rules is about 90 percent of the job," Cinch says. "Another 8 percent is talking to people and answering the same questions over and over, and the last 2 percent is the ugly stuff. It's nice that the smallest part of the job is the physical side. Actually, bouncers cause most fights. At the slightest sign of trouble, they start throwing their weight around. That's why I choose to manage my boredom by keeping a slight buzz—just enough to keep me entertained, but not so much that I lose control."

Astrid says, "Keep in mind that Cinch's version of control is bedlam."

"You got to do something to keep it interesting," he says. "People think the job is one long party, that you get all kinds of women. Overall, it's monotonous. A customer trying to be clever will ask you a question, and two days later a different person will be in the same spot asking the same question. I just stroke 'em—answer like it's the first time I've ever heard their smart-ass question, then turn the conversation back on the person so he talks about himself. It's not like I'm totally jacking them off. People really prefer to talk about themselves anyway."

"Sounds like teaching," I say. "Trying to deal with the same questions and annoying problems day after day with sincerity and enthusiasm. If it's not the students giving you a hard time, it's the administrators or the parents hassling you."

"Last call for alcohol," Birch says over the PA. "Grab someone close."

I scan the room, still feeling numb. "Wow, this night flew by."

Cinch says, "The whole season will. From this point, bands will roll in one after another three days at a time until after Labor Day. You'll be surprised how quickly time passes when you live in three-day cycles."

In unison, or at least as close to unison as three hundred drunk people can achieve, the crowd sings along with Whiplash to an original song: *Hello, friends of the Bay. Thank you for coming today. Hello, water so blue. I'll always remember you.*

Birch holds the mic out to the crowd to sing along while he stands and gazes with satisfaction. To have his words and his music sung back to him must get him through the endless covers of Jimmy Buffett tunes.

Cinch says, "Let's hang in the red barn and wait for Birch to give us a ride to the Skyway. Unless you've had enough?"

I say, "You're the cruise director. Tell me where to go."

―

Cinch leads Astrid and me back to my new room. "Might as well do it back here," he says. "It'll be the groundbreaking ceremony for Brad Shepherd planting roots on South Bass Island."

I go to the window. "Whoa, look at this: a room overlooking

the world-famous Round House and Park Hotel. Of course I can leave out that it's the back of both places. And is that the cooler? This is too much. I don't want to take the luxury suite. Really, I don't deserve this."

Astrid says, "Are we going to do this or what? Brad, grab some beers. Cinch, get to work. I'll shut the blinds."

Like a surgeon, Cinch repeats the procedure from earlier. But now there are six lines instead of four.

"You trying to kill me?" Astrid says. "I need half of one of those."

"That rail is just a suggestion," Cinch says. "I'm sure someone here will clean the plate if you can't finish it." He slides the plate toward Astrid. "Here you go. Ladies first."

Astrid nods at his chivalry. Compared to Cinch—who attacks the plate, seemingly trying to plant the substance directly in his lungs—she allows the tube to glide over the line, pulling up only the amount she wants before switching nostrils halfway through. "I'm an equal opportunity destroyer," she says.

The door to the apartment opens. "Hey, hey! Bus is leaving." Cinch calls Birch back. His eyes instantly go to the plate. "Didn't take you long to make yourself at home," he says to me.

"My first time," I say, and I offer some to him.

He waves it off. "Not for me. I can't sing with clogged sinuses."

When we get to the van and Birch starts driving, Astrid is silent. Cocaine seems to affect people two ways. It either removes inhibitions or it increases a person's aloofness.

We pull into the Skyway parking lot. A strobe light flashes in the front window. "A little disco never hurt anyone," I say.

Astrid breaks her silence. "Fine dining during the day, disco at night."

The inside of the Skyway resembles a hunting lodge: one stone wall and three covered with wood paneling, but with flashing lights and pumping bass instead of taxidermic trophies. Birch whisks behind the bar, a privilege he's probably been awarded for directing people to this spot after the Round House closes. We join the rest of our group in a narrow area between the DJ booth and the bar that Cinch refers to as the "loge."

Cinch asks, "How's the Lady treating you?"

I say, "Awesome. I lost track of time hours ago. Today has had so many different beginnings and new experiences that it seems like several days."

Cinch puts his hand on my shoulder. "On the island, the recipe for an entertaining evening is drink this, smoke that, snort this, eat that. How do you feel? Well, try this and some of that."

"Don't you worry about overdoing it?"

"I've made my share of blunders, but another opportunity always emerges to apply what I've learned. A night of partying is like a night of sex. All the rising action is foreplay leading to a peak high. A person can't be in too much of a hurry but also can't wait too long, because if he does, everyone else will be spent by the time he gets there. He then has to party by himself, which is never a good idea, mentally or physically."

I say, "That's not an option this summer."

Cinch points to the man talking to Haley at the end of the bar. "Come meet Stein, the chef at Kelley's restaurant."

A thin, braided goatee sprouts from Stein's distended face like a string hanging from a balloon. The light ricochets off his cobalt eyes, and although he's looking directly at me, I don't feel like I'm getting closer as I approach.

Stein says, "I hear we got a newbie in our midst. Let's go swimming afterward to christen Brad in the Lake Erie waters."

"Ride with us in Birch's van," Cinch says.

Stein shakes him off. "I got my bike. I'll meet you there."

"Cool, you ride?" I say. "We should go sometime."

"There aren't very many good trails. My bike's more for

transportation. I can get around faster on my bike than I can in a car. Plus, with the way I abuse my body, I need all the exercise I can get."

Birch drops off three Jell-O shots, giving one to Cinch, Haley, and Stein. Each person removes the cap, pops the alcoholic red gelatin in his or her mouth, turns to a person close, and embraces as if kissing while thrusting the shot into the other's mouth. Haley grabs Birch, Stein grabs me, and Cinch goes right back to Stein.

"Again, again," Stein says with a mouthful of spiked gelatin.

I pull Astrid from the dance floor and deposit the substance in her mouth, enjoying the contact. Her skin is like silk, especially compared to Stein's scratchy chin. Stepping back with a scowl, she swishes the 2 ounces in her mouth, looks me in the eye, and swallows, releasing a satisfying, "Ahhhhhhhh."

The overhead lights come on.

Haley says, "Time for West Shore. Birch, you get alcohol, and I'll stop at home and get towels."

Cinch turns to Stein. "Throw your bike in the back and ride with us. There's a lot of idiots out there."

Stein says, "Something tells me I shouldn't refuse."

Now there are five.

Inside the van Cinch asks, "Who's up for one? Birch, you got anything to chop on?"

"Grab one of my CDs from that box back there. At least they'll be getting some use because they sure aren't selling."

The negative comment surprises me. Birch is usually so upbeat and positive. It's probably just his way of dealing with the poor sales. He might have assumed that once the album was finished, everything else would take care of itself. And why wouldn't

he think that? Isn't that what's supposed to happen when someone pursues a dream?

"The recording is awesome," Cinch says. "It doesn't even
sound like Birch."

Astrid refuses this time, passing the CD to Stein. "I've had
enough. You take mine."

Stones hit the underside of the van as we turn off the road and
travel down a dark driveway. Stein says, "We're at West Shore,
which is technically the whole west side of the island. Years ago,
this concrete ramp was a launching spot for boats, but now it's
just a convenient walkway for a late-night dip."

Astrid's soft voice tickles my ear. "Stay close. I'll show you the
way."

Her words shoot straight from my brain down my spine to
my groin and travel back up carrying a different interpretation. I
grab her hand.

Others make the plunge. Water laps against the rocks, calling me. Astrid and I disrobe. The darkness provides convenient
cover. The water is the safest place for me now. Even if we were
alone, in my heated state I'd probably just end up doing a lot of
apologizing.

Moss covers the rocks like fuzzy ice. I plant my foot, but I
still slide clumsily into the water and scrape my thigh. I'll have a
souvenir from this excursion.

I paddle out away from shore. The waves splash against my
face, carrying a message: *Welcome, you belong here.* The undulation
of the water rocks me. The silence wraps around me like a grand-
mother's hug. I do belong here. Floating, I drift from the others.

Astrid swims toward me, breaking my trance. "You sure don't
look like any teacher I ever had. Probably drove the young girls
wild."

I splash water at her. "Good thing you weren't in my class

because I may have gotten in trouble. What brings you to the island?"

"Summer job from Ohio State. I decided to stay in the US and work instead of going back to Norway for the summer."

"Norway? How did you ever end up at a university in the middle of Ohio?"

She dips underwater, then surfaces immediately. Slicking her hair back, she blows the water from her lips. "My father got a finance degree there, so I grew up with Buckeye stuff all around me. Seemed like the logical choice. Now it's just one more year before I finish my master's in psychology."

"Figure me out and they may give you a Ph.D."

Haley's voice booms from shore. "Jesus, Shep. Are you guys okay out there? It's too cold. Let's go."

Astrid laughs. "Uh oh, your girlfriend is getting jealous. The last thing I need is Haley mad at me."

"Don't even go there," I say. "We're just friends."

"Keep telling yourself that." She floats on her back and kicks toward shore. "Follow me. I know an easy way out. Just try not to stare at my ass."

"No promises. It would be the perfect ending to the perfect day."

CHAPTER THREE

MOST SIGNS OF THE REAL WORLD ARE MISSING ON THE ISLAND: THERE'S NO STARBUCKS, NO MCDONALD'S, NO WALMART. But the ubiquitous beer signs remind me that not everything is made here. The corporate filter is just stricter. Why not? If a person doesn't like his options, he can't drive ten minutes to the next town and have different choices.

Satisfaction is a powerful sleep aid, and after the day I had yesterday, how could I not be content? Uncertainty has returned to my life, and I welcome the possibilities.

I leave the hotel and make the short walk to the Round House. On the porch Cinch sits on a stool sipping lemonade. Judging from his eyes and his level of excitement at seeing me, he must've started the day ripping tubes of smoke. "You ready? Nervous?" he says. "We could really use you tonight."

"I think I can work it into my schedule. All I have planned is to meet Stein here to go for a ride and check out the monument at some point."

"Take this." He hands me the lemonade. "I'll go get us another."

I replace him on the stool and take a pull from the drink. Wow. Stiff and strong. I hold up the cup to the light. There's hardly any color. I take another drink. Or tartness for that matter. It must be all the vodka.

Golf carts pass us at regular intervals. The periodic motion of children on swings in the park hypnotizes me. My eyes follow the straw-shaped mandolin player I saw yesterday as he picks his spot for the day. He's meandering, but he knows what he is looking for, and occasionally he stops to check the angle of the sun and scan the four directions. Eventually he chooses the ground in front of a pyramid of cannon balls constructed as a memorial. He lays his backpack on the ground along with the mandolin, spreads out the blue, white, and black Navajo blanket, removes a container from inside the backpack, lights the contents, and marks the ground around him. He then digs out his tip jar, places it in front of the blanket, and positions himself directly in the middle.

Cinch returns with another lemonade. "Another beautiful day."

I motion toward the mandolin player. "What's the deal with that guy?"

"Caldwell?" Cinch pulls up another stool. "No one knows. He first appeared on the island in the winter of '78 during the blizzard cleanup and helped dig out the school so classes could resume. Some say he's an ex–Vietnam vet; others claim he's just an ordinary burned-out musician. And of course there are those who worry he's a fugitive from the law. As far as the government is concerned, Caldwell doesn't exist because he never takes a job that requires him to pay taxes."

"Being here for so many years, people must have asked about his past."

"He just always says, 'It's past,' and no one really questions him. He lives day to day—camping at the state park all season and during the winter, looking after people's houses until they return in the spring."

Although I can't hear the music, the rhythmic strumming of his right hand combined with the precise fingering of the left still sends a comforting message.

Stein cruises up on his bike. "Did you think I forgot about you?"

"Another drink and I wouldn't have cared."

Trails may be scarce on the island, but hills are abundant. The climb is taxing but the descent is exhilarating. I stand on my pedals, lean forward, and close my eyes. I'm free.

Stein veers off the road toward a white, barn-like building: the Island Bike Shop. Within fifteen minutes he's equipped my bike with a headlight, taillight, and combination odometer and speedometer. He says, "After we finish up here, let's grab a cold one at the Presshouse next door. I can show you my apartment on the second floor."

Judging from the building, the same architect responsible for the red barn must have designed the Presshouse as well. But the inside of Stein's apartment is much smaller than our setup. It has no living room, only a tiny bedroom, bathroom, and kitchenette.

Stein flops down on his bed. "Home sweet home." Within arm's reach are a guitar, a stack of books, a pad of paper, and an ashtray.

"Cozy and functional," I say.

"It gets the job done." He glances at his watch. "Ooh, I need to get to work at the restaurant. Want to come by for lunch?"

"No, thanks. I think I'll ride to the monument."

"Good idea." He gets up from the bed. "It's a clear day. You'll have great visibility."

"What's the best way to get there from here?"

His brow furrows and he smirks. "Just look up. The monument is always there."

Five mph—7—9—16—20—coast. The clicking from my knobbed tires on the asphalt transforms to a hum as I gain speed. A tour train is ahead. Passing on the left will be too close, so I go right, through the grass.

Perspiration builds on my forehead and sweat streams down my back. The humidity from yesterday has diminished, but my body still reacts to the exercise and to my extreme indulgence since I arrived.

Perry's Monument, which appears white from a distance, radiates a pinkish hue as I approach. It stands on a narrow tract of land that connects the west side of the island with the east. The surrounding acreage is flat, providing ample space for the four teenagers throwing a Frisbee, the two kids who have brought their kites, and the numerous sunbathers. Closer to the monument, the ground slopes up toward a square cement plaza that surrounds the base of the column. Four large stone urns decorate the corners of the plaza.

A breeze drifts from one side of the water to the other, drying my sweat. I dismount. The hair on the back of my neck stands up and a shiver rifles down my spine as I ascend to the plaza and circle the pink granite base, counting the bevels: twenty-seven.

The interior is tomb-like with domed walls and a limestone ceiling, stained in parts from the moisture seeping in. The inscription on the floor divulges that three American and three British officers are buried in the crypt beneath the white and black marble floor of the rotunda.

American
Marine Lieutenant John Brooks
Midshipman Henry Laub
Midshipman John Clark

British
Captain Robert Finnis
Lieutenant John Garland
Lieutenant James Garland

The quiet penetrates. I stare at the names. The letters form other words, names from my old life that I want to forget. Breaking my trance, two children rush in and trample the inscription. They don't care about what the silence might teach them. I follow them up the stairs, dragging my hand along the cool tile.

The elevator returns and drops off fifteen people. A park ranger at the controls greets us from behind his handlebar mustache. "Good afternoon. Welcome to Perry's Victory and International Peace Memorial. You are about to travel 340 feet above lake level. The observatory is the highest open-air platform in the country. The total distance to the pinnacle of the 11-ton brass urn on the top of the monument is 352 feet. The urn was designed by Joseph Freedlander, one of the monument's architects, and built by the Gorham Company of Rhode Island. It was dismantled and sent to the island in sections. Upon arrival, it was taken to the top of the memorial penthouse and reassembled. If you were to start at the upper plaza and take the steps all the way to the top, you would climb a total of 467 steps. The monument was equipped with an elevator from the beginning. The present elevator went into service in 1939 and ascends at a rate of 256 feet per minute, or 2.9 miles per hour. On the return trip, you will be moving slightly faster at 325 feet per minute, or 3.7 miles per hour. I look forward to seeing you on the way down to answer any questions you may have. Please refrain from throwing objects from the gallery. It is slightly windy today, so hold onto any loose articles. Enjoy the view."

At the edge of the observation deck, only a four-foot concrete wall separates me from an attempt at flight. In just one motion I could be over the side. It would be so easy—too easy. I have to step back.

In each corner of the gallery, a map and recording describe the naval battle that took place in the waters below: "Put-in-Bay was Perry's base of naval operation in western Lake Erie. During the decisive battle, Perry's ship was badly damaged. Fleeing an ailing vessel, Perry moved to *The Niagara*, where he formulated a counterattack. Knowing the lake well, he baited the British into a shallow section, rendering them defenseless, as they could not turn around to position themselves for the fight. Perry then levied extensive damage on the British fleet, leaving them minimal opportunity but to surrender and thus leading to Perry's elevation to hero status."

Was he a hero, though, or just lucky? Did he win the battle, or did the British just fuck up? What a bunch of crap—just another tale passed down generation after generation to justify bloodshed. Who was Oliver Hazzard Perry really? Does anyone know? Does anyone care? Yet here in his honor is a 36-million-pound column.

My discontent has accumulated over the past months, searching for a leak in the dam I've constructed to separate my true feelings from the situation closing in around me. I just want it all to fucking stop. I'm tired of blaming society, my job, and my family for making me into the person I've become.

The tape I was listening to has stopped, but I continue to stare at the water below, still picturing the battle and thinking of Perry. I guess it's better to be lucky than good any day. Regardless of how it happened, though, the battle was won, leading Perry to send the famous correspondence to William Henry Harrison that

Robin mentioned on the trip to the island, reproduced on the plaque in front of me:

US. Brig *Niagara*, Off Western Sister Island head of
Lake Erie, Sept. 10, 1813, 4 p.m.

Dear General–
We have met the enemy and they are ours, two
ships, two brigs, one schooner and one sloop.

Yours with great respect and esteem,
O. H. Perry

How I wish I could encounter my true enemy.

The same ranger operates the controls for the return trip. "I hope you enjoyed your visit. Does anyone have any questions?"

A young boy asks, "How long did it take to build?"

"The monument was built in thirty-two months, from October 1912 to June 1915. It was built to commemorate the centennial anniversary of the conclusion of the War of 1812. It has undergone several renovations over the years, one of them being the addition of a lightning arrestor system. In July 1920, lightning struck the northwest corner of the observation gallery, knocking off a 200-plus-pound piece of granite. It fell through the plaza below and into the foundation room."

As I imagine a sizable chunk of granite plummeting from the top, the elevator's abrupt stop startles me. A smirk creeps out from behind our guide's mustache. How many trips has he made to perfect that delivery?

The steps from the elevator platform dump me back into the

rotunda. In between me and the outside world stands nine-and-a-half feet of rock. I know this feeling. This is my life.

———

I lay out my uniform for the night, the creases in the chest and midsection still visible in the new shirt. Am I really qualified to be a bouncer? I haven't been in a fight since the third grade, when Charlie Watters teased me about having a crush on the teacher. Not to mention I've spent most of my adult life in a classroom. But to go from prepubescent adolescents to drunks may be a lateral move.

I stare at the postcard of the monument that I bought for my parents, unsure of what to say. I feel bad about the way I acted the last time I saw them. Too late for apologies now. Just keep it light. *Got here safely. Having a blast. You can reach me at Brad Shepherd, General Delivery, Put-in-Bay, OH 43456. Will call soon. Love, Brad.*

Cinch is on the other side of a knock at the door. He enters with his work shirt draped over his shoulder. "Ready to hit the employee lounge? There's a small bar tucked away upstairs at the Boardwalk where I go for cocktails during my break. It's owned by another one of the main families on the island. Ya gotta love the setup of Put-in-Bay. A few families own most of the businesses, hire people to come to the island to work, house them in cramped living conditions, and don't give them anything else to do, so they go out and give their wages right back to the owners. Fucking goldmine."

The Boardwalk stands opposite the Jet Express, across the four strings of public docks. It appears to be more of a restaurant than a bar, but I've already learned, regardless of the façade, most establishments do a significant share of bar business.

Cinch and I pass through the restaurant to a flight of stairs by the back patio. Upstairs, two people wearing matching shirts are at the bar hunched over cocktails, obviously preparing for work just as we intend to. Bob Marley's "No Woman No Cry" plays softly from speakers behind the bar, which is lined with candles that fill the air with the smell of vanilla.

Cinch motions to the bartender. "Give me two of the usual, T-Bone."

T-Bone ices two glasses, puts several oranges through the juicer, and adds vodka and a splash of cranberry.

I ask, "Do you have a different drink for each bar?"

"This is the only place with fresh-squeezed juices. Most places have that shitty bar mix—gives me heartburn. I could drink these all day. Especially when I'm partying. They're refreshing, yet extremely potent when made correctly."

Nodding to the bartender, Cinch guides us to a table overlooking the public docks, away from the other people in the room. "Since you're living in the red barn," he says, "I need to explain something about the drugs."

"You seem to have it under control," I say. "Drugs and alcohol are a nice place to visit, but you don't want to live there."

Cinch raises his eyebrows. "What if someone were to work there?"

I lower my voice to a whisper. "A dealer?"

"Drugs cost money. I've got the connection. Everyone who wants to play has to pay his share. I risk bringing it here and holding onto it, so I deserve to pay nothing and to make some money on the side."

"What if you get caught?" I say, wondering if the "you" really means "we," since I'll be living with him.

"I only deal with people I trust. I sold spring break trips in college to pay for my trip. Did that make me a travel agent?"

Later, on the sidewalk in front of the Round House, a line of people winds through a portable tape maze.

Cinch says, "I love this time of evening. Everything is clean, and the customers haven't gotten their second wind yet. When we charge cover, people first enter through the maze, show their ID, and pay cover to get a wristband. After that, they can enter through any entrance or exit. All you have to do is direct them to the side to get a wristband and keep the entranceway on the porch clear." Cinch steps through the entrance and leads a man in his fifties onto the porch, fastening a band around his wrist. "Good evening, Senator. How many in your party tonight?"

"Senator, hah!" the man says. "With what I've done on this island, my political career was over before it started. Four should cover me for the night."

Cinch says, "Is that it? Must be a slow night on the docks."

The man slides twenty dollars in Cinch's pocket. "Won't be slow tomorrow. Stop by my boat for a beer."

Cinch will be my entertainment for the evening. He's the politician here—a lot of handshaking and smiling. This is his constituency.

Finished for the day, Caldwell strolls through the park toward the Round House. The mandolin hangs from one shoulder, his backpack from the other. He crosses the street and stops on the sidewalk, peering inside at the crowd. His face glows from being in the sun all day.

I ask, "How were the tips today?"

He shakes the jar. "Sixty-four dollars and thirteen cents. Pretty good for this early in the season."

A man like Caldwell can live for a while on sixty-two dollars. Cinch told me that because of Caldwell's long tenure and year-round presence, beers come pretty cheap and no one ever expects a tip. It's not out of pity; everyone just appreciates having him around. With only a few hundred year-round residents, what other choice is there but to take care of each other?

I hold out a wristband. "You coming in?"

He removes his black baseball hat and tucks his thin, silver strands behind his ears. "Nope. You're Shep, aren't you?"

"Have we met?"

"Nope, just heard and seen you around. Name's Caldwell."

He is tranquil when he speaks, making the fugitive stories difficult to believe. I say, "Oh yeah, Cinch told me you used to play in bands or something."

He smiles. "That's one of the stories."

Regardless of what his words actually are, everything he says feels like he's patting me on the back, saying, *It's okay, I understand*. His past doesn't matter to me. I marvel at the free man standing before me.

He stares into the Round House again then shakes his head. "Think I'll go down the street. Stay out of trouble, Shep."

The people flow in and out like the tide. When Whiplash starts a set, they wash in, and when the band takes a break, they retreat onto the porch and into the park for fresh air. During one of the intermissions, a pair of hands reach from behind me, shielding my eyes. Their smooth texture and jasmine fragrance divulge their owner's identity.

I say, "If you'd like to come in, the cover is three dollars. Right around to your left, miss."

Cinch emerges from inside and ends my game by fastening a band around Astrid's wrist. She says, "At least one of you is a gentleman. What's up for tonight?"

"Let's drink here for free and move the party to the red barn," Cinch offers.

"Always the planner." She turns her penetrating stare on me. "Brad, how was the monument today?"

"Kind of eerie—like last night in the water. I felt connected and detached at the same time."

"Wait until you go there in the dark," she says. "It's spooky but comforting. Definitely special."

—

At close, it takes us thirty-five minutes to clean the mess that took six hours to create, including using a wet vac to suck up the liquid that stands an inch high in some parts of the floor. Judging from the pungent smell, it's not entirely beer. Afterward, we all quickly catch up with the rest of the island. I've never seen anyone drink Cuervo straight up with a Coke back, and I've never seen anyone consume as much tequila as Haley does in the short time we're at the bar. In Key West, she drank whiskey and only did shots with the group. Tonight Cinch keeps her shot glass full, and she finishes each one regardless of whether we're drinking with her or not.

Both elbows on the bar, Haley slumps over her empty shot glass. "If you want to go meet the others, don't feel like you need to stay here with me. Won't be the first time I've been drunk alone on this island."

"Come upstairs with us," Cinch says, pouring her another tequila. "Was hoping to snag a case of beer from the cooler and replace it tomorrow."

"Don't worry about replacing it," she says. "Consider it a welcoming present for Brad. I'd join you, but I'm opening tomorrow."

To Cinch, a case of beer translates to a case and a half and two bottles of wine. Taking the alcohol appears more like entitlement than stealing. His carefree attitude represents everything I wish I could be.

But the refrigerator in the red barn poses a dilemma: sacrifice the food or drink warm beer? Cinch solves the problem by clearing the takeout boxes from the second shelf. "Food, like sleep, is optional. Now I just need to make a drop at the Park Hotel and we can start this party."

I say, "Do what you got to do, but I don't want to be present for the transaction."

Astrid says, "Me neither."

Cinch removes a calculator-sized digital scale from his pocket. "No big deal. You guys wait here. No one will even know you were wise to it." He tears off a corner of a magazine page, creases the paper, and places it on the scale. Scooping out a few pebbles from his bag, he adds some dust until the digital readout oscillates between 0.7 and 0.8. He picks up the fold of paper and pours the contents into a one-inch square green resealable baggie. "Be back in a flash."

I rearrange items in the room, avoiding eye contact with Astrid. She confronts the awkwardness. "Just be careful with all this."

"What do you mean? It's got nothing to do with me. I just live here."

"For now." Her eyes narrow then soften. "It's only your second day."

Cinch returns and slaps a hundred-dollar bill on the dresser. "Thanks for shopping. Let's party."

The blinking beacon on the monument encourages me like a flirtatious wink. The comfort I felt last night at the boat ramp is with me here as well.

Cinch reduces his voice to a whisper. "Let's climb up in one of those stone urns on the plaza."

I hand the bottle of wine to Astrid. "If I'd known there would be a physical challenge, I wouldn't have drunk so much."

From the base, I grab the top lip and pull myself up, resting on the edge with one leg inside and the other outside, and I admire the view the twelve-foot elevation provides.

Cinch's leg comes over the side and I guide him until he is able to straddle the edge. He gasps, "Ooh, that's a little tough on the jewels."

I place the wine from Astrid in the middle of the pod. But before I get back to help, her leg is already swinging over. I say, "Maybe you should've come first. Some view, huh?"

Astrid stands. "How about another five feet?"

I rise, but I don't trust my balance, and I immediately sit again.

"Yeah, fuck that," Cinch says. "Sit down. You're making me nervous."

Astrid says, "Nights like tonight are so liberating. We need to do more of this."

I take a drink of wine. "That's why I came here. I need to be free. The longer you stay in one place, the more the world closes in around you."

Cinch says, "Who cares, as long as you feel good?"

"But if you don't have hope," Astrid says, "your life is empty."

Cinch guzzles more wine. "You always have your buzz. That's a man's true best friend."

"Even the best buzz wears off," I say, "and you wake up more trapped than the day before."

Astrid asks, "What are you going to do at the end of the summer?"

I close my eyes, turning my face skyward. "I'm staying right here."

"You're nuts." Cinch passes the wine. "You might as well enroll in AA now. There ain't much else to do but drink."

"Where will you go after this summer?" I say. "Home to live with your parents?"

"It may be time for me to get a real job," Cinch says.

Astrid laughs. "Who's going to trust you with kids?"

"My dad has so many hookups in education," Cinch says, "I can write my own ticket."

I take another drink. "You're not really going to teach, are you?"

"What else can I do? I'm not the type of person to go down to Florida to work, and I certainly can't stay here."

Astrid nods. "I'm with Cinch."

"Don't give up so easily," I say. "We can finish the season here, and if we don't want to stay, we go west for the winter: Las Vegas, California, Colorado. We'll have fun wherever we go. If we like it, we'll stay. If not, we'll go somewhere else."

Cinch says, "Fuck that. Time for me to grow up."

"Believe me," I say. "Work as anything more than a hobby is overrated."

"It was for you," Cinch says. "Maybe it's exactly what we need. If not, we can always quit like you did. Nothing's permanent. We can always walk away."

"You better be ready for it, though," I say. "Once you start working, everything slows down."

Cinch snatches the bottle from me. "Listen to Mr. Heavy over here. Lighten up. Just because you didn't like it doesn't mean we won't."

"I look forward to the slower pace," Astrid says. "And having some control."

I take the wine from Cinch and shake my head at her. "You think you have control, and you think you're making a difference. Then one day you realize it's changing you."

"Screw it," Cinch says. "If my parents had their way, I'd already be married with kids, living in the house right next door."

"Yeah, fuck it." I chug the rest of the wine and drop the empty in the pod. "Who cares, anyway?"

CHAPTER FOUR

THE WEEKDAYS ON THE ISLAND VARY FROM THE WEEKENDS BUT EASILY COULD BE THE SAME. Each day, each night, people stand in my doorway urging me to indulge with them. To exist here, I'll have to become skilled in saying no—an art in which I was once well accomplished, but one I no longer care to practice.

Throughout the week people steadily accumulate like carp for a feeding. Thursday night is supposed to be as busy as last Friday, and each of the three weekend nights is considered a Saturday due to the volume of business for the Memorial Day weekend. For as unpredictable as Put-in-Bay appears on the surface, things seem to transpire exactly as forecast. Even chaos takes on a consistent form over time.

Down the street in front of the arcade, a group of skateboarders occupies my attention for the afternoon. While they all look the part—baggy pants, vintage band tees, and Vans—only two even attempt to skateboard. The others prop their boards up against a park bench and heckle passersby between trips into the arcade.

From the tattoos and piercings so conspicuously advertised to their adolescent philosophy of *I make noise, therefore I am*, these kids are familiar to me.

It was only a short while ago that I was being hassled five days a week by ones just like them, and not all that long ago, I was one of them. The only difference is that somewhere along the way I bought into the bullshit being fed to me. I got the grades, went to college, and got the job, while they're still fighting it. Just one big lost generation. Too smart to learn anything and too naive to do anything—wandering without going, wondering without knowing.

After a while, the two oldest-looking boys, obviously the leaders of the group, walk toward me. One of the boys has ten-inch dreadlocks that resemble a chief's headdress. The other has a nose ring and both eyebrows pierced. Without slowing down, they try the classic "walk by like you know where you're going" strategy to attempt to get into the bar.

I prop my leg across the opening. "IDs, boys?"

The boy with dreadlocks hands me an ID.

"Twenty-five, huh?" In the picture he has a beard and a shaved head. "You've changed."

"I look different with the dreads."

I turn to the other boy. "How about you?"

"I left mine on the boat." The silver barbell pierced through his tongue clicks against his teeth when he talks.

"Sorry guys, no ID, no enter."

Dreads says, "Go back to the boat and get it. I'll meet you inside." The ease with which he deserts his wingman further establishes his youth.

I say, "Nice try. Now go back to your gang over there and heckle someone else."

Did they not realize I'd been watching them? With a better fake ID, Dreads could maybe pass for twenty-one, but not twenty-five or twenty-six. He barely looks nineteen now.

The two boys plod back to the group, where the others receive them as battle-proven warriors. There is no ridicule, only admiration for pushing the limits.

Maybe rebellion is the right path. At their age I was so worried about having a career that I weighed myself down with commitments before I even knew what I wanted to do. What's the big rush after all? Why not drift? I admire their defiance. I wish I'd had more courage to disobey and do what I felt like. If I had, maybe I wouldn't have had to press the reset button and begin again.

I feel a tap on the shoulder. "Hey stranger, don't you love me no more?"

It's the middle of the afternoon on a Wednesday, and Haley's already plowed. "Don't be ridiculous," I say. "We see each other every day."

She brushes a strand of hair from my face. "You just don't have time for me. You wouldn't want your new butt-buddy Cinch to get jealous."

I pull back. "If I remember correctly, you were the one who declined our invitation last time."

"And what's up with you and Astrid? I hear you two are an item."

"Sorry to dash that rumor, but we're just friends."

"That's not what I'm hearing." Her drunken grin broadens.

I look out across the park. "Is this how we're going to spend our time?"

"Geez. So sensitive." She leans in and kisses me on the cheek. "Meet me at Skyway after work. Maybe we can actually hang out for a bit." She steps off the porch and weaves toward the Boat House.

Cinch comes out from inside, watching Haley's winding path. "She needs a hobby other than drinking."

"Is it always this bad?"

He clears empty cups from a nearby table. "If the bar's not busy, she's an absolute train wreck."

I shake my head. The person I felt closest to when I arrived—the person who convinced me to come here in the first place—is becoming a stranger. Have things changed so much in a week?

A group of twenty-somethings ready to show IDs steps onto the porch. Cinch just waves them through to the bar and turns toward me, putting both hands on my shoulders. "You up for a little adventure tonight? It's a tradition to kick off the season at the cove."

"What's the cove?" I ask.

"A cliff sticks out over the water on West Shore. I saw it one day coming back on the Jet Express. It'll be a cool hangout. We can take a twelve pack, jump off the cliff, then build a fire on the beach."

"I thought you said it was already a tradition."

He winks. "It will be—after this year."

"What about Haley?"

"We'll stop by the Skyway, but she'll never last. You saw how polluted she was already."

I look down toward Haley walking into the Boat House. "I just feel bad. She's a big reason I'm here, and I've hardly spent any time with her."

Cinch says, "Don't expect to. She runs on bar hours. When the bar closes, she goes home to pass out."

⁂

After work at the Skyway, Cinch and I find Haley tucked in the loge with Stein. I sneak up and put my arms around them. "Just what I like to see: two of my favorite people together. What are we having?"

"Nothing for me," Haley says. "I only stayed until you got

here so you wouldn't think I stood you up. Come and give me a kiss." She pushes her tequila-soaked tongue in my mouth.

I jerk my head back. "I guess you *have* been here awhile."

"Walk me out to my car." She stands awkwardly. "I'm done."

Stein grabs her keys. "You aren't driving. One of us will take you home."

Her words slur together. "Ahhh, you guys take such good care of me."

Cinch takes the keys from Stein. "Let's all go to the cove after we drop her off."

"But I want to go, too," Haley says in a drunken mumble.

Stein stands and helps me guide her toward the door. "We're both going home. The holiday weekend starts tomorrow. You don't need to make it any more difficult than it already will be."

On the way to her Jeep, Haley notices Astrid, walking across the lot on her way to join us. "What's she doing here? Just friends, my ass."

"Come on, don't be like that," I say.

"Just shut the fuck up, you pathetic drunk," Cinch says. "Like you'll remember any of this tomorrow."

Astrid hesitates before getting into the Jeep with us. "Maybe I should just meet you guys there."

Stein laughs. "Don't worry. Cinch is right. She'll have to call the last person she remembers being with to ask how she got home and where her car is."

Astrid climbs in the back seat. Stein and I position Haley in the front. She clings to my arm. "Just ride up here with me."

I squeeze in. Stein closes the door. "You're on your own. Now you understand why I ride my bike everywhere."

Cinch drives onto the main road. Haley maneuvers onto my lap and kisses my neck until she passes out. Astrid is silent in the back.

Once we're at Haley's house, Astrid waits in the car while Cinch and I carry Haley inside and put her to bed. I scan her languid body, asleep under the sheets. "Good thing she didn't drive."

Cinch takes a beer from the fridge and opens it. "Yeah, too many people drive drunk around here."

"What was up with her kissing me? That's the first time that's happened."

Cinch dumps some coke on the counter. "Be careful with Haley. She has ulterior motives."

"Are you sure we should do this here?" I walk back toward the living room to watch for Haley.

"Don't worry. She's out cold. You could have sex with her and she'd never know." He divides the pile into two thick lines. "You know, she and I didn't talk for an entire winter once because I got sick of her nagging me all the time. It was like we were a couple, and then I realized that was what she wanted. At least now I got you to take her off my back."

I hand him a rolled-up bill. "No way I'm going there."

Ssshhhump.

Ssshhhump.

—

Back on the road the cool night air rushes through the open Jeep. Neither Cinch nor Astrid says much, which feels fine with me right now. My heart races, but I'm relaxed. The trees dance with the wind under the glow of the sky. The road turns sharply to the right, and the vineyards to my left offer the sweet smell of Concord grapes. Crickets chirp as we race by. Are they welcoming us or telling us to leave?

Cinch pulls off the main road and parks in front of a vacant cottage next to a wooded area. We enter through a gash in the foliage. The sound of water splashing against rocks directs us. Trickles of moonlight straggle down through the trees. A fallen poplar is the final obstacle before the brightly lit clearing.

Cinch arrives first, his face beaming in the moonlight. "Ah, check this out."

The water, which beckoned from a distance, crashes against the rocks fifty feet below. White foam bubbles on the shore.

Astrid peers over the edge. "No problem. I've jumped from higher back in Norway."

"There's a way down over here," Cinch says. "Give me your shoes and socks and the backpack."

Astrid removes her shirt and drops her shorts. "If we're going to do this, we might as well do it right."

Cinch follows. "Now we're talking."

I look over the edge. "Uh, I think I'll keep my shorts on."

"Probably a good idea," Astrid says. "They could use a good washing after the past week."

Cinch collects our things and disappears down the path. The moonlight follows every curve of Astrid's lean body. "Second time in a week you've stripped in front of me," I say.

"Gives you something to think about later when you're alone."

"What makes you think I'll be alone?"

"Oh, that's right. I forgot about Cinch. Or are you stopping back at Haley's?"

Cinch returns from the beach, his bulbous, pale body emerging from the darkness like a puff of smoke. "Who's first? Just remember to jump out as far as possible to avoid the rocks, and pull up your knees when you touch the water or you'll hit bottom."

"See you boys on the beach." Astrid takes a deep breath and leaps. Seconds of silence, and then a splash. Her excitement echoes through the night. "Wow, so great. Let me swim around and check it out."

"Screw that," Cinch says. "I'm going now. Kowabungaaaa—" His voice trails into a splash. His hand smacks the surface. "Come on down. You're the next contestant on 'The Water is Right.'"

I curl my toes on the rocky surface. I don't want to repeat another poor dismount like the one at the boat ramp. I watch the outlines of Astrid and Cinch wade out of the water and convene on the beach. With my left foot planted, I rock back but can't push off the cliff. Staring at the water below, I stand frozen. My discomfort builds, and I remain there like a statue. I can't do it.

Astrid's voice radiates up. "Don't worry about it. Climb down and have a beer with us."

I eventually disappear from the edge, but not the same way the others did. Cinch hands me a beer on shore. "Here you go, ya big baby. Maybe I should put a nipple on this."

"I'm just a lot bigger than you guys and not that graceful," I say, downplaying my embarrassment.

Astrid piles some brush from the beach into a stone fire ring. "It's okay. You just have to work up to it. I grew up jumping off cliffs into the fjords. First time is always the toughest."

Cinch says, "Don't coddle him." He turns toward me. "You think you can manage to dig the lighter out of the backpack and start this fire? Or are you afraid of that, too?"

"Somebody do it," Astrid says. "I'm freezing."

I fish around for the lighter in the backpack. "I think I can manage."

"Good. I'm going up for another jump." Cinch hikes up the path to the cliff. "Watch carefully, you big sissy. Ooh, I'm scared to jump off a cliff. The water may hurt me."

Astrid drops several pieces of driftwood next to the fire ring and bends down to block the wind. "Hope you know that most of what he says is meant to be ignored."

I spark the lighter. "I just consider the source." The flame ignites the brush, and we cup our hands around the struggling fire.

She says, "Must admit, you have been on my mind quite a lot lately."

The flame spreads and burns strongly. I place a piece of the driftwood in the middle. "You too. This week has been pretty incredible. I'm excited for the rest of the summer."

Astrid crouches by the growing fire. She's put her shorts back on since coming out of the water. "That's the thing. It's a long summer. This island is great for friendships, but it's tough on relationships."

"Is this about Haley in the Jeep?" I step back from the fire. "Because there's nothing going on."

"Yes and no." Her voice stammers. "It's just—this is my last summer, then I graduate. After that, who knows?"

From the cliff Cinch sings in a high-pitched voice. "Come on, Vogue. Let your body move to the music." His rotund physique strikes exaggerated poses against the star-filled sky.

I shake my head at his antics. "Exactly. Do you think I ever thought I'd be standing here doing this? I had never even heard of this island until three months ago."

Cinch stands erect on the cliff. "Watch now. Not that tough. You stand on the end, take a deep breath, and jump." He disappears from the edge. "Geronimooooo—"

Splash.

I put another piece of wood on the fire. "I'm never going to hear the end of not jumping."

Astrid takes my hand. "Listen, I really like you, but I need to keep my life simple right now. I just want to be free."

I mask my disappointment. "We're just having fun. No hassles." I turn toward the water looking for Cinch. "Do you see Cinch? He should've surfaced by now."

She walks to the water. "Cinch? Quit messing around."

The darkness swallows her words, and only the sound of the waves returns.

I rush into the water. "Cinch! Oh fuck! No!" I swim toward the landing spot. Astrid searches closer to shore. I dive underwater. Can't see anything. I run my hands along the rocks, searching for something I really don't want to find. The panic shortens my wind. I push to the surface. Still no Cinch. I kick back to the bottom. Each smooth stone I feel is another moment that Cinch might be okay. I push upward, staying above water only long enough to fill my lungs and check with Astrid, each time hoping to see the two of them together.

After three dives, from a cave under the cliff, Cinch's voice slices through the commotion. "Looking for me?" He swims toward us. "Oh man, that was great. You should've seen your faces." He splashes in the water, imitating us. "Cinch? Oh no. Where are you?"

Astrid swims toward him. "You think that's funny, huh?" She dunks him repeatedly. "I'll really drown you."

"Okay, okay," he says each time she lets him catch a breath above the surface. "I'm sorry."

I trudge back toward shore. "Let's just go."

Cinch swims away from Astrid. "Don't be mad at me because you were afraid to jump. There's still hope you might grow a sack one day."

I push back toward Cinch. "Everything's a big joke to you, isn't it?"

Cinch stands in the waist-deep water. "Just relax, tiger. No need to get your panties in a bunch."

"Fuck off." I shove Cinch back into the water.

Astrid steps between us. "Just cool down. Both of you."

I spin away and head toward shore. "I'm out of here."

"Come on, man. I'm sorry. I was just joking." He trails after me.

I slog through the water. I know I've overreacted; now the question is just how to save face. I can't embarrass myself twice in one night.

"I don't know what I was thinking coming here," I announce. The splashing behind me increases. I emerge from the water and lengthen the separation between us. His pace quickens. I let him catch me by the fire while I search for my second shoe.

"Just wait a sec." He's panting from the exertion. "The jump might not have killed me, but this chasing shit might."

"Let's just forget it. I'll move my stuff out in the morning." I drop down on the beach to put on my shoes, still not looking at him. "Maybe one of the other places is still hiring."

"I said I was sorry." He walks over and stands in front of me. "What more can I do to make it up to you?"

Astrid joins us by the fire. "Let's all just take a deep breath and go home and get a good night's sleep. We'll laugh about this in the morning."

I stand, and finally I look him in the eyes. "You really want to make it up to me?"

His body straightens. "Just name it. Whatever it takes."

"On your knees." I unbutton my shorts and let them fall around my ankles. "I need a good blow-dry."

Cinch doesn't react. Astrid is the first to laugh. "You know, you two really are made for each other. Somebody put another log on the fire. My clothes are soaked."

I mimic the sarcastic voice Cinch was using earlier. "I'm sorry. What can I do to make it up to you? Please don't be mad at me."

"Okay. You got me. Game on. I see how it's going to be." Cinch slips on his dry shorts. "Who's the one with wet clothes, bitch?"

Astrid removes her soaked shorts and smacks them against Cinch's bare chest. "One of you jokers better find a way to get those dry. I'm not wearing wet shorts the rest of the night."

I pick up her shorts and position them next to mine on the rocks by the fire. "Let's stay until the clothes are dry or the fire goes out. Whichever comes first."

"Who's up for one?" Cinch pulls a plate out of the backpack and dangles the bag of coke between his fingers. "This could be a long night."

Astrid clenches her teeth. "Oooh, I wasn't planning to have an all-nighter. Maybe I'll just stick with beer."

"Does anyone ever plan to stay up all night?" Cinch sits down to perform the chopping ritual.

"I'm in," I say. "The sooner I go to bed, the sooner tomorrow comes."

"Oh hell, why not?" Astrid says. "Guess the first session of the season had to happen sooner or later."

"Session?" I laugh. "Is this research for your psychology thesis?"

Astrid says, "It's like group therapy. While most of the island sleeps, we'll be whoever we want to be. For the next few hours, we won't exist."

"Buckle up your chin straps, kids." Cinch passes the plate to Astrid. "Cocaine, alcohol, and new friends amount to more than a few hours, because everyone will have fresh lies to tell."

The first hour of the session consists of Cinch performing his best bits from Jimmy Stewart to George Bush. Whenever he runs out of material, either Astrid or I willingly takes over. No one moves except to reach to the right and pass to the left.

There's a drive in a lost soul—in one that is searching for acceptance, companionship, belonging, whatever you want to call it. The slightest coincidence ignites a spark that one hopes will lead to something meaningful. That's why I'm here—for the slim chance that at some point in the day, whether it be four in the afternoon or six in the morning, I might have a conversation during which I honestly connect with someone.

Astrid stares at the pre-dawn glow above the tree line on the cliff. "It's getting light out. Tomorrow has officially arrived."

After all the chemicals we put into our bodies, a flash of morning light overrides them all. Cinch passes me the plate. "Put the rest of that back in the bag. Too conspicuous to be here at sunrise. Astrid, get the empties. I'll take care of the fire."

I clean the plate and put it back in the backpack. After twisting and tying the bag as I have seen Cinch do on other occasions, I extend it to him. "Here you go. You probably want this back."

"Just keep it," he says. "That way you don't always have to rely on me."

I nod and slide the bag in my pocket.

We leave the beach as we found it and slink back to the Jeep in silence. I guess after hours of unbridled conversation, there's nothing more left to say.

We drop off Astrid at her place and park the Jeep behind the Round House. Cinch says, "How about another hour? Let's go watch sunrise at the monument."

"You don't have to twist my arm. The walk will help me sleep."

"If that doesn't work, just masturbate. Works every time."

I force a laugh. Even that takes effort at this point. "Here I thought that bottle of lotion next to your bed was for dry skin."

A thin layer of dew massages the freshly trimmed grass, prepping it for the day ahead. The tip of the sun peeks over the horizon as we sit down on the cement seawall. Why am I not here every morning?

Cinch stares at the glimmering horizon. "Supposed to be a nice day, which means that starting in four hours, the Jet Express will roll in every thirty minutes, filled with tourons whose pockets are stuffed with money to leave on the island."

My head slumps forward. "Don't remind me."

"There'll be so much going on today that the sheer energy will keep you going. We'll just party all day with them."

We sit in silence. The sun, now fully exposed, makes my sweatshirt uncomfortable, as does the time of day. "We should probably head back soon, huh?" I ask.

"Yeah, a few hours of sleep might make a difference later in the day."

We walk back along the seawall. A police car stops at the

intersection. I bury my hands in my pockets. "Heads up. We've got company."

The turn signal on the right flashes, and the wheels point in our direction. Cinch says, "Relax. We've just been up drinking all night. We do it all the time. Are you carrying?"

I brush my hand against the bag Cinch gave me earlier. I forgot to leave it with the backpack in the Jeep. The car rolls toward us. There are only two reasons it would turn left down this dead end: to watch the sun rise or to see us.

The car stops as we pass. The bulge in my pocket feels like a baseball. Producing a smile requires all my concentration.

The window lowers. "Morning, boys. Awful early for you, isn't it?"

CHAPTER FIVE

CINCH PEERS INSIDE THE POLICE CRUISER. "Skip, what the fuck? Trying to give me a heart attack?" The painted smile on his face fills with sincerity.

"If you're not doing anything wrong, why worry?" the officer says.

"You know some of those pricks you work with just look for people to hassle. Brad, Skip works the door for us now and then, whenever he isn't playing Barney Fife. Dude, give us a ride back to the red barn. We have to work in a few hours."

"One up front and one in the back," he says, unaware that if he drove straight to the station, he would have a pretty significant collar.

Cinch opens the back door for me, enjoying the situation. "Watch your head, young man."

My sweaty legs stick to the vinyl seats. I gaze through the mesh wiring separating me from Cinch and Skip, trying to connect with their conversation. The deeper I gaze through the small holes, the farther away they sound.

Skip pulls the car behind the red barn. "Cinch, you'll have to let him out from the outside. Get some sleep, boys. Going to be a long weekend."

"Thanks for the ride," I say. "Sorry—I'm a little out of it. Never been in the back of a cop car before."

Skip laughs. "Let's keep it that way, mister."

In the red barn I toss the bag of coke on the table. "Man, that was stupid. One fuckup and it's over. What if you hadn't known him?"

Cinch says, "But I did. I know about 80 percent of the cops, so I wasn't worried. Plus, we weren't doing anything wrong. Of course, I didn't know you had a bag of cosmic charlie in your pocket."

After three hours of sleep, Cinch and I begin the next day as we ended the previous one. At the cove we had passed around a dinner plate; now our breakfast comes on a mirror. Sometimes things should be more difficult than they are. It would probably save me from trouble down the road if I feel worse than I do.

On my way to work, a man wearing a pink tank top and snug khaki shorts stands by the back door of the Round House. Must be Mad Dog. His long, stringy hair is pulled into a ponytail that extends through the back of a baseball hat that says *Every day above ground is a good day*.

Cinch had explained that Mad Dog plays at the Round House on popular weekends. The first two hours of his show are stand-up comedy while he smokes and drinks. For the last few hours, as his buzz takes over, he plays rock and roll on his acoustic guitar, sometimes until six thirty, when he leaves the stage barely able to stand. He drinks only Pink Catawba wine from Heineman's Winery and shots of peppermint schnapps, consuming on average three bottles of wine and ten to twelve shots per show, all while smoking three packs of cigarettes. His tributes to excess are legendary, just like the sales on the registers as people attempt to keep up with him.

He pops a cigarette into his mouth. "Got a light?"

Fumbling through my pockets, I surprisingly find two lighters. Must've picked these up cleaning the bar. I toss one to Mad Dog. "Keep it."

Cinch rounds the corner, yelling, "Every day above ground is a goooooooood day."

"Cinchy! It's about time," Mad Dog says. "I thought I was going on without you. Get on stage and introduce me."

With only a microphone and Mad Dog's black Takamine guitar, the Round House stage looks barren. Cinch steps behind the mic. "Ladies and gentleman, I am pleased to announce that despite spending the night in jail, Mike 'Mad Dog' Adams is here to continue spreading his gospel on the international 'Every day above ground is a good day II' tour. Please welcome the Mad Dog!"

Side by side, Mad Dog and Cinch are as visually appealing as two contestants in a hot dog eating contest. Mad Dog says, "Damn, anytime I think I'm getting too old and fat to do this, I see Cinch, who is younger, fatter, and balder than I am. It's the little things, folks, that help you through the days. By the way, Cinch, I'll get that bail money for ya after the show. Drink up, folks—I got bills to pay, and I guarantee not one damn dime will go toward charity. Every bit will go toward my alcohol and drug addictions. I feel good, though, folks. I really do. I feel a lot better than you guys look. What an ugly crowd. You guys are going to drive me to drink. We better start out slow, though. It's going to be a long weekend. Haley, how about a shot? And crack that first bottle of Pink Cat. I think it's gonna be a three-bottle day."

All focus is on Mad Dog. He may be having a liquid lunch, but the screams and whistles are his nourishment.

"You know, folks, life is short. It really is. My grandfather was eighty-nine years old when he died. He smoked two packs of cigarettes and drank a fifth of Jack Daniels every day. And then the other day I was reading about some twenty-eight-year-old health nut who left his house for his morning jog and *boom*, he got run over by a truck. You just never know. At least I'm killing myself slowly. You got to take life slow, enjoy every minute. That's why I say, 'Every day above ground— '"

The crowd finishes his statement: "Is a good day!"

Mad Dog guzzles from one of the three wine bottles perched within arm's reach. "Sounds like you guys have been here before. We have some repeat offenders."

By two o'clock, Mad Dog has finished one bottle of Pink Catawba and downed four shots. Regardless of when people join the show, they always seem able to catch up with everyone else when it comes to drinking. Song by song, as Mad Dog's eyes narrow from the alcohol, the crowd's actions become clumsy, almost embarrassing to watch. So I move out to the porch. Ferries filled with sheep and cattle ready to graze on the island roll in one after the other. The more people that come to the bar, the better I feel. I'm a vampire feeding off the energy of others because I have very little of my own right now.

Robin from the ferry crosses the street with three girls and introduces Dawn, Lea, and Brooke, who are visiting for the weekend. Lea stands closer to Robin and seems to have more confidence than the others, so it's obvious that she's with him. Dawn and Brooke appear unsure of their roles, and quiet anxiety oozes from behind their polite smiles.

Robin turns to Cinch. "What time should I be in tonight?"

"Just be here by the time the band starts," Cinch says, never taking his eyes off Brooke.

I say, "Robin, you work here, too?"

He smiles. "Might as well get paid to hang out and drink."

"Ladies," Cinch says, "just ask for me at the door when you come back later. We always have room for three pretty faces. We'll throw out ten drunks if we have to."

Only a short time on the job, and already much of this is routine. After the Mad Dog show we kick everyone out, clean with push brooms, shovels, and a wet-vac, then we take our break at the Boardwalk before the evening shift begins. To show me what "busy" means, Cinch decides to position me inside by the side door.

Just before we go back to work, Haley motions me over and slides a shot across the bar. "First of all, drink this," she says. "Second of all, stand on the stool so you can see everything." She swirls the shaker and pours the rest into my glass. "Get with the program, rookie."

I put the flashlight into my back pocket and stand on the stool, placing my hand over the door to monitor who comes and goes. The two bouncers perched in the opposite chairs flash their lights to welcome me. Haley finds the matter more humorous. Every glance in my direction elicits a smile. One day I'm not here, the next I'm a fixture in her daily routine.

The pool of humanity pulses and moves with the music, flowing as one body. Within the small pond, individual puddles bubble, each having its own purpose and mission but connected in this common space.

The door shakes. I extend my wrist to prompt the people to show me theirs. Instead, two smiling faces, appearing much more relaxed than at our first meeting, shine through the glass.

I open the door and step down. "Ladies, please come in. Where's Lea?"

Dawn says, "She's with Robin getting us wristbands."

I remove two from my pocket. "I can take care of that."

I've already learned that a bouncer is more concierge than security personnel. The role entails making sure the guests are comfortable, getting them what they need and dealing with any problems that may arise.

Brooke says, "Such gentlemen around here, Dawn. What did we do to deserve this treatment?"

I say, "Ladies, I learned long ago that life is about service. Serve the women in my life, and I'll have a much more rewarding and happier one myself."

The innuendo, glances, and smiles remove all the mystery about where the night is heading. How convenient. Lea has her friends when Robin is busy, and her friends have us when Robin and Lea are busy.

Robin returns with five shots and drinks. Dawn turns to me and offers a toast. "To new friends."

Our touching of shot glasses officially begins the games for the evening. These games will not be centered on pride, individual achievement, or self-respect, but instead on blatant sexual conquest. The only question is this: who among us are the hunted and who the hunters?

These roles fluctuate as the night progresses. It's always the three women with two of us entertaining them. The other is either on the porch attending to business or—at least if the other is either Cinch or me—in the red barn having our own private party.

By midnight the foundation has been set. The shots, the dancing, and the superficial conversation have already transpired, so no one finds another bar appealing. The red barn might be appropriate to entertain at three in the morning, but not now, not with this crowd. The only thing we need is some one-on-one time to provoke physical contact.

Robin says, "I ran into Captain Rick today. He brought the boat down from Detroit a week early to get a good spot for Memorial Day. He told me to stop by after work."

Dawn turns to me. "Rick's a friend of ours who's also the captain of a seventy-five-foot boat called *Moderation*. His job is to take the boat wherever the owners request and make sure it's clean when they arrive."

Cinch says, "It'll be my first trip to *Moderation* in some time."

Moderation, which is docked at a private club next to the Board-walk called the Crew's Nest, has two guest cabins, a master suite, a dining area with a full bar, a galley, crew's quarters, and two bridges, one inside and one up above.

Rick is the host now. Cinch, Brooke, Dawn, and I go to the upper bridge. Looking at the stars reminds me of last night, and of Astrid. Why do I feel guilty? She's the one who said she doesn't want a relationship. The reason I am here is to indulge my appetites, wherever and whatever they are.

We go up to one of the bridges, and I sit next to the wheel. After a moment, Brooke coerces Cinch to escort her to the restroom. Cinch recognizes it as an excuse to go for another drink.

Dawn moves in between my legs and leans back against the steering wheel. I lift my legs to the dash, trapping her. "I thought girls always went to the restroom together."

She kisses my left cheek, following through to my ear. "Not when we have ulterior motives." Her lips are soft and gentle. She continues down my neck and back up to my mouth. Her tenderness paralyzes me. Releasing a stunted breath, I pull her close to steady myself.

"Uh, sorry to interrupt, folks." Cinch extends a drink as an apology. "I told Robin and Lea we would see the girls home. Judging from what I see here, I think you agree. Are you ready to go?"

Dawn turns to face him. I wrap my arm around her waist, keeping her close. "I think we'll stay here for a bit."

Cinch is indifferent to her suggestion. Probably because he has his own agenda, one that doesn't involve us. Before he leaves, however, he tells Dawn that Brooke wants to talk to her downstairs. She lifts my hand to her lips, promising to return with another delicate kiss. Cinch waits for her to depart. He says, "Let's hit one before she gets back."

I say, "I'll pass. Think I've had enough. I don't want to go overboard."

"Consider me your life preserver." Cinch dumps out a mound and divides it. "You watched too many after-school specials. Trust me. It'll help during sex. Right here on the dash."

Ssshhhump.

Ssshhhump.

Cinch leaves when Dawn returns. I try to think of a smooth line to recapture the mood, but all I come up with is, "Where were we?"

Dawn follows the script. "Right here."

We both know it is cheesy, but the whole night has been. The flirting, the lines, the games, all of it leading to a meaningless one-night stand. It's a trade-off, a barter of services for services. Morals and values are cast aside for the pleasure only another human being can provide. The last thing I'm going to do now is fumble around waiting for the perfect moment. This deal is done. I know it and she knows it.

Dawn pushes me back on the seat and climbs on top of me, thrusting her tongue in my mouth as the waves lap against the side of the boat. Her tenderness transforms to wanton thirst. She claws off my shirt and devours my chest, moving down to my abdomen, stopping at my belt line. She slides my pants to my ankles then drops to her knees, embodying my words about service.

I am getting close. Need a distraction. I reach down and lift her sweatshirt. "My turn."

"No, it's too cold," she says. "Just the bottoms." She lifts her right leg to allow me to slip her shorts and panties off, leaving them anchored around her left ankle. She shudders as her ass touches the chrome steering wheel. And again I return to my commitment to service. After a while, she pushes me back on the seat and climbs on top, carefully choosing her resting point. I taste the sweat on her lips and feel the vulnerability in her skin.

Finally she turns around and places one hand on each side of the wheel. I slide in behind her. Gentle rocking escalates to fevered thrusting, until I drop back into the seat in exhaustion, and Dawn falls back on top of me. I wrap my arms around her and squeeze for no other reason than sheer appreciation. What else is there? I really don't know her at all.

The next morning Cinch is sitting in the recliner with the bong between his legs when I return from dropping off the girls. He says, "How'd your night go?"

"Full steam ahead, Captain." I flop on the couch. "Man, I feel like shit. Let me hit that."

"Whuuuht? Mr. Non-Smoker, I thought you didn't do this one?"

"It's bad when you gotta party just to stand yourself. You know they're coming back next weekend? I had fun, but the last thing I want to do is get involved with someone. If I wanted that, I'd be with Astrid."

"So what's going on there?" he asks.

I pass back the bong. "Nothing. We don't want to ruin it."

"Then what's the problem? You haven't hooked up with Astrid because you wanted something like last night to happen. You just got the post-party blues. Nothing worse than someone who goes to the dance, is excited to dance, dances all night, and then complains all the next day about his feet being sore."

"You're right—screw it," I say. "I'm entitled to have some fun. I'll go punch us in while you get your game face on."

———

At work Haley stops me on the way to the porch. "Shep, you trying to break up a marriage?"

I do an about-face and head back toward the bar. "Dawn, engaged? How would I know? No one told me. Nice, really nice." I continue to the back room and confront Cinch as he comes through the door.

"I didn't know," he says, laughing. "She didn't say anything? Oh man, you got played."

"I don't care about that. I don't want to deal with an angry boyfriend. I don't need that drama. That little bitch."

———

Mad Dog cracks his third bottle of wine by four thirty, predicting it might be a four-bottle day. If excess leads to the palace of wisdom, Mad Dog is the supreme ruler. And he surely won't disappoint this weekend. If people have fun, they'll return throughout the season.

I move out to the porch. The second hand doesn't move fast enough. People come and go. I only reveal what I want them to see because I've returned the veil to my face, the one I've been trying to remove. Only time spent sober will dispel this mounting chaos. Fun is fun, but when fun becomes work, a person needs to take a time out.

Stiffness seizes the back of my neck as the heavy partying from the past days catches up with me. I roll my head from left to right, listening to each crackle and pop as if it's a cryptic message.

"You look like you had a rough night."

It's Dawn. I don't even look at her. I mutter an emotionless, "Hey."

"What? After last night all I get is 'hey'?"

"Oh, I'm sorry. You're right. Where are my manners?" I walk over and embrace Brooke and Cinch standing next to her. "It's good to see you both."

"Very funny." She turns to Cinch and Brooke. "Will you two excuse us? Brad and I need to talk."

"I'm working," I say. "In case you haven't noticed. I wouldn't come to your job and bother you." I walk back on the porch and sit on the stool. "You lied last night. Plain and simple. Spare me the drama and keep your distance. I don't need to catch heat from your fiancé."

"Things have been over with him for a while." She steps up on the porch and stands in front of me. "I needed last night as a way out. Lea recommended that Brooke and I come with her to get away, which is exactly what I expected. What I didn't expect was that I'd meet you."

I say, "Let's just pretend the whole night never happened."

"No. I don't want to forget it," she says, not letting me off the hook so easily. "Our time together was wonderful. Don't get the wrong idea about me. Before last night I've never had sex with someone I just met like that. I know I have changes to make. Granted, you figure into the whole situation, but I'm making those changes for me. You just provided a push. You made me feel special again and showed me there's more to life than what I was settling for."

I try to avoid eye contact but she is too close. I stare impassively at her. "Glad I could be of service."

She clutches my hand. The electricity of her embrace escalates the emotion. "Listen, I don't need anything from you. I don't expect anything from you. The last thing I want is to get into a serious relationship again. I have fun when I'm with you.

What's wrong with that? Besides, I know one area in which we seem compatible. Any chance of you sneaking away for fifteen or twenty minutes?" She leans in and touches her forehead to mine. Our eyes lock. I glance away, but our close stance and her penetrating stare offer no chance of escape.

Game, set, match. How can I argue with that? In a matter of minutes she has changed my outlook from never wanting to see her again to wanting to take her up to the red barn and reconcile in a more suitable way.

"Do you realize the position you put me in?" I say to her. "Last night you had every opportunity to tell me the truth, but you didn't. I don't even know your fiancé, but no one deserves to be cheated on. That's got nothing to do with me, though. I'm in a weird place right now, but I'm allowed to have fun. Still up for that hug?"

Cinch returns with drinks. "It's good to see you kids getting along again. It was a little chilly out here before. What do you want to do for our break?"

Dawn says, "We'll catch up with you. Brad and I need to run up to the barn for a few minutes."

The day I have been laboring through becomes easy, and the night stands poised, ready to accept and conceal me. Once darkness falls and the band starts, my energy will increase and carry me through. Unfortunately I'm not quite there yet. Post-release, I scrutinize my actions. There's nothing like an orgasm to force a person to think—and, more often than not, to think too much.

At the Boardwalk every sip of my drink pulls more alcohol than the last. The faster I get to the bottom, the sooner an answer will come, or the sooner I won't care. Either way, I will resolve the problem for now.

Since new people are working on the porch, Cinch positions me inside for the evening in the front chair opposite the band. Seniority after only one week. At this rate, I'll be managing by the Fourth of July.

The space between people diminishes. With their elbows tucked in and drinks held to their chests, patrons stand shoulder to shoulder in groups of three to four, hovering around their buckets, allowing just enough room to raise and lower their elbows. Not only is the bucket of beer economical, it's also functional: people can carry one large beverage rather than three or four smaller ones. Although the bucket might spill, three-quarters of a bucket lasts longer than four half-full cups.

Robin flashes his light, directing me to turn on the jukebox. I descend the chair and weave through the crowd. AC/DC's "You Shook Me All Night Long" blares out when I flip the switch.

A girl stops me on the way back to my post. "You should be more careful how you sit, or wear tighter shorts. With your leg propped up, it's obvious that you don't wear any underwear."

Her friend says, "Not that we're complaining, but you could scare somebody. I looked over Meadow's shoulder and there it was, staring back at me. Anyway, I guess introductions are in order—that is, unless you want to be known as Rod."

"No, but you're close. Brad."

The girl who stopped me introduces herself as Meadow and her friend as Lynn. In the fifteen minutes before the band returns, I learn as much as I can without really knowing anything at all. It's last night all over again, only instead of Dawn and Brooke, these talking heads are Meadow and Lynn. I know where they're from, what they do for a living, where they're staying, and where they went to school, but I can't say I feel any closer to them than when I first walked up. It isn't really conversation; we're merely exchanging words. True conversation is its own experience, and experience, not words, is the thing that brings people closer.

I direct our talk to a topic that is always well received. "You know, I used to be a teacher."

"Does that mean I have to call you Mr. Shepherd?" Meadow asks.

"Only if you want to be excused. Besides, you've seen my penis. There's no reason for formalities."

Cinch strolls over, and I relay the event leading to our introduction. He says, "At least our training program is paying off. It takes just the right positioning to execute a successful flash."

I now understand his comment about the faces changing but the roles staying the same. Tonight I'm following the same protocol: flirting, attempting witty innuendo, trying to determine which girl might be interested in me. So primitive. Worse yet, I didn't even notice these girls before they singled me out. Is that all it takes for a girl to snare a guy? Just pick him out of a crowd and make him feel like he matters, and from there, just get him talking about himself. A man is so self-absorbed that a woman doesn't even need to steer the conversation in his direction. He'll do it all on his own. He might as well say, "That's nice, but what about me? No seriously, what about me?" or "That's funny, the same thing happened to me. This one time I . . ."

"Let's not mess with this," Cinch says after the girls go to the restroom. "We're just asking for trouble. We've got our hands full with Dawn and Brooke."

"Do what you want with Brooke," I say. "But I think Meadow is my way out."

"Well, before you get too involved, I need a favor. I forgot to make a delivery to the Beer Barrel, and I can't break away."

No way. I'm not ready to turn my new hobby into a part-time job. I say, "Just go. I'll cover for you."

He says, "Can't. Have to shut down the front and count the money from the cover. I'm the only one who can do it."

"I don't know." My eyes scan around the bar. "I don't want to get involved in that side of things."

"Wouldn't ask if it wasn't important." He hands me a Marlboro Lights box. "Give this to that fat bouncer at the front, and he'll give you a buck-ten."

I stare at the box. "That's all there is to it?"

"It's a simple drop," he says. "In and out."

I slide the box in my pocket. "No problem. It's the least I can do."

—

The intended recipient looks like a boxer after a ten-round fight. I remove the package from the box and cup it in my right palm. I say, "Cinch couldn't make it."

My mention of Cinch is like smelling salts. *Ding, ding, ding.* He's ready for another round. Leaning forward, he says, "One-ten, right?"

I nod then scan the area for spectators. "Got it in my right hand." He slaps the money in my left. I shake his right hand, but I can still feel it in my palm when I let go.

He shakes his head. "It's stuck to your hand. It better not be all fucked up."

I switch it to my left hand and drop it in his breast pocket. "I'm sure it's fine. Catch you later."

Back at the Round House, Cinch asks how it went. I hand him the money. "I won't win any awards for that performance."

"Nothing is ever smooth with that guy." He thumbs through the money once, twice, then a third time. "That cocksucker shorted me fifteen dollars."

I say, "Maybe I'm not cut out for the business side."

"Don't be ridiculous," Cinch says, playfully slapping my cheek. "Just need more practice."

CHAPTER SIX

OTHER THAN THE FEW HOURS OF SLEEP THIS MORNING, I HAVE PARTIED FOR ALMOST TWO DAYS STRAIGHT, AND IT DOESN'T APPEAR TO BE SUBSIDING ANYTIME SOON. I am two people. One goes through the motions, rolling from one thing to the next; the other is withdrawn, watching a complete stranger.

It probably would've been more mature just to talk to Dawn, but look where maturity got me before. How pathetic. I used to go straight ahead and overcome whatever was in my path. Now I weave through obstacles, allowing them to dictate my course. I'm like a fish in a pool, turning quickly to avoid what challenges it. My only decision is whether to go right or left to sidestep confrontation. I barely recognize myself anymore.

Stein cruises up on his bike on my way back to the red barn and reveals a cigarette cellophane containing five small pills. He says, "This ecstasy should provide a nice boost tonight." He hands me a pill. "Rollin', rollin', rollin', keep them doggies rollin'."

In the red barn we split a beer to wash the ecstasy down and do a bump to carry us through until the roll begins. Why wait? At this point I have to flow from one buzz to the next and not let myself come down.

A warm tickle spreads through my torso; my fingers relax and lips tighten; my thoughts and movements become concise. The red barn is no longer a suitable environment. Time to head back to the Round House.

The activity in the street energizes me. Stein pulls up a stool next to me on the porch. We're at the top of the big hill, looking over the edge, ready to rush down.

Meadow emerges from the crowd, fanning herself. "I think I've sweated myself sober."

"We purposely turn off the air," I say. "The more you sweat, the more you drink. It's all about selling alcohol. Where's Lynn?"

"She wants to go," Meadow says. "I know you're busy, have work to do, people to see, blah, blah, blah, but after work come to the Skyway. If it's too crowded, we can go back to the pool or to our condo."

On the same seat six hours later, falling for a similarly direct approach. I'm so easy.

At the Skyway, Stein and I enter through the back door into the kitchen. Randy, the owner, whips around. "Oh, it's just you, Stein. I thought I was going to have to get physical with somebody. People from the condos think the back door is an entrance. Since you got such a sweet ass, I'll let you slide."

"You're so good to me." Stein says. "Do you care if we bring some girls back?"

"Are you sure they can handle you?" Randy asks. "You better bring them back just in case they need me."

Stein and I fish the girls from the dance floor. They beam and glisten with sweat.

"We need to freshen up," Meadow says. "Where's the restroom?"

Randy takes her by the hand. "Come on, sweetie, I'll show you the back way."

"Always the back way with Randy," Stein says.

I wait for them to exit. "Whew, I feel awesome. This is my first time on this stuff. Do you think we got time for a bump?"

Stein says, "Maybe a small one, but I usually don't mix the two. The coke overrides the ecstasy."

Cinch isn't here, so it's up to me to assume his role. "Who cares?" I say as I remove the small baggie and stick the straw inside. "Be careful. Don't inhale too hard. You'll blow the back of your head off."

Stein takes his turn, and then I inhale mine. I slide the bag back in my pocket as the girls return with Randy. My eyes begin to water, and I break into a sweat. I should have followed my own advice. "I need a drink. Anybody else?"

Randy says, "First round's on me. Stein, give me a hand."

Stein has a distant look in his eye. He probably overmedicated himself as well.

Meadow walks over and leans up against me, splitting the distance between my legs, helping me focus. "You are coming back to the condo with me, aren't you?"

"Do I have a choice?" I ask.

"No, but we want to dance more. Whatever you do, just get me before you leave."

Stein returns with cocktails and Jell-O shots. We slurp down the shots, and the girls take their drinks to the dance floor.

Randy says, "Aren't you guys the charmers?"

I gulp down my vodka on the rocks. "They'll come back. They always come back."

My feet anchor to the floor and my body is numb. If the place were on fire, I would die in the flames. Randy refills our drinks. The tingling subsides. By the time the girls return I can feel my toes again.

Finished with the Skyway, we get a twelve-pack from Randy and walk back to the condos. My supplemental fuel still powers me, but I probably only have another hour or so before my body finally rebels and shuts down.

In the condo the couples quickly separate. Stein and Lynn go out on the balcony, and Meadow and I wander back to her bedroom.

At this point I'm functioning solely on instinct. All meta-cognition has ceased. Whatever thought flows through my mind comes out of my mouth. I go to the restroom for one final refueling.

When I return, her body, stripped to bra and panties, glows in the soft light from the candle flickering on the nightstand.

She removes my shirt and shorts. "I was hoping I would get to use this candle tonight."

"Does that mean I should expect the hot wax treatment?" The filter is definitely out. I love it. Free to do and say whatever I want. I straddle her and reach behind to undo her bra.

She grabs my hands. "Hey genius, try the clasp in the front."

After a few more seconds of fumbling, I remove the bra and slip my arms through the loops.

"Is there a history of this?" she asks.

"It looked so good on you, I thought I might give it a try." I saunter over to the full-length mirror on the door. "Come stand with me. Let's see how we look together." I position her in front of me and kiss her neck. It smells like coconut. She leans forward and puts her left hand on the door for support. I trace the imprint the bra left with my lips while removing her panties. She places her other hand on the door and widens her stance. My hands descend to her hips with my thumbs resting in the dimples on the small of her back. I control her movement, rocking her back and forth.

My legs begin to ache. I turn her around. "Let's move to the bed."

She climbs on top of me and does all the work. I feel close at times, but then nothing. Eventually she stops in frustration. "What do you want me to do? Is there something wrong?"

The truth is I've pushed my body to the point where a release is probably out of the question. It doesn't matter, though. Right now, I don't care about anything. I pull her near. "No. You feel incredible."

She coerces me to stay until she falls asleep. We lie together naked except for the bra I'm wearing. After she drifts off, determined to take home a souvenir, I slip on my clothes over the bra and blow out the candle.

When I get to my bike behind the Skyway, people are inside cleaning, so I walk it to the road to avoid drawing attention. Once on Langram I flip on the lights and pedal home. The aerobic activity at the condo combined with my pedaling has given me a second wind, or maybe a third, or a fourth. I've completely lost count.

In the red barn, noise from Cinch's room draws me into the bathroom to listen through the common wall. What at first sounds like conversation is now clearly moaning as Brooke alternately proclaims her faith in God and Cinch. The X must be working for him as well.

I move to the locked door. "Is everything all right in there? Let me in. I have something to show you."

"Show us in the morning," Cinch says. "There's a surprise waiting for you, too."

I shake the door to test its strength. "You better let me in." Not hearing any movement, I push with my shoulder and pop open the door.

"Aaahhh!" Brooke hops in the middle of the room, pulling her panties up with one arm while reaching for a shirt with the other. Cinch is propped up in the bottom bunk with his back against the wall, lighting a cigarette.

"I guess I'd be lying if I said I was sorry." I don't even bother turning away while Brooke gets dressed. "Why was the door locked?"

Now fully covered, Brooke says, "Silly me. I thought it might give us some privacy."

"Are you ready for my surprise?" I flash my new undergarment. "I guess I should've loaned you this when I came in."

Cinch asks, "Where in the hell did you get that?"

"Stein and I went to a party, and some girl was talking how she only wears black bras and black thongs. Stein asked her to prove it, which obviously she wanted to or she wouldn't have brought it up in the first place, and then I asked her if I could try it on. She agreed and I didn't want to give it back, so I gave her twenty bucks for it."

Cinch takes a long drag and exhales. "Don't tell me you have her thong on, too?"

Brooke says, "If you do, we'll take your word for it."

"No, just the bra." I sit down on the bed next to Cinch. "I think I look good in black."

Brooke says, "I guess since you're staying, I might as well get something to drink. Anybody else?"

Cinch and I both request a beer. I try to tell him the real story, but Brooke returns too quickly. She asks, "Did you tell him our surprise?"

Cinch shakes his head. "You better go check your bed."

The smell of familiar perfume mixed with alcohol conveys the answer before I get there. Blonde hair strewn across the pillows confirms my assumption.

I say, "Oh, that's nice. She feels she can sleep over whenever she wants?"

"It's my fault," Cinch says. "I didn't want to take her home, so I said she could crash there. I didn't think you would care. Sorry."

"As long as it was your doing, it's okay," I tell him.

"Why don't the two of you date?" Brooke asks.

I kiss Cinch on the cheek. "Good night, dear. It's time for me to go to bed."

I disrobe except for the bra and climb into bed. I can deal with the discomfort just to see the reaction from Dawn.

She stirs when I get into bed. "Sorry, must've fallen asleep." She slides next to me and rubs her hand across my chest. I lie still, waiting for a reaction. She grabs the bra. "What's this? What the fuck is this?"

I relay the story I told Cinch and Brooke, but she doesn't find the same level of humor in the story as I do. I unhook the bra and fling it toward the dresser. "Christ! Why don't you get a sense of humor?" I turn away from her. "I didn't ask you to be here anyway."

She curls up behind me. "I'm sorry. I guess I was a little surprised and disoriented. And just for the record, I didn't ask to stay here. Cinch invited me because he didn't want to take me back to Robin's. I admit, when I didn't see you before, I was upset. But it was only because I missed you, not because I was mad at you. We're just having fun, remember?"

Her warm body presses against me. I turn toward her to acknowledge her advance. Our lips connect. She climbs on top of me. What began at the Skyway is finished a few miles away in the red barn.

Memories of last night linger like a pungent odor. The bra draped across the dresser represents another experience. I shake my head to dispel not only the vertigo from the ecstasy but the guilt as well. I know the dizziness will pass; I'm not so sure about the self-reproach. This morning should not be spent alone. It *can't* be spent alone.

After taking the girls back to Robin's, I find Cinch in the living room in his usual position. "One more day," I say. "Even after only a few weeks, I feel like it's been years."

He releases the remaining smoke from his lungs. "Today things might get ugly. After partying hard for several days, not sleeping enough, people will be strung out. The hard-core drunks will come out. Maybe we should go down to the docks for an hour before we punch in. You can see some of the tools we'll be dealing with today."

The sunlight revitalizes my tired body, and retelling the story from last night invigorates me mentally. If I had done it for the story, then telling it gives my actions purpose. I begin the story with Dawn in the bedroom yesterday afternoon and bring it back full circle to end it there. It awakes my ego and quiets my conscience. I can't believe Cinch and I are beginning the party all over again, but it's easier to keep going than change. I have to get through the day to get through the weekend. Monday will bring order.

Cinch gathers three regulars from the bar and has me share the story again. The same tale that triggered disgust when I awoke now lifts me to heroic status on the docks, and I willingly accept their admiration. The more description I add, the more they enjoy it. The only complaint is that I don't have the souvenir with me. How many times will this story be passed on? Hopefully not so many that it gets back to the other two participants.

"So are you glad you came this summer?" Cinch asks on our way back to the red barn.

"It's kind of strange," I say. "My favorite parts of being here are the times we have at night at the monument, or the cove, or the boat ramp. None of which I even expected."

It's a rare serious moment for us. Not that our relationship

is complete frivolity, but most things are understood. You don't
have to spend years together to have a bond like Cinch and I do.
You earn brotherhood—the purest friendship, trust, love, whatever you want to call it—moment by moment through how you
treat others. Whether people admit it or not, they're always keeping score. Little by little, you either build a friendship, destroy
one, or maybe just hang out never really knowing if you can trust
the other person or not. It's probably this uncertainty that causes
most people to talk seriously. They require continual affirmation
of feelings and thoughts because the spoken word is all they have
to share. Most are afraid to give up anything more.

In the red barn Cinch locks the door behind him and retrieves
the lock box. "Probably time to survey my supplies. We've been
partying pretty hard. A trip off the island might be necessary
sooner than I planned."

On one side of the lock box is a stack of twenties, tens, fives,
and hundreds, totaling $1,570. Scattered throughout are small
bags, several straws, a scoop spoon, a scale, a bag of mushrooms,
and a bag of pot.

I say, "There's an American portrait Warhol should've done."

To make light of the excess is the only way to downplay the
potential consequences. To abuse the indulgence is the only way
to rationalize the risk.

Cinch fans himself with the stack of bills. "It's been a busy
weekend. We have twenty-five grams left and almost the whole
investment returned."

"Is twenty-five grams a lot?" I ask.

Cinch holds up the golf ball–sized bag. "A little under an
ounce."

I use the opportunity to ask another question that has been
bugging me about why coke is measured in both grams and ounces.

Cinch says, "Not sure. It's a weird US/metric hybrid system
for coke. A kilo is equivalent to about thirty-six ounces, and things

go down from there. A half of a kilo is eighteen ounces, and a quarter kilo or 'quarter bird' equals nine ounces. I usually stay within the one- to two-ounce range, or twenty-eight to fifty-six grams. Consumer levels begin after you get below the half-ounce mark: a quarter ounce is seven grams; an eighth or 'eight ball' is three and a half grams; a sixteenth or 'teeter' is anywhere between one and a half and one and three-quarters. From there it's all metric: a gram, a half-gram, even a quarter-gram."

"I thought I was the math teacher. They never taught me those conversions in college." I still don't consider Cinch a drug dealer—not really, anyway. He's not pushing coke to kids on street corners or anything. He's pooling money, buying in bulk, and distributing to acquaintances for no other reason than to keep the party going and have a good time. I say, "Don't you ever worry about all the hand-offs?"

"People are always giving and receiving. Transactions define our society. It doesn't matter whether it's a newspaper, money, or information. People interact with one another only to gain something or give something. From the outside, no one knows what exactly is being transferred—unless the people involved act strangely. Remember, the key is to act natural."

All afternoon the Jet Express arrives with passengers ferried on all three levels. The waves catch the sunlight, juggling it momentarily before throwing it back toward the sky. The island has suddenly become small. When compared side by side, my days can barely be distinguished from one another. The only difference is what I do after work and with whom I do it. It's not déjà vu; I've literally already lived the moment, and probably only twenty-four hours before.

When I return from break, Haley confronts me by the side door. "Are you dealing drugs?"

I remain composed, reminding myself what Cinch just taught me, that people only know what you let them know. "What? Get serious."

"I know you've been partying pretty hard lately, but while you were gone, that fat bouncer from the Beer Barrel came in all coked up looking for you and Cinch. You guys can do whatever you want, but if you're selling that shit, I don't want anything to do with you. I can't have that associated with this bar. I have too much to lose."

"Relax. We were at a party the other night where there were drugs. Cinch knew the guy that had it, so he hooked that dude up with him. I do the stuff once in a while, but is that what you think of me? I mean, really, can't you at least give me the benefit of the doubt?"

She backs off immediately. "I'm sorry," she says, her posture relaxing and the attack disappearing from her eyes. "It's just that I haven't seen you much, and you and Cinch have been running around like crazy people since you got here. When that guy came in, it all fell together. Please don't be mad at me. I guess the weekend is catching up with me. Promise we'll have dinner this week. I just miss you."

After all the superficial party chatter I've heard the past few days, Haley's sincerity dissolves my disdain. But watching her slam shot after shot behind the bar during her shift transforms the warmth to acrimony. Who is she to judge me? I'm not the one who needed help getting home the other night. Fuck her. I can do what I want.

Knowing tonight's going to be a wild night, I prepare extra to take along. I pack five grams into one of the baggies and form the remaining pile into two six-inch rails.

Cinch walks in as I manicure the lines. "We need to get a bigger mirror. What's gotten into you tonight?"

"Guess who stopped by all bug-eyed looking for us while we were on break? Fuckin' fatass from the Beer Barrel. Haley jumped my ass about dealing and partying. What should we do?"

Cinch snorts his line except for an inch, which he rubs on his gums. He shakes his head, unable to speak. Undeterred, I do mine. The roof of my mouth goes numb. Cinch's laugh is like a forty-five record played at thirty-three speed. I read his lips: *Are you okay?*

I say, "Whoa, that's the line I've been looking for. We better hurry back. Put this stuff away. I already have an adequate care package for us." The surging endorphins launch another topic. "Hey, did you hear something running around above us this morning? Was that on the roof or in the attic?"

"Probably just squirrels or mice. Hope they don't fall through. Can you imagine being asleep and fucked-up when a half-crazed raccoon drops through one of the ceiling tiles into your bed?"

"As long as they stay out of our stash," I say. "Do you think we should move it?"

"Don't worry about it. It's safe in the box. You know, tonight there's an after hours at Bean's. His parents own a big house on the water on the east side of the island. They left today, so he's having people over. Since tonight could be a long one, I picked up two more pills from Stein." He pops one of the hits in his mouth and gives me the other. "About our visitor: We cut him off. We cut everybody off and just chill for a while. We're getting low anyway. We don't want to leave ourselves short." Cinch takes a final swig and drops his beer in the trash can on our way out the door to head back to work. "You take the side. I'll check the front."

Inside the bar, familiar faces surround me, two of which are fortunately foreign to each other despite their indirect connection. Dawn and Meadow have moved from opposite sides of the bar to directly in front of me, where they face one another with their friends at their sides. Robin and Stein stand back-to-back between them.

The meeting materializes like a car crash. Stein inadvertently bumps into Robin, then they both turn and laugh at the coincidence, followed by introductions. It's just a matter of time before they move past the pleasantries and talk about what they did last night.

A beam of light slaps me in the face as Cinch motions me to the front. I gladly flee to the porch.

Cinch says, "As much as I enjoyed watching you squirm, I need you to help throw somebody out. He keeps bumping into people and spilling his beer on them. Just watch my back." Cinch approaches the man, who is in his fifties, short and stocky, with a sun visor on backward and thick, curly salt-and-pepper hair sticking up through the top. He is wearing white shorts covered with so many stains they look like camouflage, women's flip-flops, and a sleeveless T-shirt that, judging from the fresh rips around the shoulders and the distinct tan lines around his biceps, he must've created himself not too long ago. Cinch says, "Sir, I think it's time to move your party somewhere else."

"What? I'm not doing anything wrong." His movements are slow but hostile, his speech lumpy.

"Sir, we've had several complaints," Cinch says. "You need to take a break."

"I'm going to finish my beer." He sways side to side with some back and forth. "You had no trouble selling them to me all day."

Cinch's tone strengthens. "Sir, I'm giving you a choice. Either walk out, or two of my friends with badges will take you out. No difference to me. It just seems easier if you leave and go somewhere else so you don't ruin your evening."

His body straightens. "Fuck you. I ain't leaving."

Cinch grabs the beer from the man's hand. "You're done. Either walk out, or the cops will drag you out."

As Cinch turns to throw the cup in the trash, the guy takes a swing. Cinch never sees the punch, but the guy never sees me. I rush him off the porch and onto the sidewalk. The police charge across the street. Cinch helps me get the guy to his feet.

"What's his story?" one of the officers asks.

"Too much to drink and took a swing at me," Cinch says. "It's no big deal. Just get him out of here."

The officers walk the guy over to the park and sit him down at a picnic table to evaluate his condition.

"I owe you one," Cinch says. "I never even saw the punch. I guess that's why they call it 'under the influence.'"

"Him or you?" I say. "Besides, I couldn't let it ruin your buzz."

Isn't that all anything is about anymore?

———

After our shift Cinch and I walk out the back door of the bar, both of us beaming from the ecstasy. The empty kegs in front of the cooler glisten like an elaborate ice sculpture.

He asks, "So what are your plans? I'm meeting Stein upstairs and we're going to Bean's. You want a ride?"

I point to the empty kegs in front of the cooler. "There must be one hundred kegs there."

"Hey, space cadet, you coming or not? Stein wants a package, and then he and I are going to Bean's."

"I feel too good to go in a car. I'm going to ride my bike to the Skyway and then to Bean's. Give me directions."

Cinch explains the way, but I don't write it down. After all the biking I've done, how tough can it be? Even if I choose the wrong driveway, I'll find where I'm going eventually.

CHAPTER SEVEN

EACH TWINKLE OF STARLIGHT CORRESPONDS TO SOME TINGLE INSIDE ME.
With each revolution of my pedals, the tension regarding Dawn
and Meadow fades. I'm free again. Goosebumps on my legs feel
as big as dimes, shrinking as they travel up my body to my head,
where they feel like tiny electrical shocks. I begin to sweat and
can feel my heart pumping through my shirt. My mouth goes
dry. Maybe I'm pushing too hard. Three cars pass. An eerie feeling swells inside—I'm being watched. I pull over to the edge of
the woods. The darkness attacks. Someone is standing up ahead.

I call out, "Is someone there?"

No one answers. I walk my bike forward. The figure doesn't
move. The lights from an approaching car chase away the darkness. The person is only a shrub. Two more cars pass: police. I
remember what's in my pocket. Cinch isn't with me to save me
this time. I must keep going. The Skyway's ahead. I need to be
around other people.

Twigs snap in the woods. Someone is following me. I pedal on, but the eeriness remains.

The sight of the Skyway lights calms me. I hide my bike in the back. A group of strangers are in the kitchen. I step up on the stairs but withdraw. I'm not ready to deal with unknowns. No one from work is inside because they're at Bean's. Why didn't I go there when I had the chance? Maybe Meadow is back at the condo. If I see someone I know, I'll come out of this state.

I leave my bike and walk. A couple approaches. I wander off the path to avoid contact. The soft lights in the parking lot comfort me. People by the pool stare as I pass. Maybe they're expecting someone. Are there always this many people around here?

Meadow's condo is dark, pushing me back toward the Skyway. I'll go to Bean's. I need to keep moving; I need to find Cinch. Maybe I should stash my bag somewhere. No, I'm not ready to part with it. Everything will be okay once I'm at the party.

I start fast but coast after a half mile, afraid to overdo it again. I stop and rest, but the environment overwhelms me. Someone, something is fucking with me. The monument is ahead. I ride around front and step off the pedals, straddling the bar while bouncing the bike back and forth between my legs. I can't stay here. My destination is only a little farther.

What am I running from? What am I running to? Perhaps the drugs are fucking with me; perhaps it's something else. Even the monument's friendly, protective stance can't help me tonight.

The stars and the occasional house provide the only light. Unfortunately most of the houses are dark. My bike light will draw too much attention. I know people are at Bean's, though. I just have to find the place. The landmarks Cinch conveyed don't match the picture before me. Silence has built walls, walls that I attempt to break by pedaling faster, only to be imprisoned a hundred feet down the road.

A car pulls out of a driveway ahead. The lights blind me,

concealing the passengers. I stop at the driveway and turn my light on. If this is the place, now I want people to see me.

For every twenty feet I ride, another twenty open before me, revealing nothing, only increasing the space behind me. Probing stares from invisible specters replace the comfort I've felt other nights. Noises from the woods, now on both sides, call out to me. What were once soothing whispers are now screams of terror. Nothing is back here. I should turn around.

My light catches a reflector on a car parked off the road. Several other cars sit empty in front of it, none of them familiar.

The path opens into a clearing that extends to the water. People are sitting around a fire on the beach. The smell of burning pine and the sound of laughter ease my fear, but a dark cottage to the left startles me. It's not the house Cinch described. Yet I can't turn back now. I stash my bike in the woods with a glance at the foreboding structure, eager to move away from it. I rush toward the beach. Something knocks my feet out from underneath me.

Daisies caress my face. I put a hand on each side of the rowboat-turned-flowerbed and push myself up, trying not to cause further damage.

"Can I help you?" a voice asks.

It is posed as a question, but the tone imparts dismissal. I move toward the voice, but the person remains out of sight.

"Uhmmm, I'm just, uh, here for the party. Is this Bean's?"

"There ain't no Bean here."

"Do you know where Bean lives?"

"There ain't no Bean here," he says. "You should go."

I feel him on my right and left. Maybe he's not alone. The edge of the flowerbed grazes the outside of my calf as I rush by.

I struggle to get my feet into the toe stirrups of my bike. My right foot locked in, I give up on the left. The stirrup scrapes the ground as I pedal. I keep going until I'm safely in front of the monument. I no longer care about the party. I just want to be home. Cinch will notice I'm not there and come to the red barn looking for me. If not Cinch, someone else will. I don't care if they're only looking to keep the party going. I'll give them the drugs. I'll use them just as much as they use me.

The red barn is as deserted as everywhere else I've been. Faces from the weekend flash into my head, intensifying my loneliness. I try sitting in the living room; I try sitting on the porch. Inside, something calls me outside; outside, something forces me back in. I lock the door. What if something bad happened? What if Cinch got busted? Maybe that's why I haven't seen anybody. Maybe that's why that guy chased me away. Maybe they're watching me. Maybe that bouncer from the Beer Barrel got in trouble and turned us in. I left before the cops got here. Cinch and Stein got arrested. The police must not be able to come in without a warrant. They're waiting for me to do something stupid like leave with the drugs. Otherwise, they'll wait for the warrant and come in the morning. I'm not crazy. There really is somebody out there. I open the door. At least now I know.

I smile into the darkness outside. "You're not going to get me."

I just have to get rid of the evidence. The money is not a problem. The bar business is a cash business. I'll flush everything else down the toilet.

I go back inside, lock the door, and pull the drapes. I'm not going down easy.

I can see outside my bedroom window even with the curtains pulled, which means they can see inside. I can't allow them to know what I'm doing. It might give them reason to break in. I gather all the towels and turn out the lights. Methodically, I cover each window with towels. If I eliminate all traces of the outside world, I'll disappear from their view as well.

Standing on a chair I remove the panel and reach my hand into the attic space, which is still warm from the day. But nothing is there except four dried leaves and an old sock. I turn on all the lights. What do I have to be afraid of? Nothing is here.

They must have pinched Cinch with all the stuff. The only thing saving me is that he probably didn't turn me in. He probably said I didn't have anything to do with it. Why did we have to be so stupid? I should just turn myself in. I can't leave him hanging. I can't let him go through this alone. But what good will it do if we both get busted? It's not like they'll lock us up together.

Stay calm. Don't do anything rash. Get this place clean and then relax. Maybe everything is okay.

I wash the mirrored surface and any plates with residue on them. I gather all the empty baggies and paraphernalia. I go into the bathroom and empty the contents of my pockets: a bag of coke, three bottle caps, a lighter, a pack of matches, a piece of a bagel, two credit card receipts (one is not even mine), a rolled-up twenty, two straws, a balled-up fifty, sixty-three cents in change, two empty baggies that have been torn open and licked clean, and four business cards from people I met in the bar. This is what my life has come to. This amalgamation of miscellaneous shit is the summary of my life.

I sort the stuff into two piles. One pile can go in the trash; the other, down the toilet. I scrape the first pile into the trash. *Whoosh*. There goes half my life. Now for the other half.

One by one, I drop the items in the toilet. *Plop, plop, plop*. Ripples travel away from each splash, reminding me of my first night here when I was in the water, free from my past but not yet imprisoned by this reality, simply existing in the moment.

The only thing left is the full bag. I rub my fingers across it. What a waste. I open the bag and dump the contents into my hand. Squatting down with my hand over the toilet, I wiggle my fingers, allowing the coke to fall into the water. The rocks dissolve before they hit the bottom. I return to the sink, splash cold water on my face, and peer into the eyes of the stranger in the mirror. "If I get out of this, no more fucking around. I promise," I say. "Please don't let anything bad happen."

A loud banging noise wakes me. I want last night to be a dream, but I'm waking into this nightmare, not out of it.

I stumble to the living room. On the porch the silhouette of a man leans on the door. His head rests on his left arm, which extends up the wall. His right hand is still managing to pound with force, although somewhat tiredly. I open the door. The sunlight and fresh air rush in as if I am being released from a coffin.

"Man, it's about time," Cinch says. "I've been knocking for fifteen minutes. Why'd you lock the door? Oh shit, you cleaned the place. What happened to you last night?" Still confused by what's happened, I stare back at him in silence. He barrels on. "You missed a great party. There were about fifty people there until sunrise. I went to Robin's with Brooke and crashed for a few hours. What the fuck is wrong with you? You still drunk?"

I force out a response. "You wouldn't believe what happened to me last night."

"Better than the night before? Bring it on."

"Definitely different. I freaked out last night. I thought the police were out there. I heard voices and thought I was being watched. It seems crazy this morning, but it was so real. Why didn't you come looking for me?"

"After Saturday night I figured you were with those chicks at the Skyway." He sinks into the recliner. "That would've been cool: Me, Brooke, and Dawn all go looking for you. You already dodged that bullet earlier in the night."

I flash back to last night. I know I didn't imagine the missing lock box. "Where's the stash?"

Panic seizes Cinch's face, and then he laughs. "Oh shit, I'm sorry. After you left, Stein and I were partying here, and I started thinking about those squirrels running around. By the time we were ready to go, I was so amped, I couldn't get it out of my mind. I hid the box behind a loose piece of paneling in my room."

"Good move," I say. "I was ready to flush it all down the toilet. Instead I only flushed the five grams I had in my pocket."

Cinch says, "Look at the bright side. One, nothing bad happened, and B, we still have ten grams left. Don't ever forget: it's just shit."

"But it's your shit."

"Don't worry about that. Can always get more. You actually should feel good about last night. You have things in perspective. When given the choice between getting caught and flushing drugs down the toilet, you chose ditching the drugs. You could've sat there and done it all because the thought of wasting it tortured you. I don't know if most people would have done what you did."

I'm not sharing his optimism. I say, "Most people wouldn't do drugs in the first place."

"But we aren't most people." He reaches under the recliner and pulls out a plate with coke on it. "Ah, there it is. Looks like you missed one."

I shake my head. "You're unbelievable."

"Screw it." He walks toward the table. "Let's do a line and get ready for work."

I step in his path, not ready to forget about last night. "It's so easy for you, isn't it? *Fuck it. Who cares?*" He shrugs his shoulders and moves around me. I grab him by the shirt. "You know what? I fucking care."

He pulls away. "That's your problem."

I knock the plate from his hands. "Yeah, well, I don't have Daddy to fall back on."

"Fuck you." He shoves me back into the couch. "You don't know me."

I scramble up and get in his face. "What's wrong? Daddy's boy getting mad?"

"Better back off." He pushes past me.

I grab his shoulder and spin him around. "Why? You going to tell Daddy on me?"

He lands a punch on the left side of my jaw. I fall back into the coffee table. He shakes his hand. "Damn, man. Why'd you make me do that?"

I spring up and tackle him. Intertwined, we roll around on the floor.

He pins me. "Are we done?"

I struggle to free myself, eventually surrendering. "Just get off me already."

He releases me. "You act like you're the only one going through shit."

"I never said that."

"You don't have to. It's obvious."

I stand up. "At least I'm trying."

He pushes past me toward his bedroom. "Congratulations. Invite me to the awards ceremony."

—

Clouds roll in off the lake, and an algid dampness fills the air. The patches of sky that have been visible for most of the day are now gone, and a dark cumulonimbus cloud has parked itself over the island.

Even Caldwell has given up for now. From the porch I watch him gather his belongings and amble toward me. I ask, "Calling it quits?"

"There's a nasty storm coming. Tonight's a good night to be

indoors." He motions toward the bruise on my face. "Looks like you need to duck."

"Good advice," I say, eager to change the subject. "What is it that you light and rub on the ground before you play?"

"Sage. It wards off evil spirits."

"Are you superstitious? You always go through the same ceremony."

"Not really. It's more like a ritual. Helps me find that comfortable place inside myself."

"You're a lucky man, Caldwell. You really are. I hope someday I find something I enjoy as much as you enjoy playing in the park."

He projects his trademark grin. "Most would look at me and think otherwise."

"Fuck 'em. They're the same ones who kept telling me how lucky I was to have such a good job."

"I just try to keep things simple."

"That's not really a secret formula."

"Doesn't have to be. Have what you want and want what you have."

"You just have to know what you want."

He shakes the change in his tip jar. "Variety may be the spice of life, but consistency pays the bills."

"Not when you're consistently wrong."

"Maybe you're looking in the wrong places."

I look back through the bar. "Don't have a lot of options here."

A crack of thunder sounds. Caldwell looks out across the lake. "It only takes one thing to give your life order and some purpose."

"And it only takes one lottery ticket to be a millionaire. Not much probability there, either."

Fat raindrops fall, accumulating on the sidewalk. He tilts his head back and catches a few in his mouth. "Tell you what, if you're interested in a new hobby, I'll give you some guitar lessons. Never know where it could lead."

I consider the offer. I've always wanted to learn to play but never had the opportunity. "Definitely have the time."

"Allow me to share a verse with you." His voice becomes rhythmic. "*The journey is lonely, and it's long. Keep your focus, and you'll be strong. Trust your heart, you can't be wrong. Find your meaning, sing your song.*"

"Who wrote that?"

"Caldwell." He looks back up at the sky. "I better get home. Let me know about the lessons, Shep."

The storm hits fast and hard. The streets empty. The heavy rain and wind pushes people to whatever shelter they can find. I stay out on the porch and watch the storm roll through. Going to be a slow night. Haley tells me to punch out. Not sure if she knows what happened between Cinch and me. I'm just happy not to be in the bar.

To avoid Cinch I steer clear of the red barn. I'll go back when I'm ready to sleep. The rain has stopped, and the clouds depart as quickly as they arrive. Walking on the seawall on the back side of the monument, I spot Astrid sitting alone on the slope leading to the plaza. I haven't seen her since our night at the cove and my nights with Dawn and Meadow. I hop off the seawall and stroll toward her.

"Looks like you caught me at my hideout." She pats a spot beside her on the raincoat spread across the ground. "I love it here at night—especially after a storm. So peaceful. Sometimes, I like to lie here on the hill and scan the sky for a shooting star, imagining the monument is watching over me, protecting me. The cool grass, the spongy ground, and the quiet absorb all my fears." I flop down next to her. She looks at the bruise. "Whoa, what happened?"

"Cinch and I got into a fight."

"With who?"

"Each other." Even the words feel strange coming out of my

mouth. "Not sure I agree with what you said the other night about the island being good for friendships."

She laughs. "I wouldn't pay too much attention to anything I said the other night. I'm not sure what got into me."

"Don't worry about it. I don't have too much faith in my decisions and actions lately, either."

"Seriously," she says. "We hang out a few times and then I start talking about relationships and being free. I mean, what's up with that?"

I lie through my teeth. Anything to protect myself from further embarrassment. "You were right. We both need to figure out where we're going and what we want to do. How can we be true to each other if we have no clue what we want?"

Astrid stands and straddles me, extending both hands. "Come here. I want to show you my favorite view."

We climb over the wall leading to the plaza. At the base of the monument she lies on her back with her legs extended at a sixty-degree angle, her feet resting on the column. "Lie down and stare up one of the flutes. Look up at the top. Inhale when the light comes on, exhale when it goes off. Blow away your fears, let go of your problems."

The fixed stare of the stars comforts me. I direct my eyes to my feet and follow the channel upward. I synchronize my breathing with the light and melt into the concrete. "What do you have to be afraid of?" I ask her.

"I don't know. Life, I guess."

"I've never felt more alive than the past few weeks."

Astrid drops her legs and sits up. "That's a load of crap. You're just running away."

"Easy for you to say."

"No, it's not. I think I do the same thing. I come here to hide. I avoid getting involved with you to hide. If I don't try, I can't lose."

"It won't be like this forever."

"It will be if we don't change."

I focus on the beacon flashing against the starry sky. "I'm doing the best I can."

"If you really believe that, there's nothing more to talk about."

I drop my legs and sit up. "What the fuck do you expect from me?"

"I don't know. I just can't accept that liking someone is really a good reason not to be with them."

"You were the one who said the island is tough on relationships."

"I was just protecting myself." She takes my hand. "Either it's going to work or not. If it's not, let's at least have some fun ruining it."

"What do you suggest?"

"Not to worry about the future. Let's just go out one night this week."

A wave of excitement rifles through me. I say, "Our choices are somewhat limited on the island."

"I don't care what we do." Her voice bubbles with hope. "We can go to dinner, hang out, whatever. Just the two of us."

I turn toward her. "I'm willing to try if you are."

She fastens her arms around my neck and pulls me close. "Does this mean we're going steady?" she asks. "Won't the other kids tease us?"

"I don't know if there'll be anything steady about it, but I think we're finally going."

———

The red barn is dark when I return. The smell of marijuana lingers in the air. Hoping to avoid Cinch until the morning, I leave the lights off and creep back toward my room. His voice cuts through the darkness. "Where you been?"

"Oh, hey. Thought you were in bed or still out." I turn on the light. "Was over at the monument hanging out with Astrid."

Cinch says, "What do you think? Did she hear about Dawn?"

"I don't know what to think. She wants to go out this week."

"Don't think. Fuck her. Give her what she's asking for. What's there to be nervous about? Pussy is pussy."

"But what if it goes really well? Or what if it goes poorly? I don't know if I'm ready for anything serious."

"Man, you're fucked up. Just go on the damn date. Quit trying to predetermine everything."

"I wish it were that simple. Life is a lot easier when you don't care about the outcome."

He tilts the recliner forward. "I'm sorry about before. I shouldn't have hit you."

"It'll heal." I continue back toward my room.

His tone is soft and warm. "You know, I cared once."

I stop and face him. "That's your problem, right?"

"I guess I deserve that. If you don't want to hear this—"

His usual sarcastic edge is filed away. I stop and walk back to the living room. "No, go ahead."

"It was high school. I worked my ass off to play football because my dad was a coach. But it was never enough. He just pushed and pushed. He would wake me up on Christmas morning to work out before we opened presents. Know why? Because no one else was working out then, and that's how I was supposed to get ahead."

I get us two beers from the fridge. "So what happened?"

"Blew out my knee senior year." He extends his left leg. "One pop and my future changed. All the colleges dropped me."

"Things seem all right with your father now."

"Not really. It's never been the same. It's like he thinks I did it on purpose. In some ways I'm glad it happened. I hated football, and I hated him for making me play it."

"At least he was involved in your life," I say.

"Could've used a little less involvement. Sometimes no one being there is an advantage."

I take a long pull from the beer. "Fuck it. Who cares?"

He rises from the recliner and tosses the half-full beer in the trash. "I do. And you do, too. Let's get a good night's sleep for a change."

CHAPTER EIGHT

THUUUNG. The keg I'm pulling off the truck nearly lands on my toe. Bob says, "You better be careful. That's the second time you've almost taken off your toe. Sometimes you get the kegs, and sometimes they get you."

The week after the storm, Bob approached Haley to recommend someone who could assist with delivering beer in the mornings because Bob had to unload all the beer himself whenever his helper didn't show up. After working with him I'm not sure which he values more, the physical help or the company.

For me, although the money is good—fifty dollars cash per day for three to four hours of work—it's more than the money that gets me up every Monday to Thursday at seven-thirty. I can make easy money in other ways. Working for Bob gets me out of bed and moving. If I go out the night before, the hangover is gone by noon. It is also a welcome distraction for me from the fight with Cinch, the impending date with Astrid, the uncertainty of what my life is becoming.

Every morning Bob and I make different stops to replenish the stock and cart out the empties. Some mornings are more difficult than others, as some places take kegs, some bottles, some cans, and some all three. Today the stops are Tipper's, the Castle, the Presshouse, the Beer Barrel, and the Skyway. Although the job is repetitive, it's satisfying because progress is evident in each trip from the truck to the cooler. Regardless of whether I'm carting in beer or hauling out empties, one stack always decreases and the other increases.

After we finish at the Beer Barrel, I hand the owner a copy of the order receipt. He stares at the five stacks of papers on his desk. "Oh, I don't even know why I try to stay organized. Someone just comes in and shuffles everything around anyway."

The interaction is soothing. Even though my conversations with the owners and managers are brief, they continue from visit to visit. The combination of what Bob tells me and what the people divulge provides plenty of material from which to build a story, and having the breaks in between allows ample time for me to formulate questions.

Bob stresses the importance of maintaining good relationships with his customers because he's also the salesman. While most distributors have one person for each job, Bob does both. He's been associated with the island for so long that he really doesn't have to sell anything. He merely tells people what they need, and they trust him. The customer contact feeds me in an entirely different way, though. The two or three minutes I spend with each person are often the most meaningful ones in my day.

"How are your kids?" I ask the owner of the Beer Barrel. "They're probably excited for the summer. I remember when I was a teacher, I—"

He looks up. "You were a teacher? What on earth are you doing carting beer? Summer vacation?"

"I retired. After five years I decided to see what else might be out there for me. The only thing I really miss is the interaction with the students." Honestly, I don't know if I believe that or not. I haven't really second-guessed any of my decisions. If the school didn't want me, I had no use for them. I'm learning quickly, once you quit one thing, it gets easier and easier just to leave situations rather than deal with shit. If I really cared, I probably would've stayed and at least tried for a fresh start in another school. But there's nothing fresh about that image. It would've been the same job filled with the same faces pleading for me to do more and me falling short.

"If you stick around here," he says, "the school's always looking for substitutes. Most of the full-time teachers either ride a boat or fly to school, so you can imagine how difficult it is to find subs. It'd be good for the kids to see a young professional person. Most of the young people around here are drunks or drug addicts." The irony of his comment forces me to look away. Guess I fooled another one, at least for now.

Bob walks up and puts his hand on my shoulder. "You ready to hit the Skyway? We can have lunch there when we finish."

Knowing little about Bob, I'm curious to see his interaction with Randy. For some reason I expect it to be awkward. Will Randy initiate his usual banter? Stein told me he thinks Randy is gay, but also that no one really knows because Randy never has a boyfriend. He appears to play the part, but he also seems to like fucking with people. If someone's not romantically linked to a female around here, everyone else's gay-dar goes off.

Due to the busy Memorial Day holiday, the orders have been large. Bob warned me not to let the extra weight scare me off. That the week after a holiday is always hell.

I lift a keg onto the pushcart. "Nice to do some actual work for a change." It's probably the most honest statement I have made in a long while. I have pushed myself so far over the line since I got here that I don't even know where the line is anymore. I feel cut off from my surroundings, but I have nowhere else to go. The island is now my home. I hope the new work and the fresh start with Astrid will ground me.

At the Skyway, Bob positions the truck by the basement door. "Wait for me here. I have to go through the front to open it." After a few minutes, his round, smiling face appears on the other side of the door. "Randy sure is an interesting bird, isn't he? He was all a-flutter when I told him you were helping." He walks back through the basement. "Let's see what the cooler looks like. Sometimes those other delivery guys leave it a fucking mess."

As predicted, food items block the entryway inside the cooler, and a stack of milk crates with assorted dairy products stands in front of Bob's designated spot.

Bob says, "You see? Some guys just drop their stuff in here and take off. They think somebody else should arrange it for them. The way I see it, there's only so much space in the cooler. If you don't take care of yours, there's no guarantee you'll keep it." He stands and readjusts his pants. "Why don't you handle the Lite? I'll straighten this and get the other stuff."

The Skyway doesn't sell draft beer, so only cans remain. Bob taught me that if I stack correctly, I can fit ten twelve-packs on each cartload. After my fourth load, I stop to wipe the sweat from my eyes. Randy barrels down the steps. Wearing only briefs and a kitchen apron reversed and tied around his neck as a cape, he stands confidently with both fists clenched on his hips, like a superhero. "Enough screwing around down here; let's get some work done."

A lady yells from the top of the stairs, "Randy, get some clothes on. What if the health inspector shows up?"

Bob restacks the beer on his cart, which he dumped due to the surprise. Still laughing, he says, "Come on, Randy, can't you wait until we're finished? We only have a little more to do. You're making us hungry. What's for lunch today, anyway? Italian sausage, maybe bratwurst?"

Randy simply turns and bounds up the stairs.

Bob can't help but smile and shake his head each time we pass during the remaining trips. After we finish, he pulls me aside. "You know he did that only to get a laugh out of us, right? I don't want you to get spooked."

"Oh, I know. It's all about shock value. I wonder if he's even gay."

"You might find out. He's never come down in his underwear for me before, or for anyone else who's worked for me."

My part-time job with Bob is only one of several changes that occurred after Memorial Day. Cinch's brother recently graduated from college and wanted to come for the summer to keep his parents off his back about finding a real job. Griffin of all people probably deserves a break, though. He graduated in four years with an engineering degree while playing football each year, achieving what Cinch failed to.

It's easy to tell that Cinch and Griffin are brothers. They share the same hairline and carefree disposition. But the more I'm around them, the more opposite I realize they are. Cinch always takes the easy route; Griffin likes a challenge. Cinch is a history teacher, Griffin an engineer. Even if they share a common interest, they hold opposing positions. Both played football because of their dad, but Cinch was a running back while Griffin was a linebacker.

I'm not sure if it's the athletic training or the way Cinch and Griffin were raised, but Griffin handles delegation well, while Cinch is definitely in charge. An obvious respect resonates between the two brothers. Griffin is grateful for Cinch pulling him on board and is willing to do whatever it takes to carry his share, whether in the Round House or the red barn.

What Griffin doesn't realize is that Cinch didn't have to pull any strings to get him a job. Actually, Griffin is better suited for the work than either Cinch or I. He is six feet two, but with a shirt on, his muscularity is well concealed, and his experience playing linebacker has taught him how to leverage bodies. The only strike against Griffin is that he's Cinch's brother. Everyone loves Cinch, but one is more than enough.

Griffin's arrival has pumped energy into a situation that even after a short time has become stale. Together, Cinch and I made one trip on the roller coaster and safely arrived back to the station. I'm not completely sure I want to go again, but Griffin makes the decision for me. *Please sit back, riders, fasten your seat belts, and make sure the safety bars are pulled down and locked in a secure position.*

For Griffin's first night on the job, Cinch makes up a new position called *floater*, which translates to *person who does anything Cinch doesn't feel like doing*. Watching Griffin from the porch, Cinch says, "I love new employees. They're so prompt and responsible. They come to work sober, showered, and clean-shaven. It doesn't take long for this place to change that, though. You want to stay out here tonight?"

"For a while at least," I say.

Cinch pats his pocket. "Well, I got something to entertain us if it's too slow."

"Uh-oh, I don't know if I like the sound of that."

"You ever done Special K?" he says. "It's liquid cat tranquilizer that is cooked down into a white powder. You do little bumps. Pretty intense. It's like you just walked into a fun house with the floor tilting; your head and feet feel as if they're five times their actual size. You just have to be careful you don't do too much. It can make you sick, or knocks you into a K-hole. I saw a guy do a line of it thinking it was cocaine, and he wigged out. He was on all fours trying to smash all these invisible ants. He kept saying 'the ants, the ants.'"

I tell him to go up to the barn and serve it up. Instead he reveals a small glass vial with a rounded red plastic top. "Why leave when we can do it right here with this bullet?" He cups the vial in his palm. "See this little handle? Turn it so the arrow is down to open the chamber. Now flip it over, bang it a few times until the chamber is filled, turn the handle a quarter turn to lock in the hit, and flip it back over. When the coast is clear, turn the handle so it's pointing up, place your finger over the carburetor, put the rounded part in your nostril, and inhale, taking your finger off the carb to allow air through so it pushes the hit into your nose."

With the bullet in his right hand between his index finger and thumb, Cinch lifts it to his right nostril, inhales, and then releases his thumb, allowing air to whistle through.

I mimic the stealth technique, only I inhale with much greater force.

"You don't have to suck that hard," he says. "Takes a few seconds to absorb into your system." His stare lengthens. He looks like he's in a trance. "Oh fuck, here I go."

A few seconds later, everything slows down for me, too. I stand on the steps in front of the bar and lean back, squeezing the railing to keep me upright. I'm stoic but erupting on the inside. I focus on the people coming across the street toward us, thinking it might help to reattach my legs, which feel as if they're floating beside me. Cinch, having both more experience with the drug and a head start, regains his composure and performs our duties.

The evening passes quickly as we take turns administering doses of the cat tranquilizer. It ends slightly before the band does, providing just enough time for us to organize the closing.

After work, we again choose the boat ramp for Griffin's christening, expanding it from a seasonal kickoff to a ritual for all new hires. Many names exist for what we are attempting to form.

Some call it a fraternity, some call it a club, some call it a gang; to me, it's a family.

At the boat ramp the wind off the lake swirls, seemingly unsure of whether to push us back or pull us into the water. Cinch serves up a blaster to each of us. Griffin passes one of the bottles of wine. Stein crouches down with his head between his knees, trying to light a joint. He says, "Come on, man, you got to hit this. Tonight's about brotherhood."

I don't know if it's the sharing, the forbidden quality, or the chemical effects of our actions that pull us together, but on the ramp in the moonlight, fears and doubts fade. Silence paralyzes us. They must feel it, too. They have to. How else could everyone be so quiet?

We all plunge into the water then reconvene on the ramp. Stein and Griffin go for a second dip. I stare out over the water, waiting for them to emerge. The moonlight reflects off the water on their skin, radiating a soft glow.

We pledge to stay until the wine is gone. The conversation bounces from work to women to stories from our pasts. I gaze wistfully at each face as the words and underlying promises flow. All that remains is to forge the commitment. Regardless of how right everything feels, words never last.

I walk down by the water and watch the waves wash onto the ramp. Tomorrow our words must become actions. I whisper, "Please, don't let me down. I need you guys. I have nobody else."

⁓

The next morning after helping Bob, I return to a locked door at the red barn. I shake the handle and pound a few times. Cinch peeks through the blinds. Opening the door, he ushers me inside and locks it. The lock box is open on the table with the digital scale and empty bags next to it. He reaches in his pocket and hands me a wad of cash. "This is for all the help lately."

"No way." I extend it back toward him. "Between what I flushed and what I've used, we're even."

"Consider it an advance," he says. "Things are going to start getting busy."

I thumb through the money. "There's two hundred bucks here. That's way too much. I just busted my ass for three hours for fifty."

"What can I say? Life isn't fair." Cinch sits down and scoops a spoonful of coke onto the scale. "Also, I think I need another favor. I have to go to the mainland to meet my guy, and Haley has me booked all week."

"Why doesn't he just come here?"

"He doesn't deliver," Cinch says. "I was hoping you could make the run for me. It's just in Cleveland. Would have Griffin do it, but I need someone I can trust. He always seems to fuck things like this up."

His vote of confidence does little for my apprehension. I survived one scare. Do I want to go deeper so soon? I say, "I have to work all weekend, and I'm supposed to go out with Astrid Sunday night."

Cinch counts the full packages next to him. "We're good through the weekend. You can leave Monday morning and come back that night or Tuesday."

I remain silent. This is a whole other level.

"I already checked with my guy. He's totally cool with it." He scrapes the last spoonful out of the bag onto the scale. "If it's too much to ask, I understand."

My gut tells me no, but I feel obligated. Right or wrong, we're in this together. I nod at him. "I can do it. Might be good to get off the island for a day."

"Exactly. You're new to the area. No one will suspect anything." Cinch flips me a package. "For the weekend."

—

Two days of thirteen-hour shifts with no breaks, six to seven hours of partying, and four hours of sleep elevate the already accelerated pace we have set all summer long. Cinch knows only one speed, and that is *Go*. Griffin came at the perfect time. I'm not sure we could've made it through the weekend without him. So much for slowing down and taking it easy.

Preparing to open the bar Sunday morning, Haley says, "You know, last week during the storm was like the fall and winter here. You always run the risk of being stranded, and you almost look forward to it because there's nothing you can do about it. It's as if Mother Nature raised her hand and forced you to realize you're not in control of your world."

I say, "Yeah, right. It's just another excuse for people to tie one on."

"Seriously, what are you planning to do for the winter?" she asks. "It gets pretty lonely here. All there is to do is drink and go ice fishing, and you don't seem like the ice-fishing type."

"I'll probably end up staying here unless something else comes along."

"If you're interested, a few of us plan to go to Key West again for the winter. We're leaving right after Labor Day to scout out living arrangements and line up jobs."

At least her offer provides a default plan if nothing else arises. But will I really be ready to pack up and go to a new place?

The side door opens behind me. "Are we still on for tonight?"

I know it's Astrid, but I turn around with a confused look on my face to make her think I need to check who is there.

She says, "Who else do you have plans with tonight? Are you planning another doubleheader?"

My legs weaken. "What? What do you mean 'another'?"

"Relax. We weren't together. You forget that you're on an island. A story like that travels fast. I have reservations at the Crew's Nest at eight. Let's meet here and walk over together."

I wonder who else knows that story. Does either girl know? I doubt Meadow does, but Dawn might.

I say, "Uh, yeah, that sounds good. I get off at five and some of us are going to the winery after work for an hour or so."

"You ought to be in good shape, then," she says. "Don't be late."

"Stein and Griffin have to work, so I don't think we'll get too fucked up."

"I didn't say anything about not getting loaded. What I said was, 'Don't be late.' I just hate waiting."

After work Cinch, Stein, Griffin, and I pile into a cab for the short ride to the winery. All I really know about Heineman's Winery is that Mad Dog drinks their Pink Catawba wine, the Chicken Patio uses their Sweet Concord in its barbecue sauce, and people are totally pickled after visiting there.

Excluding the vineyards, Heineman's consists of a long, wooden single-story building with three different points of entry, all with signs on the doors to guide tourists. Wine is made in the far left section of the building. The middle door leads to the gift shop, which is also where tours convene. To the far right is the tasting room, which has a long bar staffed by several tenders. Round wooden picnic tables provide seating.

Stein directs us to the rear of the building. "Go back in the wine garden and get a table. I'll get the wine."

The tasting room empties onto a covered patio, beyond which is a courtyard with stone tables arranged around a fountain. People occupy only three of the tables, but multiple empty bottles convey that they have been here a while. They are at the social stage of drunkenness when their separate groups have begun to intermingle. Several of them have discarded the small plastic cups served with the wine and are drinking directly from the green-tinted bottles. One girl has removed a label from a bottle and wears it stuck to her forehead.

I point to a nearby table. "Let's stay here in the shallow end."

Stein returns with two bottles of white and a bottle of sparkling wine. Bean accompanies him with a tray of meats and cheeses. Seeing Bean reminds me of the night when I tried to find his party. It seems like a bad dream now. Stein proceeds to fill our glasses with three-fourths Vidal Blanc, a semi-sweet white, then tops it with sparkling wine. The small 4-ounce wine cups encourage rapid consumption.

Griffin says, "How about some medicine to go with this wine?"

Cinch leans forward to the middle of the table, prompting us all to angle in. "On the back of the toilet, I'll throw down two lines for everybody and lay a piece of toilet paper over them just in case someone else walks in." He illustrates the plan using the scraps lying around the table. "I'm the wine cap, Stein's the cigarette butt, Brad is the cracker, and Griffin, you're the salami. I'll go here." He moves the wine cap in the direction of the restroom. "I'll do the work, then after I emerge, Stein will come in." He moves the cigarette. "Everyone know the order?"

Griffin says, "Why do I have to be the salami? Why can't I be the cracker? I hate being the salami. Salami is all greasy and smelly."

"Fine, you big baby, you be the cracker," Cinch says. "Brad will be the salami. It's just like when we were kids. Griffin could never just go along with the play."

One by one we file into the restroom, each going in slightly loopy but coming out stone-faced. We really don't need to be so discreet, because the people in the courtyard are oblivious. The alcohol has shrunk their universe to their immediate surroundings. The more they drink, the smaller their world becomes, which is fine with me because my tolerance for drunks when I'm off duty has eroded considerably.

Stein says, "It's time for a winery tradition called the Name Game. Everyone fill your cup. One person starts the game by saying the name of a famous person. It has to be somebody most people know, such as an athlete, an actor, or a musician. It doesn't have to be somebody nationally famous. The person can play at the Round House or somewhere else on the island. If I start it off with 'Oedipus Birch,' we go clockwise to Cinch, who would have to come up with a person whose name begins with the first letter of the last name I said. In this case it would be B. If you can't think of anyone, you drink while you think. So Cinch drinks, drinks, and then says, 'Bryan Adams.' That means it's A to Griffin. The only other thing you need to know is that if the first letter of the first and last name are the same, such as Donald Duck or Adam Ant, the game reverses, and single word names, such as Madonna or Prince, call for a 'social' where everybody drinks."

My self-induced anxiety resulting from our trip to the restroom takes over. I blurt out, "I'll start. How about John Lennon? L to you, Stein."

"Lenny Kravitz."

Cinch says, "K . . . uhmmm . . ."

"Drink while you think," Griffin says.

The wine barely touches Cinch's lips. "Kanye West."

Griffin says, "W to me, huh?" He drinks before anybody spits the rule back at him. "Winston Churchill."

"Charlie Brown," I say. "B to you, Stein."

Names flow freely when the game is on the other side of the

table. I drain the last of the Vidal and go to the bar to get more. Cinch and Stein are locked in a doubles-war on S when I return.

Griffin says, "They'd rather drink to think of a double than admit defeat by using an easy name to pass it on."

"Sammy Sosa," Cinch says.

Stein pauses. "Sam Shepherd."

"Susan Sarandon."

"Stephen Stills," Stein replies.

Cinch, stumped, drinks an entire cup of wine. "Sinjin Smith."

"Who?" Stein asks.

"Well done." I high-five Cinch across the table. "Famous pro volleyball player."

"Okay, okay," Stein says. "Uhmm . . . Simple Simon."

Cinch says, "Sergeant Slaughter."

"I see your Sergeant Slaughter," Stein says, "and counter with Sergeant Schultz."

Cinch holds up his cup to the middle of the table. "I think it's time to end this with a social: Sinbad."

Everyone raises his cup. Whether Cinch was thinking of the pirate or the comedian is irrelevant; he has successfully ended the battle without anyone losing.

I say, "Let's hit the head one more time, finish this wine, and take off."

When the game resumes, Cinch begins with Neil Diamond to Griffin, who follows with Denzel Washington. I reverse with Walt Whitman, but Griffin is ready with Willy Wonka. I pass it to Stein with Wes Unseld, which stumps him for a moment until he comes up with Uma Thurman. The wine must be kicking in. The names used are more random and our volume increases. Tom Jones—Jimi Hendrix—Hank Aaron—Albert Einstein—Eli Whitney—Wilma Rudolph—Randy Travis.

"Tiny Tim," Cinch says, reversing it to Griffin.

Griffin's probably the drunkest, but he still manages to push it back to Cinch with Tanya Tucker.

"Tina Turner," Cinch says.

Griffin drops his head forward, takes a deep breath, and returns the cup to his lips while he searches for a name. Drinking has become sipping. "Ted Danson. D to you."

"Daffy Duck," I say.

"Davy Crockett, C to you," Griffin says to Cinch.

Cinch smiles. "Sorry, bro—Cindy Crawford."

Griffin says, "Carl Reiner."

I say, "How about Richie Rich?"

Griffin chokes down his last sip of wine. "Come on, can't you let me go? I don't even have any wine left."

Stein adds some of his wine to Griffin's empty cup.

Griffin slumps forward with both elbows on the table. "Gee, aren't you a pal? What letter is it?"

The best thing for him to do would be to hit the stall again, but this time to discharge the wine.

I say, "It's R to you, buddy, going toward Cinch."

"R . . . R . . . R . . . Rodney Dangerfield. F to you."

We all hesitate, contemplating his logic.

Cinch says, "Nice try, dumbass."

"What? What's wrong with Rodney? You guys know him, don't you?"

Cinch puts his arm around his brother. "Think about it: Dangerfield, F to you? That's a good one to end on."

Griffin stands motionless. His face crimson, the glassiness in his eyes transforms into a blank stare. The buzz previously restricted to his head must've moved south. Getting drunk, the kind of drunk that Griffin is, on this sweet island wine means that the drinker either gets sick or goes to sleep. The former, although usually not desirable, is the best-case scenario right now. It's better to dispel the liquid than to have it absorbed into the body.

"Don't fight it," I say. "Just go to the restroom."

Cinch says, "Yeah, don't fucking puke in the red barn. The stench will never go away."

Griffin disappears into the restroom. "Hoo-awl!" I follow to ensure he is okay. The splash splatters like emptying a mop bucket. He blows out a deep breath and spits repeatedly. "Much better."

I say, "Throw some water on your face and let's go."

In the cab, Cinch says, "Tonight might be a good night for those mushrooms. What do you say?"

"When should I propose that to Astrid? She'll say, 'What did you want to do?' I'll be like, 'Well, I thought we could go back, eat some mushrooms, and hang out with Cinch. Nothing too special, just your average first date.'"

"She won't care," he says. "She loves 'shrooms. Besides, it'll take the pressure off you. We'll trip, then when we come down, if something happens, great. If not, so be it. What do you think?"

I drain the rest of my wine. "No promises."

CHAPTER NINE

STEIN AND CINCH TAG ALONG TO MEET ASTRID AT THE ROUND HOUSE. I can't remember the last time I wore clothes other than work attire, let alone a shirt that buttons up the front. I say, "When Astrid gets here, you two clowns have to take—" Her entrance clips my words. I'm not the only one who hasn't been out of island clothes in a while. The gray and white wave pattern on her sheer drawstring dress undulates with each step. The translucent material flows around her like a fitted cloud. Underneath, a strapless slip hugs her trim body. To avoid leering I raise my eyes to the sun-streaked hair framing her golden face. "Wow, you clean up pretty well. Do you want a drink, or should we get going?"

She says, "Let's go. You spend too much time in here. I want a piña colada at the Boardwalk." She turns to Stein and Cinch. "You guys want to come?"

Stein says, "No, you two love birds go ahead."

I no longer care if they stick around. Seeing Astrid has wiped away my nervousness. I say, "It's just one drink. Come along."

Trivial concerns fade when I'm engaged and content. The opposite is how I knew leaving St. Louis was the right move. Once the school district turned on me, every little thing made me petulant. Things that never bothered me before instantly became signs telling me to move on. Now I feel free, and hope is creeping back. Maybe because I'm paying attention to what I have rather than what's missing. It could also be because I can't remember the last time that I've been sober for more than a day.

One problem with living on an island is that it's impossible to go anywhere without knowing people. Between the people having dinner and those working at the Crew's Nest, Astrid and I don't spend much time alone.

"Next time we should leave the island," I say during a brief intermission between visitors.

"At least the company is good," she says. "What do you feel like doing tonight? Not that we have all that many options."

I stab one of the mushrooms that accompanied my New York strip and wave it at Astrid. "What do you think about breaking into those 'shrooms Cinch has? We can go listen to the band at the Round House, or maybe just wander around the island. It'll be nice and mellow. I don't want to be up too late since I have to leave the island tomorrow."

"Sick of it here already?"

"Just heading up to Cleveland for the day. Haven't been there before."

"I wish I didn't have to work. I would go with you," Astrid says. "Unless the Indians are playing, there's not much more than the Rock and Roll Hall of Fame and the Art Museum." She plucks the mushroom off the end of my fork. "The 'shrooms sound like a fun idea. I haven't done them since last summer."

We decline dessert, opting for an after-dinner drink on the porch. The building is the same Victorian style as most of the older structures on the island. A wraparound porch borders the front three sides, providing a magnificent view of the shimmering lake. We find two open chairs. I say, "I hear the island is most beautiful in the fall, but I can't imagine it being any better than this."

Astrid leans back in her chair and straightens her legs, drawing attention to her toned thighs. "I love it here in the fall. It's so peaceful. Most people are so busy all summer that they don't take much time to enjoy the island, then fall hits and things slow down. People know winter is coming, so they really soak up everything."

I sink into the chair, using the back edge to massage my neck. "That dinner was fantastic. It's the first non-bar fare I've had since I came here." An elderly couple in a golf cart passes in the street fifteen feet away. I say, "Could you ever live here year-round?"

"Oh, I don't know." She pulls her feet under her knees and leans forward. "What would I do for a living? I would need to have a real job. I couldn't work in a bar all summer and collect unemployment all winter like a lot of people around here. I'd go crazy."

"I don't know if I agree with your order. Maybe it's better to find somewhere you want to be and just figure out a way to make it work. Too many people let their jobs dictate their lives. I want my job to be secondary, to fit me, rather than me having to conform to it. Even if a person spends ten hours a day working, he's still away from work for fourteen. And there're weekends, too."

"But if people aren't happy during those hours at work, that will spill over into their personal life. Always searching with no satisfaction can be quite frustrating."

I identify with her words because that's what pushed me here. Whether fulfillment comes from work or something else is irrelevant. I say, "I just don't want to wake up one day and have only my career to show for my life. It's so typical to expect happiness to come from work because doing is being in America. The more you do, the better you are. 'Early to bed, early to rise...' What a bunch of bullshit. Is it the same in Norway?"

"Work is definitely secondary. Very family-oriented and much more liberal. People have more of a sense of duty to help one another rather than hoarding everything for themselves. They're more active, too: skiing, hiking, biking."

I laugh. "Not fat, lazy asses like here?"

"We're definitely born with skis on our feet. But it's changing there, too. You see it in the younger generation. There never used to be overweight kids."

"Do you think you'll move back?"

"Probably some day. I really miss the closeness to nature. In minutes you can be out of the city and into the forest. Just away from everything."

"That's why I like it here so much. I feel detached but connected at the same time. It's really strange. I guess I'm not making much sense, huh?"

Astrid stands and slaps my knee. "Not really, but I'm used to it. Shall we go?"

We follow the sidewalk along the front edge of the park. Griffin is sitting alone on the porch of the Round House. I'm surprised he's not passed out in the barn, considering the condition he was in after the winery. Cinch must've provided some powder to level him out. Although only the park separates us, I'm far away from the world he represents.

Astrid reaches for my hand. Her warmth and softness melt me. I recall students walking down the hall holding hands, beaming with pride and excitement. A subtle touch can be so powerful. The first girl whose hand I held—Sandy—comes to mind. We were in seventh grade and had arranged to meet at a movie. I remember sitting in the dark, staring at the movie screen, not even paying attention, simply feeling this tremendous rush of energy and heat.

First I let my leg flop over to the right so it was barely touching hers. Since she didn't react, I gradually let more and more of the weight of my leg lean against hers. I enjoyed that for a while.

Just being next to her gave me a raging hard-on that lasted the rest of the movie and half the ride home.

For my next move I put my hand on my knee so that it was close to her leg but still not touching it. It was all so casual. It had to be, though. One wrong move would have been disastrous. Sandy had the power to go back to school and ruin me.

Without moving my head I kept checking her knee, hoping she would place her hand there. The whole time I repeatedly pressed my palm to my knee to absorb the oozing sweat. Did I mention how hot it was in the theater?

To advance the situation I eased my hand over until I was touching her leg with the side of my pinky. Then I extended it like a bridge until it was resting completely on her leg. There was no turning back. I waited to see if she would push my finger away. No movement. Did that mean she liked it or that she was afraid to do anything? I could feel her leg connected with mine from our feet to our thighs. If she was uncomfortable, all she had to do was swing her leg over to the other side. She must've liked it.

I moved the other three fingers and my palm onto her knee, cupping it with my fingers on one side, my thumb on the other, my palm resting on top. She placed her hand on top of mine. I carefully turned my hand over and intertwined my fingers with hers. Relieved, I tried to catch up with the movie, but it was useless. How could I concentrate? There I was, sitting in the dark with a girl, and we were holding hands.

I squeeze Astrid's hand, remembering the feeling of that first contact. People consider first-time exhilaration a product of the innocence of youth, but it's just benchmarking. The more unique the experience is, the greater impact the memory will have. That's why first times are memorable, regardless of whether it's sex, driving a car, doing drugs, whatever. The first time marks an experience at a previously unattained level.

I know this all too well. The same thing is happening here on the island: I'm perpetually searching for the bigger, better buzz. Yet hopefully things are different now, and I'm moving on to something better rather than attempting to suck more out of the same stale situation.

Astrid weaves her fingers with mine as we approach the monument. Sweat forms in the palms of our hands, but I don't want to let go. I never want to let go.

I grasp her other hand and face her. "You know, I think a lot about the first night we went swimming at the boat ramp. Sometimes I wish we could go back to that point. Now all of a sudden, I don't want to go back. I'd rather be here."

I lean in and press my lips against hers, feeling the warmth from our hands spread through my whole body. Our lips linger. Seconds or maybe minutes pass. I don't know. I don't care. I am free.

Astrid moves her lips to my right ear. "It's about time you kissed me. It's only taken a month."

Climbing the steps to the red barn I question whether I really want to go through with our mushroom plan, but once I see Stein and Cinch acting like children on Christmas morning, I know retracting is not an option. It's easier to go along than explain why I don't feel like putting on a new buzz.

Cinch asks, "Are we making tea or what?"

Astrid says, "Of course—I always trip on the first date. I might not sleep with you, but I always trip."

"Tea is the only way to avoid the crappy taste," Stein says. "Just throw the mushrooms in six cups of boiling water for several minutes, toss a tea bag in a glass, pour the liquid over the tea bag, and it's tea time."

Cinch tosses the bag of 'shrooms to Stein. "Cook up a quarter's worth. Once we start tripping, we can eat another cap to really get us going."

Tonight is full of firsts: my first decent meal on the island, my first kiss with Astrid, and the first time we've used our stove to cook anything.

Cinch pulls out a plate from under the couch. "We might as well keep ourselves busy while we wait."

I pat my stomach. "It's been over forty-five minutes since I ate. I think it's safe to dive back in."

"Only a small one for me," Astrid says. "And I call first rights to the toilet. Just like that morning cup of coffee, it's one taste and off to the bathroom. Such a glamorous drug."

The boiling water rattles the lid on the pan. Stein drops in the mushrooms. A caramel hue clouds the water. The mixture returns to a boil. A pungent smell emanates. He presses the pieces against the side of the pan with the spoon. More of the intoxicant oozes into the water. Satisfied with the potency of the potion, he dumps the steaming contents into a pitcher. The mint from the flavored tea covers the odor of the mushrooms. He says, "Ladies and gentlemen, tea is served. No crumpets, but I left the remnants in the pitcher if anyone wants a snack."

As the liquid cools, the size of gulps increases until the last drink, which I must force down due to the earthy sediment swimming in the bottom.

Cinch slurps down one of the long stems. "Astrid, you want one of these?"

She shudders. "I try to stay away from anything limp."

Stein throws the empty pitcher in the sink. "Let's go to the bar before the 'shrooms kick in."

I nod, already incapable of speech. The special brew is taking over. I feel warm. My hands are clammy as well, and by the time we walk into the Round House the buzz has swelled within me. Objects at the periphery of my vision distract me. First a mosquito, then a flash of light from a golf cart passing in the street. My sinuses clear. I breathe deeply through my nose, something I haven't done since I arrived due to my perpetual Colombian flu.

The lights and sounds from the stage wrap around us like we are part of the show. Cinch goes to the bar to retrieve drinks, but he returns empty handed. Astrid reminds him about his intended mission. He just laughs and shakes his head.

Stein intervenes. "I'll go. Head over to that empty table and try not to stare so much."

Astrid leans over. "Watch the bass drum. It pulses with each beat."

I nod without seeing what she's talking about. "I'm going to walk around."

A burly biker over by the restroom is leaning with his back against the bar and his arms wrapped around a girl. He squeezes her ass as he shoves his tongue down her throat.

Making his rounds, Griffin walks by and does a double-take when he sees me. I don't know how he is even still standing after the shape he was in, but I'm in no condition to evaluate anyone. I say, "When did you get here? I didn't even see you come in."

I stare at him, trying to focus on his words, but instead I'm distracted by the size of the pores on his face, each one a separate canyon.

I say, "Man, I'm fucked up. We made some 'shroom tea." I point to the table where the others are sitting without taking my eyes off the couple. The man's hand is up the woman's shirt, rubbing her tits. "You been watching this?"

"They've been going at it since the band started." He looks into my eyes. "Dude, your pupils are huge. There's hardly any color around them."

I go into the restroom and turn on the water. Splashing water on my face, I stare at my reflection, giggling at how fucked up I feel in contrast with how peaceful I look. Three days of stubble

poke through, softening the angle of my jaw. Thoughts I'd nor-
mally keep to myself, I say aloud as if another person is present.
"Need to go. Need to be by myself." I flex my eyes and smile in
the mirror. "Yeah, fucked up."

Back outside, Griffin walks over from the couple at the bar.
"That son of a bitch had her bra off. I told 'em if they wanted to
keep at it, they had to go somewhere more private."

His words pass over me. I'm in my own world. I say, "I'm
going for a walk. Tell the others I'll catch up with them later."

I head out the front and hop down the steps. Which way?
I turn right toward the Crescent Tavern. "Yeah, let's just walk."
Another right at the Depot. "Time to get the fuck out of Dodge."
I go past the boarding house where Astrid lives. People are on the
porch, but I look away. I can't be around others right now.

Up ahead a snake lies half in the road. I creep forward. No
movement. Only a block out of town and dead silent like the
inside of a closet. I throw a rock at the snake. No movement.
Three steps forward my right foot nudges it. It's only a stick. I
pick up the three-foot piece of wood. It is damp and soft. "Just
me and my stick."

I press on, hesitating when I reach the spot where I first
wigged out that night. How could I be afraid out here? There's
nothing that will hurt me. Of all places, I'm safe here.

A gust of wind whistles through the trees. Questions race.
I don't have time to answer. I repeat the same words over and
over. "Why, where, what, when, how?" So many questions but
no answers. A car approaches. My eyes follow the taillights. Why
must I travel this road? I don't have a destination.

I angle into the woods. The weeds at the edge are thick, seiz-
ing my ankles as if waiting for a command to release me. A fallen
tree lies ahead. I rub my hand along the bark, still able to feel life
in the tree. "We all have our time, don't we, old friend? Why did
it happen for you? In the middle of all these trees, completely

safe, how did you fall?" I look around at the other trees. "Why didn't you protect him?" But as I sit on the fallen trunk, I feel no sadness. "You lived your life, huh, old timer? There's nothing to be sad about as long as you lived your life."

I place both feet on the tree and lean back on my hands. The neighboring trees conceal the sky. I recline and allow my hands to dangle. All the trees are so different, yet all so majestic. Each could meet the same fate as this one tomorrow.

A weeping willow stands twenty yards away. I approach. Sorrow penetrates. Faces appear in the leaves, gloomy, tired, old faces. "Why so sad?" I say.

A message comes back to me: *Don't be like us. Don't get trapped.*

I stare into the leaves. Is this really happening? The faces linger. I offer a response. "Who are you? How did you get trapped?"

No answer, just more pain and sadness.

I ask, "What happened?"

Again there's no answer. I peer deeper into the leaves, attempting to extract an answer with my desperate pleading. With each step, their warning presses more strongly. I reach for one of the faces, but it disappears.

You can't help us, but help yourself. Don't end up like us.

My hands touch the trunk. It is cold and dry. I try to picture the faces again but see only leaves.

A breeze on my back urges me forward. Lights filter through the brush ahead. My trek is ending. I question whether to turn around and go back. A few more steps land me in a parking lot. Still confused, I follow the side of the building in front of me. Around the corner, the back of Kelley's Restaurant is a familiar sight. I must've walked through the center of the island.

The stones compress under my feet, grinding and crunching together. The parking lot is empty. The dinner rush ended hours ago, but the late-night crowd hasn't arrived yet. A friendly face sits alone at the end of the bar.

Feeling more social now, I go in for a drink. "Hey, Caldwell, mind if I join you?"

"Pull up a stool," he says. "What'll you have?"

"Whatever you're drinking. Bud? That's fine with me."

His tone and cadence provide instant comfort. "Out by yourself tonight?"

"Just walking around the island." The beer is thick and grainy, but the cold liquid soothes my throat. "Caldwell, excuse me if I seem out of it tonight, but I'm kind of in another place. I ate something to enhance my mood."

"Ah, there's a little fungus among us. Man, it's been a lot of years since I've done that."

"I've got more. That is, if you want to, or maybe some other time. Uh, you know what I mean."

"Thanks, but I just stick to alcohol anymore," he says. "I noticed you guys been partying pretty hard this summer up in the barn."

"Is it that obvious?"

"Let's just say I know the signs, and I see things and hear people talking. Just be careful."

I press the cold beer to my forehead. "I know I'm fucked up right now, but the weirdest thing happened to me on the way here. Actually, it's not the first time something like this has happened. I hear things when I'm around the island, like someone or something is trying to communicate with me. I felt it the first night I was here. Something reached out to me as if to say, 'Welcome.' I know it sounds crazy, but it's like there are voices in the wind, faces in the trees."

Caldwell smiles. "Its water speaks and wind shows; what is possible, no one knows."

"It freaks me out," I admit. "Just now I was in the woods behind Kelley's and saw this weeping willow tree. When I looked closely at it, I saw faces. They were tired, old, sad faces, and they were warning me. The other trees looked so vibrant, but the willow seemed tired. It was like it was filled with souls that had lived unfulfilled lives. I could feel them urging me not to end up like that."

"The world communicates subtly. Most people don't hear or see the signs because they're so wrapped up in their day-to-day lives. We have to keep ourselves open. That's what I think drugs do for you initially. They open new passageways, so we perceive our surroundings differently and are receptive to new messages. Notice I said 'at first.'"

"Which drugs did you do?" I ask.

"What didn't I do? Pretty common story, I guess. I started with pot and alcohol and moved to coke and pills, eventually dabbling in some heroin. It didn't matter after a while—anything to give me a buzz. At first I only partied with my band mates. It was a bonding thing, almost a ritual. We partied only on Saturdays because we never had gigs on Sundays and would carry on well into Sunday morning. Sometimes we'd keep going all through Sunday to Monday, then sleep all day Monday and be ready to play Tuesday night. Eventually we started drifting apart. Our only friends were people who we did drugs with, and our Saturday nights began to occur on Friday, then Thursday, and so on. Before I knew it, the drugs completely took over. One night I was at a party, looked around, and didn't even know any of the people there."

I try to picture Caldwell as he describes himself. I just can't imagine him out of control. I say, "My thing is that I get bored. The majority of my life is so tedious and methodical. If I'm going to trudge along and go through the motions, I might as well do it with a buzz."

"Don't let yourself get bored. Exist to question; question your existence."

The words flowing from his mouth are like an IV pumping life directly into me. "Do you have any regrets?"

"My life ain't over, so if I did have some, I still have time to fix it. Each decision I made to get to this point in my life was made independently of others. Sure, other factors influence choices, but the bottom line is that individuals have the power to choose. At any given moment, a person can make a change."

"Why is it we only realize that after something bad happens?"

He laughs. "That's a whole other bottle of vodka. I'm still working on that one."

"Let me know when you figure it out." I drain the last of my beer. "I should probably head back. I got an early day tomorrow. Going up to Cleveland for the day. See you when I return."

Caldwell tips his beer at me. "Watch out for those trees on the way home."

Three passengers exiting a cab stop me in the parking lot.

"Where the hell you been?" Astrid asks. "We've been riding from place to place looking for you for over an hour."

"Sorry, I just drifted away and ended up here. Been talking to Caldwell."

"No big deal," Cinch says. "We made a game of it. We each took turns picking the place we thought you'd be. The only one I feel sorry for is the cab driver. I think this is the only place we haven't been."

I say, "I wandered through the woods behind here for a while then stumbled into Kelley's parking lot, so I went in for a drink. I was pretty fucked up. How do you guys feel?"

"I'm coming down now," Stein says, "but for a while I couldn't even talk. That's why we left the Round House."

Cinch says, "In for a drink?"

I shake my head. "I'm not into this scene. I want to get up early tomorrow."

Astrid says, "You really are unbelievable. You know that?"

Eyes widening, Cinch steps back and motions toward the bar. "We're going to go inside and let you guys get back to your evening."

"Our evening ended when he took off on his own. I'm done." Astrid walks toward the entrance. "I knew this was a bad idea."

I go after her. "Hold on a second. You're mad at me?"

"Not mad. Just disappointed."

"But I was fucked up. We all were."

Her eyes narrow. "You were the only one who left."

She was the one who pushed for this. I was happy to keep things as friends. I say, "I told you I was going through a tough time."

"That's why I'm not mad. We tried. It didn't work. Move on."

I soften my tone. "But what about the monument? I know you felt something."

"I'm tired of talking. Just go home. You have a full day tomorrow. When you get back we'll just act like it never happened."

"But—"

She turns and walks into Kelley's. I step to go after her.

Cinch, still lingering in the wake of the drama, intercepts my pursuit. "Just give it some time. She'll come around."

I turn back toward Stein and Cinch and shrug. "I guess it was bound to happen eventually. Better sooner than later."

Cinch pulls me close. "You still cool about the trip?"

Now I'm glad I'm leaving. I say, "Absolutely. It's time for me to do my share. We're partners, remember?"

Cinch kisses my cheek. "Three thousand dollars and a hundred miles isn't a simple hand-off."

"I'm just getting off the island for a day. Hold down the fort. I'll be back before you know it."

His tone is one I've never heard him use. The words are sharp, the speech direct: "Remember, it's just shit. You made the right choice that one night. We can always replace money."

CHAPTER TEN

I KEEP SAYING TWO THINGS DURING MY NIGHT IN CLEVELAND: ONE IS A QUES-
TION, THE OTHER AN ANSWER. I promised I wouldn't put myself in a
position where I stayed up all night, but as the hours tick by, I
keep asking, "What's another hour?" Then once that hour passes
and Cinch's guy Van puts down two more lines, I say the other
thing: "Okay, one more, but that's it because I need some sleep
before I head back to the island."

At five a.m. I break the cycle. I have to sleep. Van directs me
to a beat-up mattress in the basement. I close my eyes. The floor-
boards above me creak from the pacing of the people not ready to
give up yet. My brain won't switch off. I am so amped that it will
be hours before I go down. There's no sense in lying here. I can
be back on the island by noon.

To at least simulate a division between yesterday and today, I
shower and stash the purpose of my trip in the trunk of my car.
It's almost seven thirty. I'll just blend in with the morning com-
muters. No one will suspect anything.

I pass each town and each landmark along Route 2, trying to remember what I thought during my first trip to the island six weeks ago—anything to keep my mind off the three ounces of cocaine and the fifty hits of ecstasy I have in my trunk. Unfortunately I can't think of much else.

When I first met Van on Monday, his dilapidated appearance astounded me. His face was puffy, his mood erratic. He seemed like a person who was trapped inside a costume, and the people around him were indentured puppets. Desperation pervaded everyone's actions; partying had plainly lost its appeal, but they still kept pushing harder. At times I sensed them struggling to escape the macabre play they had cast themselves in, but in the next instant they would surrender and again assume their assigned roles.

Van told me that he made one trip a week out of town, usually for three days, to get a kilo, and then he would return to sell it and party until it was gone. When I arrived he still had half remaining from his last trip.

Looks like Caldwell was right about the slow decay of a person too wrapped up in the scene. Van had been up for two days straight when I saw him; he was going on three when I left. I felt the sadness in him right away but chose to ignore it. Initially I thought that maybe my perception was distorted because I'd never met a big dealer like him before, but now, driving back, I know it was because I was afraid to confront him. I was afraid that if I said the wrong thing, he might cut me off and I would have to go back empty-handed.

Van is on his deathbed. He might not be dying from anything specific, but he is dying because he has quit living, and I contributed to his death. I might not have pulled the trigger, but I pushed the gun closer so that he could do it himself.

My excitement to deliver the payload overpowers the regret

and fatigue I am feeling. Miles quickly turn to minutes, and minutes become hours. I'm almost home. It seems like I've been away a week. The anticipation, the risk, the lack of sleep, all make each minute of the twenty-four hours memorable.

Once safely at the dock I lower the windows, lean my seat back, and listen to the water splash against the rocks, waiting for the horn to signal that my boat has arrived.

Beep! I lunge forward. The car in front of me has already driven onto the boat. My car is the second to last to fit. I glance in the rearview mirror. The flashers on top of the car pulling behind me stare accusingly. My heart and stomach switch positions. It's probably a sheriff, or maybe it's a visiting officer who's working on the island for the Fourth of July weekend. It's still only Tuesday, though. Any visiting police won't be needed until at least Friday.

The crewmen release the lines. The cars on my left and right trap me. I slide down in my seat and watch the officer in my mirror. Seagulls escorting the ferry to the island circle above us. The rocking of the boat intensifies my captivity. Sickness swells inside me. I exit the car and pass the cruiser on the way to the back of the ferry.

The sun and an occasional spray of water ease my anxiety. A car door opens. Like a drum roll, my accelerated heartbeat mixes with the footsteps on the steel deck.

A voice says, "You're a long way from home. What part of Missouri you from?"

I avoid eye contact. Just act natural. He'll know only what you let him know. I release the words with a casual exhale. "St. Louis. Well, it used to be St. Louis. I'm living at the Bay now."

"You must've driven all night to get here so early. That would explain your little siesta back on the dock. I know that drive all too well. I was stationed in St. Louis at Fort Lindenwood when I was in the service."

I don't bother correcting his assumption about the drive and instead turn the conversation back on him, inquiring about the purpose of his visit to the island. He tells me he has to pick up a prisoner who was arrested for disorderly conduct on the island and has three outstanding warrants on the mainland. He says, "This jack-off will be celebrating Independence Day behind bars in the county jail."

Even after talking with the sheriff for the entire ferry ride, an uneasy feeling remains as he follows me off the boat and into town. With each glance in the mirror, I swallow harder, pushing the lump in my throat back toward my stomach to reside with the rest of the tension from the trip.

Passing the Round House, Cinch and Griffin stand agape on the porch like suspended marionettes when they notice the car following me. Almost makes the scare worth it. I park in the back, finally in the clear.

Cinch meets me in the parking lot. "How'd everything go?"

I dig out the package from the trunk. "As well as can be expected."

He rubs his hands together in greedy anticipation. "I was worried as it was, but I about shit my pants when I saw that sheriff following you."

"How do you think I felt when he pulled behind me on the boat and came to chat when I got out for some air? The whole time I'm trying not to face him because I'm worried about having a coke ring around my nose."

Cinch takes the package from me. "Were you partying on the drive back?"

"No, but we were up late, and I couldn't sleep. Waited until the morning to blend into traffic. I feel pretty good overall, but I'll probably hit the wall later."

He says, "Good thing you and I have the night off."

My legs are shaky on the stairs. I could actually use a drink and should probably eat, too, but somehow I don't see the latter happening.

Cinch locks the door behind us and opens the package at the table. "Let's have a look at the goods. We finally ran out Sunday night, so I'm jonesin'."

"You should be happy with the score. Three ounces and fifty hits of X for the low, low, low price of three G's. It's all chunk, too. I watched him take it off the block. He had a glass pie pan with literally half a brick of coke and kept breaking off chunks until the scale read eighty-four grams."

Cinch lays the largest chunk on the scale. His eyes bulge as "50.7" registers on the scale.

Tonight will be about indulgence. Plenty of time to worry about sales later. After what I've been through in the past day, I'm going to enjoy it. I have to. Why else would I put myself through all this hassle?

———

After our second bottle of wine at the winery, Cinch says, "Should we get another? We can't end on an even number."

The trip here was my idea. I needed something to allay the tension and ease me into the evening. At this point I'm not much more than a bag of blood. I surrender. "Okay, but then I need to go lie down for a few hours. If I cash in now, I'll be able to rebound later."

Cinch is not ready to let me off so easily. He says, "Why don't we just pop a tab? That'll give you a boost."

I shake my head, which feels like a twenty-pound sandbag. "Dude, I learned my lesson last time. I'm drunk, tired, and haven't eaten or slept in over a day. I need some down time. I don't want another paranoid episode like before. I'll be fine later."

"Whooh." I let out a deep breath and thrust forward in darkness. Completely covered in sweat, I remove the blanket draped over me and stand. A note stares back at me from the coffee table. *Meet us at the Skyway.* Still drunk, I fall back on the couch.

It's only one a.m. Plenty of time to rally. I debate whether or not to drop a hit of ecstasy. Cinch probably has by now. I don't want to be left out, but by the time I get going he'll be coming down. Who am I trying to fool? Whenever there's doubt, say "fuck it" and do it anyway. Rationalization is foreplay with one's conscience.

Riding my bike in a straight line is difficult. Probably should've just gone to bed. But it's too late to turn back now. I never did eat, so the ecstasy will hit quick and strong.

I stash my bike behind the Skyway and go up the back stairs, my legs burning from the ride.

Randy is inside. He says, "Shep, where you been? Your boyfriend and Astrid just left for Kelley's." A concerned look washes over him. Dizziness prohibits my response. He hands me a bottle of water. "Jesus, are you okay? You're white as a sheet."

I shuffle to the counter, trying to ignore the tiny flashes dancing around me. The water is gone in two drinks. I ask for a vodka and soda. He returns with a full twenty-ounce tumbler.

I gulp the drink. "I guess the ride took a lot out of me."

"That's why I don't exercise," he says. "Too consuming. Cinch told me to tell you to call if you got here and wanted to go to the after hours at Bean's. You don't want to repeat what happened last time."

"You know about that, too? Man, it's impossible for people to keep stuff to themselves on this island."

"Don't worry about it. I've been there before."

His comment takes me by surprise. I try to slow my roll and reconsider his words. "Do you still partake?"

His brow rises, lifting the corners of his mouth as well. "Occasionally. Why, you got some?"

I pat the side of my pocket. "Always."

"Let me help the bartenders close and then we can party. Don't worry about Cinch and those guys. I can give you a ride to Bean's if you still want to go."

"I bet you can," I say, trying to think things through clearly, but I'm rolling too hard. If things get weird, I'll tell him I need to go meet those guys.

I wait on the back steps. Sounds from the people at the pool echo in the empty night. Looking at the condos reminds me of Meadow. I'll probably never see her again. She's a cool girl, but then again so is Dawn. So is Astrid, for that matter. What the hell am I looking for?

Randy gives me the all-clear sign. "You need another drink?"

I look down at my empty cup. "I guess so. I'll get it, though. You've been working all day."

"No, you got other things to tend to. Just throw it down on the end of the bar."

The whole action takes only seconds. Repetition over the past months has standardized the process. I hand him a rolled-up bill. "Did you used to party a lot?"

"Yeah, I was your age in the late 80s, living in Fort Lauderdale." He snorts a line. "Back then, there were two things you were guaranteed to find around gay men: good music and drugs. But things had to be kept underground. Drugs were more acceptable than outward homosexuality then. You had to be a closeted gay, whereas now you need to be a closeted drugee."

"What's your deal with all that?" I ask him. "I know a lot of it is purely to fuck with people, but give me a straight answer."

"A straight answer about being gay? That's a good one. I'm

just open. I've had experiences both ways—some good, some bad. All experiences serve to pleasure. A person can have a completely satisfying sexual experience all alone. What's that, monosexual? From there one adds elements according to one's attraction toward certain attributes or features. Tall, short, blonde, brunette, thin, fat, black, white, male, female." He inhales another line. "All those things will vary from time to time. Sexuality is not a matter of orientation. More like an appetite. A person might be a beef eater and eat steak every night of the week, but occasionally he's going to crave a piece of fish or some pasta. The main thing is that a person has to be open and honest with himself, which most people aren't."

"I don't know. It just never sounded that enticing to have a cock shoved in me."

"Not for me, either. Maybe a finger occasionally, but I'm more the giver than the receiver. You've never been with a man?"

I do another line, searching for the courage to share what only one other person knows. "When I was twelve." I pinch my nostrils and sniff, releasing my nose to allow air to whistle through and pull back lingering fragments. "One of my friends and I, you know, would touch each other and stuff, and get each other off. But nothing since then."

"What makes you think you're really that different now? Back then you trusted him and enjoyed the feeling you got from it, so you did it. That's what kills me. Most guys have had the same experience, then they run from it their entire lives rather than accepting and understanding it. Sexuality fluctuates. Emotion is what complicates it all. For example, if two people are attracted to one another and they become emotionally involved, let's say married or even living together, the question surfaces, 'Do they have responsibility to each other to resist temptation with others?' If attraction is like an appetite, is a person supposed to resist spontaneous cravings? If he doesn't, should he tell the other person? If one indulges and the other doesn't, how will each react? It gets really messy."

"Don't look to me for any answers. That's the part that fucks me up every time. I deal with it by keeping my obligations to a minimum. If at some point I want to commit to another person, I will, but until then, I'll do what I want."

Randy pours more vodka in my cup. "One thing for sure, there ain't a woman around that can suck a dick like a man. It's all suction and tongue."

His proximate stance rifles a shiver of discomfort through me—not because I want to leave, but because I'm aroused.

Randy says, "Women try to use their teeth like they're teasing you, like the danger of it all adds to the excitement. When they ask me about giving head, I always tell them—"

I turn toward him, fully erect. Our lips meet. The stubble on his chin scratches my face. His lips are strong and his tongue wraps around mine convincingly. He reaches down and slides his hand down my shorts. I want to pull away but can't. It all feels too good.

I break our joined lips but still remain close enough for him to keep holding me. "What if those guys come looking for me?"

"We can stop if you want. Or we can go out to my office."

I surrender to the moment. "Okay, let's go."

I button my pants, chug the rest of my drink, and follow him out to the modular home that serves as the office. Maybe I should just hop on my bike and ride away. I don't know if it's the drugs, the alcohol, or his convincing speech, but I can't stop. Unlike my other stories, however, I already know this is one that can't be shared with anyone.

The office is divided into four rooms: two bedrooms, one serving as Randy's office and the other as a storage room; a large living room, which is equipped with two recliners and an L-shaped leather couch; and a bathroom. A big-screen TV stands in one corner facing the couch, and there's a desk in the opposite corner. Fortunately Randy doesn't turn on the lights. As long as I can't see what I'm doing, I can create whatever picture I want.

Randy and I tear off one another's clothes like reunited lovers. I fall back onto the leather sofa, completely naked. Randy puts his lips around me and sucks slowly at first, gradually increasing the force. I lean back, numb from my self-prescribed medication, yet totally invigorated by the treatment administered by Randy. The muscles in my legs and ass spasm.

I lift him from my groin. "Wait, let me do you." I take him in my hand while pushing my lips up and down, never breaking the seal, remembering what he said about suction and tongue. I rock back and forth on him while he plays with me with his foot. I feel him soften in my mouth. I increase the intensity.

Randy stops me. "I don't think it's going to happen. Sometimes when I party I can't get off. But I want you to." He leans me back on the floor, again sucking vigorously. I picture Astrid, but as his coarse hands rub me, I'm reminded that it's another man who is pleasuring me. The contractions in my legs and ass begin again. Each time he swallows, I go deeper in his throat. I'm only seconds away. Saliva runs into the crack of my ass. His finger slides inside me. I explode, thrusting my hips forward, feeling him swallow the tip and all the discharge.

Randy continues to suck, eventually leaving me cleaner than when we started. He pulls off me. "I guess I should get you out to Bean's."

The reality of what happened settles in. I can't face the others. "Just take me home. I've had enough for one day."

The drive is quiet. I stare out the window feeling like a whore who has just pleasured his sugar daddy.

"Don't worry about anything," Randy says as he pulls up behind the red barn. "We had some drinks and you went home. Nobody has to know any different, and don't think this has to happen on a regular basis. It's a one-shot deal—no pun intended—unless you want differently." He grabs my hand as I get out of the car. "I told you another man knows how to suck a dick, huh?"

———

"What happened to you last night?" The voice from my doorway is sweet and familiar. Astrid enters and sits on the edge of my bed. "Cinch kept telling me you were going to meet us out, but when you never showed, I thought maybe he was stroking me to keep me partying with him."

I try to sit up, but the axe stuck in the middle of my forehead forces me back down. "I, uh, was going to come out, but once I got to the Skyway and had a drink, I was tired, so I just came home." I look away, unable to keep eye contact with her.

"I also wanted to make sure you're not weirded out by what happened before you left." She leans over and kisses me on the cheek. "We're still friends."

I smile, but I'm not thinking about her. I'm only thinking of the real reason I didn't see her last night. I say, "I am so sorry about the other night." The shame from last night has transformed into fear that others may find out. I roll her on her back. She looks surprised, but she pulls me close. Our lips lock in a fevered embrace. I slide my hand to her crotch, pressing my groin into her thigh, attempting to prove to her, and to myself, that I'm still a man. Our breathing becomes heavier, our movements more emotional.

"Wait. We can't." She slides out from under me. "I have to go. I have to be at work."

I grab her hand. "Don't go. I screwed up. Give me another chance."

"No, this isn't right. I've got to go." She pulls away. "I'll see you around."

I wait for my arousal to dissipate and move to the shower.

Maybe I can simultaneously scrub away the physical traces and the subsequent confusion from last night. I wanted to move away from the person I was becoming by coming to the island. But in the past twenty-four hours, I've not only destroyed the person I once was, but also ruined any progress I may have made since my arrival.

I get ready for work quickly and quietly, still not yet ready to face the others. If I can be out early, I won't have to deal with them until they show up for work. I need to build some confidence around other people first. I need to convince myself of the lie I'm going to tell about last night. Strangers don't see through the cracks as easily as people who know you.

"What's bothering you today?" Cinch asks while on break before the evening shift. "You've been out of it all day."

I've been trying to act normal, or at least steer clear of anyone I know, throughout the day, but the question was inevitable. He sees the crack. We're too close for me to be able to hide anything.

I say, "I don't know what's wrong. I guess the trip took a lot out of me. Maybe my body is finally rebelling against the torture I've put it through. Tonight I should just take it easy and get a good night's sleep. Birch arrives tomorrow, so it might be my last chance for any rest until after the Fourth."

Cinch offers to find someone to work for me, but time off is exactly what I don't need. I have to stay busy and keep my mind occupied. I vow to stay on the porch and out of the mix.

He says, "Relax now—Brooke called. Things are going to get interesting around here. She and Dawn are coming this weekend. Have you talked to Dawn?"

"No, and I don't plan to. I'm not getting involved in her mess."

"Too late. She broke off her engagement."

I push my hand through my hair in frustration. "Well, have fun hanging out with both of them because I ain't going to be there."

"Whatever happens, we'll be busy. People will party to get ready for the holiday, party to get through the holiday, and party once it's all over."

CHAPTER ELEVEN

"SHEP, YOU UP YET?" Birch's voice resonates from the living room like the engine of a rescue plane. He's early, something you never expect from musicians, especially in the morning.

I wrap a towel around my waist and emerge from the bathroom, still dripping with water. He is exactly the person I need to see right now, a familiar frame of reference to regroup around. I understand the person I am when I'm with Birch. More than anything, he's someone from outside the party circle. I love my friends here, but if the drugs were removed, how much time would we really share? That's probably why there's so much false brotherhood surrounding the party scene. People don't want to admit the real reason they're hanging out, so they overemphasize the true value of their friendships.

Birch's return marks the beginning of the entertainment cycle again. Working at the Round House is like working in a tollbooth. People pass through on a regular basis, and although our interactions are brief, I learn a lot about them because of the frequency of their visits. Not to mention that reunions are always an excuse to party.

"What's happening, baby?" He hugs me, lifting me off the ground.

I catch my falling towel. "Why're you so pumped up today?"

"Dude, you're not going to believe what happened. About eight weeks ago I put together some promo packs and sent them to different record companies, but I didn't get any responses. That's why I was frustrated about my CD the last time I was here. So before we left, I was loading the van when the phone rang. Usually I let it go to voice mail, but for some reason I decided to pick it up. It was a producer from a small label in Nashville. He really liked the CD and said he's gonna pass it on to upper management. I'm not expecting much, but the toughest hurdles are over. We'll at least get a listen, which is all I ever wanted. At the very least, a few execs will make a trip to see us live. He's supposed to call me next week to set up a time when we have a few gigs in a row. It's crazy, man. Nothing happens, and then from out of nowhere, you catch a break."

"That's awesome. Which gigs?"

"Probably next time we come here. This is kind of our home. Where's Cinch?"

"Still sleeping."

"Wake his ass up. Let's grab lunch somewhere."

"It'll have to be quick. We have to work at one."

"Since when are you guys on time? Meet me at Frosty's. Time to celebrate."

Although I'm happy for him, I feel empty when he leaves. He's working toward something. What am I working toward? What do I have to look forward to?

I go into Cinch's room to wake him. Also asleep underneath the covers is Brooke. The visual itself isn't as shocking as the attached implication that Dawn is not far behind.

I put my hand on his shoulder. He opens his eyes and stares at me, obviously still not awake. I say, "I'm meeting Birch at Frosty's for lunch. Get up and meet us down there."

Cinch smiles and moves his eyes several times in Brooke's direction. "Look who showed up last night."

"Dare I even ask if her partner is here?"

"She is, but I think your troubles might be over. She was all chummy with Bean and this guy Mize from the Beer Barrel. You should've seen her. She was flirting so hard, and I know it was so that people would come back and tell you. Like you even care." Brooke stirs. "Go ahead. I'll see you there shortly."

I go for a walk to kill some time before meeting Birch. The pain and confusion from yesterday still linger but have receded. The experience with Randy is just another benchmark. Once again I have ventured into the unknown and at least for now have safely returned.

Birch is with Cinch at the bar when I walk into Frosty's. "Man, that was a quick getaway," I say. "Forty minutes ago, Brooke wasn't even awake. How'd you get rid of her so quickly?"

Cinch slides a Bloody Mary toward me. "Just told her I had to work. Put her ass in a cab and sent her to Robin's."

Birch says, "Nothing but class around here."

"What do you mean?" Cinch says. "I paid the two bucks."

I look around the bar. "Being here for lunch is a new experience for us. We usually open it with the fishermen at seven a.m. after a long night. I swear I've taken at least three years off my life in the past three months."

"Maybe that's the conversion," Birch says, obviously about to go on one of his stream-of-consciousness tangents. I welcome it, though. Having these types of conversations is exactly how we became friends. "Maybe one month here equates to one year on the mainland. That's why people typically only last one or two seasons. Think about how much you do here and how many people you see in a month. A month might be exaggerating things, but you could definitely equate four months to a year. And the place is only busy for four months, so people cram a year's worth of experience into that short time."

I say, "Time doesn't age you; experience does."

"Exactly," Birch says. "If I do in four months what most people do in a year, haven't I really lived a year?"

Cinch says, "But you're gauging your life by some other frame of reference. You're saying that what another person does in a year is the standard, which might not be true. Maybe they're not doing enough, and a year of your life is average. In the end, does it really matter how old we are anyway, or what we did at age twenty-five, thirty-five, or forty-five?"

I raise my glass. "I'll drink to that. Birch, go order the pizza. We only have an hour before we have to work. Anything but onion for me."

After Birch leaves, Cinch says, "Dude, you should've seen Dawn and Mize last night. She kept asking me about you and what she should do. I kept telling her to back off and give you space, but she kept bugging me. Finally I told her you were seeing someone else. As soon as I said that, she turned her attention to Bean and Mize. He's a buddy fucker from way back, so he was more than happy to play the game, keeping one eye on her and one on the door, hoping you'd walk in."

"At least I'm off the hook."

"And that will piss her off even more."

The conversation, the good night's sleep, and seeing Birch all serve as additional building blocks in my reconstruction. By tomorrow it will all be behind me. I don't know if it's the entertainment cycle with the bands or the Friday, Saturday, Sunday routine, but I too am living in three-day segments. Tomorrow ends another cycle, and I'll be ready to begin again.

In the afternoon, Dawn strolls into the Round House. Her smile wider than usual and her head held higher, she is ready to spar. Even if Cinch hadn't told me what happened the night before, her added confidence gives it away.

"Surprise," she says. "Sorry I didn't call, but I didn't want you to feel like you had to entertain me. We're just having fun, remember?"

I say, "I wouldn't be surprised by anyone who shows up here on one of the busiest weekends of the year. Not to mention that I saw Brooke this morning in the barn."

"I was going to come over with her, but I didn't want to intrude. So why weren't you out last night? The island starting to take its toll?"

Cinch's advice for her to give me space is transparent in her words. Equally as clear is her peacock-like strutting. I keep reminding myself that I don't care, but her smug attitude erodes my veil of indifference.

I answer her questions and continue our conversation for the better part of an hour, successfully evading each of her attempts to lead me into asking what she did last night. I talk to her about her work, life in Detroit, my trip to Cleveland, anything to deny her the satisfaction of implying that something might have happened. But she counters each escape with another assault. The final blow in the attack communicates just how far in advance she prepared for this battle. Appearing just as puffed up as his partner, Mize walks through the front door to meet her here for a drink, probably by her invitation, during his break from the Beer Barrel. How pathetic. Each of them so happy to use the other for entertainment and redemption.

I walk over to Cinch. "Can you believe this? She really thinks she's getting back at me. How far will she go to get even for being blown off?"

"Who cares? If you're lucky, maybe she really likes him."

Even though I try not to watch them, my eyes continually drift in their direction. I recognize my jealousy, but it's not because I care about her. I don't want to be with her, but I don't want anyone else to have her, either. I like thinking she's there for me, but I don't want to be there for her. I want her away from me, but not so far away that I can't pull her back when it's convenient.

Eventually the two of them walk out together. Dawn gives a casual glance over her shoulder as she steps onto the porch. But there isn't anything casual intended by her gesture—instead, it's as if to say, "You want space? I'll give you space, so much that you'll wonder not only what, but *who* I'm doing."

Over the next few days, not only are Cinch and I unable to make a trip to the Boardwalk in order to refuel, but the increased traffic also stymies our delivery business. People have to come to us.

To fill orders, we keep everything in my locker at the Round House. All the packages are pre-weighed: grams, sixteenths, and eight balls. The grams are in a Salem box, the sixteenths in a Marlboro Light pack, the balls in a Camel box. One of us takes the order, grabs the package out of my locker, and returns to the bar or patio to finish the transaction.

At the end of the shift we empty our pockets and sift through the remnants in the red barn, counting the wads of fifties, twenties, tens, and fives as we pass around a plate, each night increasing our level of indulgence.

After work I try to hook up with Birch or Haley, someone outside the crew, but either my buzz or my preoccupation with making another sale always lures me away. I can no longer deny it: we're drug dealers. Between the stuff we move at work, at late-night bars, and after hours, we have become quite prosperous. Word has traveled quickly that just because you're on an island doesn't mean you have to be stranded—as long as you have cash.

All of it only encourages us to party more, mainly so we don't have to think about how lucrative our partnership has become, but also because we can.

In St. Louis, my life changed suddenly, completely out of my control. In contrast, my metamorphosis here has been full of warning signs, ones I have ignored while convincing myself that I can always change and that tomorrow will be the day when the change occurs. Will enough ever be enough?

Just before sunrise, Cinch slides the plate toward me. "What do you say? One more to knock us out, then we call it a night?"

I laugh at the contradiction in his question. Sleep is no longer a realistic option. "I'm done," I say. "I need to wind down until I have to meet Bob."

He offers to help, but why should both of us suffer? I should just go lie in bed and stare at the ceiling until it's time to go.

Cinch does not give up. He says, "If both of us go, Bob might actually get his money's worth. Besides, look at the bright side: at least the Fourth is over. We're halfway through the season."

"And that's a good thing?" Even though technically Labor Day is still two months away, the Fourth of July is considered halfway because it's the second of the three big holidays. But the milestone means nothing to me. I don't know if one-half, one-third, or one-sixth of my season is over because I have no idea what I'm doing at the end of the summer.

Cinch says, "Don't forget what we agreed to last night when we were leaving work."

"Refresh me. I don't even remember leaving."

"We're supposed to meet at the winery at five o'clock."

"No recollection. At this point, the entire weekend is running together."

Five hours of sleep pass quickly after being up for thirty-six. My alarm sounds, but it's still not enough to wake me from my dream, in which I'm running through a forest. Branches and twigs break under my feet. The ocean calls in the distance. I accelerate, but the sounds of the sea drift farther and farther away. Dew dropping from the leaves chills my skin. My breathing becomes heavier as my pace quickens. My heart is about to burst through my chest, but I'm still not getting closer to the water. The snapping of wood and the faint call of waves are the only audible sounds.

Birch shakes my leg. "Dude, you okay? You're soaking wet, your alarm's going off, and you didn't even bother to take off your shoes."

I sit up and run my fingers through my hair, down around my neck, and together in front of my face, holding them as if I'm praying. "Fuck, what time is it?"

"Five o'clock. We got to get to the winery."

"Is Cinch up?" I go to Cinch's room and fling my wet T-shirt at his heaving stomach. "Hey, we gotsta go, bro. It's five. I'll shower. You chop 'em and be ready when I get out."

At the winery, we gather in the back around the same table as before. Haley is inside with some other islanders. Griffin must've come straight after work. He and Stein have already finished one bottle and are two-thirds of the way through another.

Griffin says, "Where the hell have you guys been? We had to start without you."

Cinch says, "Why didn't you come upstairs and get us, you selfish bastard? Try thinking about others for a change."

Griffin slumps forward like a scolded puppy.

Birch says, "The way you two were going at it, I didn't see much left for anyone else. Come on, let's get the game started. I have to work tonight." Birch looks directly at me. "Antonio Montana to you."

The game moves rapidly. Maybe because we've all played before, maybe because we're relatively sober. Regardless, the names spring easily and the wine goes down slowly. Tom Cruise—Cameron Diaz—Derek Jeter—Jessica Biel—Bill Gates—George Clooney—Chris Matthews—Michael Jackson—Jessica Simpson.

We are all down to a half cup of wine when Griffin pulls a reversal on Cinch with Shel Silverstein.

Cinch holds up his cup. "Socrates. Who's getting more wine? More importantly, who's doing the honors in the restroom?"

Birch collects the empties. "I'll get the wine while you guys do your thing."

Stein and Griffin go take care of business in the restroom. I turn to Cinch. "Have you noticed Birch acting differently today? Maybe we revealed too much over the past few days."

Cinch raises an eyebrow. "Should we rub him out?"

"No, I'm serious. Like his crack about Scarface when we started the game, and his little dig when you were busting on Griffin."

Cinch offers his typical response. "Who cares? Come on, it's our turn."

When we return, the empty wine bottles have been replaced with full ones, but Birch is gone. I ask what happened to him.

"Up front," Griffin says. "We're supposed to play without him. He has to head back shortly."

Stein says, "Screw him. Who's going to start?"

"I'm done playing," I say. "Maybe we should go hang out with the others."

Griffin says, "You go ahead. I'm way too amped to be around those folks. I might as well tattoo a big red C on the end of my nose."

"They're all pretty juiced," Cinch says. "They can hardly see past the end of their own noses, let alone worry about yours."

—

One-third of the bottle of Cuervo at Haley's table is gone, and she's the only one drinking tequila. "It's about time you quit being antisocial and join us. We're only halfway through the season, but I think you two have Couple of the Year locked up. How did you survive during the trip to Cleveland without each other?"

"Gosh, Cinch, remember how peaceful it was out back?" I say. "Why did we come in here? Oh, that's right, to hang out with friends. What were we thinking?"

"Okay, okay, how about a toast?" Haley says. "To the second half of the season. Hopefully it will be as good as the first."

We touch plastic cups and throw back the contents. Five minutes later she makes another toast, followed by several more. Birch repeatedly looks at his watch.

I hold up my cup. "To Birch not falling off the stage tonight. What time do you have to go?"

"I should leave now," Birch says. "I have to grab a bite to eat and get a shower. If I don't, I probably will take a spill."

I say, "I'll tag along. I could use some food, too."

Haley downs another shot. "Meet us later. We'll probably bar crawl back—Kelley's, Captain Tony's, the Brewery, and the Beer Barrel."

Cinch declines our invitation. "I ate Friday night. I'm good until at least Wednesday."

Birch wants a bread bowl of bisque at the Boardwalk to help soak up the alcohol. The short trip in his van is like a ride in an elevator with a transvestite. My words are blatant attempts to conceal the true question hanging in the air.

Birch parks behind the Boardwalk. I say, "Wait. Before we go in, what's bothering you? You've been different the past few days."

"I've been different? I have? How do you think I feel? You've been a completely different person ever since you came here. I should've never brought you into all this."

"How am I different?" I know the answer but am unsure of what else there is to say.

"Gee, I don't know. Could it be that the only people you hang around are your drug buddies, or maybe that you have to do drugs just to get through the day, or perhaps it's all the not-so-casual handoffs I've seen you make the past week? The worst part is that I don't think you even realize how deep you're into everything. You actually think you're in control. I know after what happened in St. Louis it hasn't been easy for you, but one mistake with the way you're living now, and your life is over. Bye-bye, see you in twenty years. And if all this happened in a month and a half, what will you be like at the end of the season?"

"Don't worry about me and don't feel responsible. If I didn't come here, I would've been somewhere else doing it. I simply need to forget while I figure things out."

"Just remember, there comes a time when the party isn't a party anymore; it's your life," Birch says. "While you're inventing the new Brad, don't completely discard the old one. He's a pretty good guy."

After our talk, I don't feel like eating, and I go for a walk instead. The wind off the lake is cold on my exposed arms. I bury my hands in my pockets. Might as well just go home. I cut through the park and pass in front of the Round House. Robin is on the front porch with Dawn, Brooke, and Lea. I pretend not to notice and continue to the red barn.

Back in my room, I hear the front door open. Thinking it is Cinch, I call out.

"It's me," Dawn replies.

I yell back, "I'm really not in the mood. Why don't you go hang out with your new boyfriend?"

She appears in the doorway. "That's not fair. What am I supposed to do? You obviously don't want anything to do with me."

"No one can call you imperceptive." I lean over to take my shoes off. "If Mize makes you happy, go for it. I have more important things to worry about."

"Like who your next customer is?"

What a bitch. I can't believe she's bringing that into this. I say, "Don't start with me. You don't know me."

She sits down next to me on the bed. "But I want to. Just let me in."

"Why don't you help yourself? Your life isn't exactly award-winning: broken engagement, slept with me, slept with Mize, who knows how many more."

"Fuck you." She slaps me and storms toward the door. "I'm trying to be your friend. You better think about that because you can't afford to have enemies. I can think of a few people on this island who would love to know the source of the new menu items at the Round House."

I go after her. "Hold on. That'll hurt more people than just me. Let's keep this between us."

She straightens with confidence. "I guess that's up to you, isn't it?"

I explain that it has nothing to do with her and that I can't be with anyone right now, but she brings up Astrid. I tell her, "We're just friends."

Her eyes tighten. "You're a fucking liar. At least be honest with me."

I go back on the attack. "Because you believe and respect honesty so much? Look, you wanted to have fun and we did, but it's over."

"It's over when I say it's over," she says, asserting the control we both know she has in the situation. "You're not going to make a fool of me and just walk away. I'll be down at the bar. I suggest you join me there, and then we're going to the Boat House for a drink."

"This is insane. I'm not going to pretend that I like you so that you can save face."

"What a shame. You know where to find me if you reconsider."

Cinch has joined Dawn and the others on the porch when I finally come down. He says, "I heard you were meeting us."

Dawn slides over in her chair. "We can both fit. Let's have a drink and go down to the Boat House."

My expression blank, I pretend to be indifferent. "Whatever you guys want to do."

"There's nothing going on there," Cinch says. "Let's just stay here."

Dawn says, "Do what you want. We're going to the Boat House."

This is going to be tougher than I thought. I say, "Why not the Beer Barrel? Isn't your friend working tonight? Cinch, let's get drinks."

At the bar Cinch asks, "Want to tell me what the fuck is going on?"

"If I don't play along, she'll blow the whistle on our side business."

"Forget that. She's crazy, but not that crazy."

"For one night, it's not worth the risk."

"Should I talk to Brooke?"

"I got myself into this; I'll find a way out. Hopefully Dawn will get drunk, we'll have sex, and she'll go home tomorrow."

Despite Cinch's continual urging, Dawn will not surrender her intention of visiting the Boat House. The look on Astrid's face when we enter is the exclamation point on Dawn's resolution.

I lean over to Dawn. "Are you happy?"

She kisses me on the cheek. "Not yet, but there's plenty of time for that later."

To apologize I try to make eye contact with Astrid, but she won't even look in my direction. She disappears into the kitchen and doesn't return.

I say, "I'm going to the bar for a shot. Anyone else?"

Dawn hands me a twenty. "I'll buy."

I ask the bartender what happened to Astrid. He says, "What do you think happened, asshole?"

Cinch comes to the bar. "Is everything cool?"

"Sure, why wouldn't it be? Just out having fun with my friends. What's next, sandpaper on my ass?"

Cinch proposes a trip to the restroom and I agree, needing something to make the situation better or at least to alter my perspective. When we return, Mize is sitting at the table with the girls. When we walk up, he says to Dawn, "I thought you said things were over between you two."

Dawn pulls over another chair. "Have a seat. We're all friends here."

Brooke takes Dawn by the hand. "Aren't you taking this a little far?"

I say, "This is where I leave."

Dawn scowls. "Did I say you could go?"

"Fuck off, whore." I turn to walk away. "You two losers deserve each other."

Mize pushes me in the back. "Who you calling loser?"

Cinch steps between us. "Mize, cool down. Shep, just walk away."

"Isn't this what the little bitch wants?" I reach over Cinch's shoulder and push Mize. "How's my dick taste?'"

Cinch faces Mize. "Drop it. She isn't worth it."

Dawn says, "Boys, boys, don't be so childish."

"Is this foreplay for you?" I say. "Well, you ought to be nice and hot."

Dawn says, "Too bad your two inches couldn't do it."

I turn to walk away. Mize lands a punch square on my nose, knocking me into a table. Cinch tackles Mize. Bouncers descend on them. A waitress helps me up. Dazed, I fall back down.

Dawn hasn't moved from her chair. She smiles. "My work is done here. We can go now."

I lie in bed with a bag of ice on my face. When I sit up, my entire face throbs. At least if I stay flat on my back, I don't have to worry about my face exploding.

Astrid's voice floats over me. "I heard what happened."

I lift the ice and tilt my head. "It's not what you think."

"I don't know what to think anymore."

"She threatened to turn us in for selling drugs. It's not me I was protecting."

She sits down on the edge of the bed. "Maybe it's time you think about yourself. I didn't leave the Boat House because you were with her; I left because I'm sick of watching you be a coward."

I say, "It's not your problem."

"It is, because I care about you." I feel her eyes on me, but I can't look. She says, "There's just not enough room for me in your life because cocaine is your mistress. She's there when you need her, and she makes you feel bigger than life. Why would you want anything else? You don't have to worry about her hurting you or about you disappointing her. And you can share her with your friends without jealousy or guilt."

I say aloud what I've been trying to convince myself of all along. "It's just a vacation. I'll stop at the end of the season."

"Why wait and waste the next few months? Stop now."

"I can't. Not here, not now."

"I guess I'll see you around, then."

She leaves, and I return the ice pack to my face. I wish it would explode.

CHAPTER TWELVE

MY SWOLLEN NOSE FORCES BOTH SOBRIETY AND WITHDRAWAL. I wake every two hours covered in sweat, fling the covers off, and then, shivering, I scramble for them moments later. The second night I eat a pinch to loosen the grip. Cocaine to help me sleep. I have to stop.

The days are even more difficult. It's not because of the physical discomfort of the sobriety, but because of the huge block of time I discover now that I'm not partying. The time I had spent hustling and indulging combined with the time I spent recovering added up to another full-time job. With the partying gone, I'm actually bored for the first time since I got here. I need something to occupy my mind and fill the free time. The bruises from Mize have shielded me from after-hours activities, but once I'm healed, I'll need another excuse. I arrange to take Caldwell up on his offer to learn to play guitar.

I ride my bike out to his campsite. He sits in a lawn chair tuning a guitar in a screened-in room he's added to his pop-up camper. I roll off the gravel road into the grass. "Hope I'm not too early."

Caldwell plucks a string and turns one of the tuning knobs. "Right on time. Just finishing getting ole Emerson ready."

"Probably should pick up one of my own," I say. "Name it after the philosopher?"

"Nah. When I used to play in a band, we had a contest every night who could spot the girl in the crowd with the biggest cans. Referred to her as Emerson, as in 'Em are some big . . .'" He cups his left pec and shakes it. "Decided to carry on the tradition with this guitar."

I laugh. This is the most relaxed I've seen Caldwell. Not that he's ever uptight. It's just usually he's so serious. I guess even Caldwell lets his hair down at home.

Patting the body of the guitar, he says, "Why don't you just keep this one? I have two others."

"That's too generous." I unzip the screen flap and enter. "At least let me give you some money."

"Pay me by practicing."

I nod in agreement, scanning the campsite. "Nice setup."

"Gets me through the summer until I can live for free taking care of someone's cottage for the winter." He looks at the bruises on my face. "Healing pretty quickly."

"Black, purple, yellow—one shade closer to normal. Why is it that a person always gets it when it's not his fault?"

He strums a chord slowly. "Cause and effect are rarely directly related. Justice has a mind of her own."

"With the way I've been living, I know I probably deserved it. Just not then, not from him."

"When you look back over the past months, what's the common destructive element?" He plucks each of the strings, listening carefully. "Remove that element."

I sit in the chair next to him. "Is lesson one tuning the guitar?"

He drops the pick inside the guitar. "Lesson one is how to get the pick out when you drop it inside." Holding the guitar horizontally in front of him he shakes it, working the pick to the center of the hole. "Maneuver it to where you can see it. Left hand loose on the neck and with the right hand flip it quickly." Caldwell spins the guitar and the pick falls to the ground. "Got it? Your turn." He grabs the pick and drops it into the guitar.

"Seems easy enough." I take the guitar and mirror his actions, but nothing comes out. I try again. Same result.

"Turn with the wrist, not the arm." He goes inside the camper and returns with another guitar. His long, bony fingers remove the pick woven between the strings and drop it inside the body. "Like this." With a couple shakes and a spin, the pick falls to the ground.

I extend the guitar in front of me. With a flip of the wrist, the pick drops into the grass.

Caldwell picks it up and drops it back inside. "Again."

This time I get it on the second try.

"Improving already," he says. "First chord is a G." He strums a perfect G. "Sixth string, third fret. Next string, second fret. First string, third fret."

My hand is a clenched claw around the neck. My fingers struggle to bend in the proper directions.

Caldwell positions my fingers. "Apply pressure without tensing. Now strum."

I strum awkwardly and the instrument emits a muted, off-key sound. Clumsy and stiff I try again, fumbling the pick into the body. "Fuck. Maybe this isn't for me."

"You're giving up that easy?"

I get the pick out on the first try. "No. It's just maybe I'm not meant to do this. You make it look so easy."

"Let me assure you, nothing comes easy to me. It's all perseverance." He strums a G. "Do you want to learn?"

I contort my fingers to reach the strings. "Absolutely."

"Then you're meant to play." He holds the G and strums a rhythmic pattern with his right hand. "Down-up, down-up, up, down-up."

With my left fingers across the neck, my strum hand jerks across the strings. The low G note rings, but the rest is muted and off-key. "At least I got one string right."

"You can't bullshit a guitar. You only get better by playing it."

I pluck each string separately. Five of the six sound. "Practicing won't be a problem. Got plenty of time now."

Caldwell adjusts my finger on the bottom-most string. "What's changed?"

"Me. Just done partying. Time to end my vacation from reality."

"People go home after vacations."

"This is my home."

"Then you're not on vacation," he says.

—

Another sleepless night. Only this time not from withdrawal. I can't stop thinking about Astrid. Why did I blow it with her? It's not like I don't care about her. She is beautiful, smart, fun, and doesn't take my shit. What am I so afraid of? I need to talk to her. I need to work this out.

Resolving to reach out to Astrid releases me for a few hours of sleep. As with most mornings lately, I am the first one up and out the door, quick and quiet. I take Emerson over to the monument and sit on the seawall to practice.

All the strings now ring on the G chord, and I am able to keep a slow rhythm with my right hand. The waves splashing against the wall offer percussion. The circling seagulls provide the vocals. I think of the many bands I have seen this summer. I have so far to go before I can reach that level. Maybe I am starting too late in life. Maybe I should devote this energy to solving real problems rather than starting something new. Don't think. Just play. The brain always gets in the way.

At work I gaze through the park from my usual perch at the entrance. The same show still goes on, but I am no longer a part of the production. I have stepped off the stage and into the audience.

The familiar picture before me is like an abstract painting. The azure sky melts into the leafy trees and back to the blue of the lake before dripping into the lush grass. A couple strolls hand in hand toward the docks. The movement is the only way I know that time is still ticking.

A child kicks a ball and chases it through the park. My eyes follow him down the diagonal sidewalk toward the Jet Express. He passes a lady wearing a red visor that matches her shorts and shoes, just like my mom would wear. Not only must her belt always match her shoes, but her shorts and hat must as well, and her shirt and socks are always color-coded, too. She thinks it looks good because people comment on her outfits. I tell her that's not necessarily a good thing and that she looks like a candy cane.

I still feel bad from the way we left things my last night in St. Louis. Other than the postcard I sent after first arriving, I haven't had any contact. I must be feeling guilty now because the guy walking next to the lady, his head buried in a map, reminds me of my dad. I've seen him bump into people, benches, and garbage cans; walk into traffic; and even pass right by his destination because he never looks around. He always follows the map, only lifting his head when the directions indicate that a landmark or the destination should be near.

At least I know where I get it from. That's exactly what I do with my life. I always want a map to navigate the chaos.

The glaring resemblances become specific as the two tread through the park. With each step in my direction, I creep backward until I am inside the Round House watching through the window.

The woman follows a few steps behind the man, who still hasn't looked up from the map. He stops at the sidewalk on the other side of the street and raises his head, finally speaking to her. My skin goes cold.

Cinch walks over. "You don't look so good. Maybe you came back too soon."

"My parents just showed up." The words sound foreign coming out of my life. How could they just show up unannounced? I stagger backward. "Can you take the front? I need to get out of here."

His face goes blank. "What do you expect me to do?"

"You'll think of something." I rush toward the side door. What the fuck am I going to do?

<hr />

In the red barn I rummage through the unopened mail on my dresser, stopping on a card in a pink envelope with no return address, but with a St. Louis postmark. My mom never puts her address on any card she sends. She thinks it makes opening the card a surprise, like unwrapping a present. There's no point in opening this one. The knock on the door tells me what's inside.

My dad's voice bellows. "Baaaah! Where's my shepherd?" When I was a kid, he always bleated to get my attention. Now he only does it when he feels uncomfortable.

"It's open." I follow my voice to the living room. "Nice surprise. You could've called."

"We would have, if you had a phone." My mother's not with him. His eyes fixate on my bruises. "Occupational hazard?"

"Something like that," I say, not ready to let up the attack yet. What the hell am I going to do with them for the next few days?

"Your mother sent a card, which you obviously didn't open. We were worried. You just dropped off the face of the earth."

"It's more like you were pissed," I say. "Mom made this about her like she does everything. She probably got tired of not being able to answer her friends when they asked what I was doing or when I was coming home, so she concocted this surprise attack to get back at me. You went along with it so she wouldn't turn her wrath on you."

He looks around the room and nods toward the bong. "Judging from this place and from the looks of you, we should've come sooner. It's a good thing your mom went to the hotel first."

"Whatever. Let's go get this over with. We can pretend like everything is okay, just like we have been for years."

My dad must've warned my mom about my face at the hotel, because when they meet me in the Round House, her first words are, "It's not that bad."

My dad says, "From what I hear, you should see the other guy."

Cinch brings over a full bucket. "If I would've known VIPs were coming, I would've given Brad the night off. Maybe Robin can fill in."

"He's off the island," I say. I'm not even sure if it's true, but I'm more than happy to stay at work. I turn to my mom. "You're probably tired from the trip anyway, right?"

She says, "We'll just stay here. Looks like we have our work cut out for us with this bucket. Good thing our hotel is right next door."

As the level of liquid in the bucket drops, the tension dissipates. *Sorry* is never spoken, but it's exchanged in extended glances throughout the night. At first my mom diverts her eyes when I catch her staring at me. But eventually our eye contact lengthens and we both let go of our anger and hurt. Maybe their coming is a good thing.

After a round of shots during the band break, my mom says, "You'll have to teach me how to make those purtle hoopers. They sure will liven up our next barbecue."

No one corrects her mispronunciation. I look at my dad and motion toward the door with my eyes. He says, "I think it's time for the old fogies to retire for the evening."

I walk them to the hotel. "I hope you enjoyed today. I still have a few hours of work left. Let's meet tomorrow for lunch."

In the red barn after work, Cinch says, "That sure was an interesting twist. I better go through my mail first thing in the morning." He extends a tooter toward me. "How's the face? You ready to come off injured reserve?"

I wave it off. "I'm officially retired."

Griffin says, "Why quit? Partying has nothing to do with Dawn, Astrid, or your parents."

"I just need to move on."

He takes the handoff from Cinch. "Wait until the end of the season."

"Yeah, fuck it. We're all in this together." Cinch brings the plate and sits next to me on the couch. "You haven't been out since you got popped. You're going to need something to help get you through the next few days."

"Take a look at me." The swelling on my nose has lessened, but the bruising under my eyes is still prominent and a topic of conversation when I'm in public. "Unless we're going to a circus, this freak show should stay home."

Cinch says, "Who cares? You've been working in the Round House all day. It'll be the same people."

"Come on. It'll do you good," Griffin says. "Just have a nibble. It all ends up in the same place anyway."

"No, I'm fine. I'll go. But don't be pissed when I want to leave early."

At the Skyway, Astrid is the first person I see. She stands by the stone wall with another girl from the Boat House and two guys I don't recognize. My commitment from last night to talk to her floods back. I shouldn't interrupt them, though. I just need some eye contact or for her to break away.

Cinch, Griffin, and I make our way to the loge. Cinch says, "You having a beer? Or are you off alcohol, too?"

"Now that's just crazy talk," I say, and I position myself so I can watch Astrid.

Griffin takes his beer and scans the room, also more interested in what is happening around us than between us. His eyes rest on a girl he was working all evening at the Round House. "Jackpot," he says and gulps his beer. "Don't wait up for me, boys."

Cinch says, "I give him ten minutes and he'll be back."

I nod, my eyes angled on Astrid. "Yeah, probably."

"Boy, you're a load of fun tonight." I don't respond. He waves his hand in front of my face. "Why don't you just go talk to her?"

I look at Cinch with surprise. "Who?"

"Astrid. That's who. You've been eye-fucking her since we walked in."

"I don't want to interrupt."

Cinch says, "So you'll just stare at her all night. Good plan."

"Why won't she look over here?" I ask, my frustration mounting.

"I don't know. Maybe because you abandoned her on your date? Or maybe it's that when she opened up to you, you said, 'No thanks.'"

I put my beer on the bar. "I'm going to talk to her."

Knowing I won't have to intrude if she sees me, I approach in her line of sight. But she never diverts her eyes from her male companions. The other girl from the Boat House does, repeatedly tapping Astrid in the hip to alert her. Even with the girl's assistance, I still don't get Astrid's attention until I'm standing right next to her.

She yields a brief glance. "Oh, hey. When did you get here?"

"Could we talk for a second?"

"I'm kind of busy," she says. Her voice is cold and dismissive.

The others shift uncomfortably. I say, "Do you guys mind excusing us?"

Anger fills her eyes. "That's rude. Now that you want to talk, everyone else should drop everything?"

The girl grabs the two guys by the hands. "Let's go do a shot."

Astrid says, "Get me one, too. I won't be long."

I dive in to preempt her rage. "I'm sorry, but I can't stop thinking about you. I don't sleep. I just keep going over and over how I screwed up."

"The lack of sleep is probably from something else."

"No." I gesture toward my face. "Haven't partied since the fight. I'm done with all that."

She lifts her chin and speaks to the crowd. "Oh my God, everyone, he stopped partying for me. I'm such a lucky girl."

I look around to check who's listening, but no one cares.

They are crafting their own stories for the evening. I say, "I don't understand. Why are you being like this? I just want to talk."

"We've talked enough."

"Come on. Let's just leave. Go somewhere more quiet."

"That's not going to happen," she says. "You must really think I'm stupid. All you've done since we met is push me away. Like an idiot, I kept coming back. Even after you embarrassed me in front of all my coworkers, I still came back. All I asked you to do was try, and you couldn't even do that. I'm done." She walks toward the bar.

I grab her by the wrist. "Please don't do this."

She glares at my hand. "I suggest you let go. You didn't want to try, and I honored that. I'm just asking for the same respect."

I search her face for any of the hope or warmth I felt on other nights. Nothing. Her icy glare cuts through me. I release her wrist.

She stares deep into my eyes. "I would say it's over, but it would've had to start for there to be an end."

She joins her friends at the bar, instantly switching back to the person I remember. I start to go after her—she just needs to understand how serious I am—when a hand cups my shoulder. It's Cinch. He says, "Let it go. That's only going to make it worse."

"If I can just get her alone and talk, she'll understand."

"It takes two for a conversation."

"She's just afraid, like I was before."

"Of course she's afraid. You're acting like a stalker. Go back to the loge and party like nothing happened. Beat her at her own game. The best way to get over someone is to get under someone else."

I know he's right, but I don't want to accept it. There's no way I can stay here after that. I walk straight out the front door. I hear Cinch calling after me, but I don't look back. I need to get as far from this place as I can, as fast as I can.

Outside, I weave through the people on the front patio. The faces and sounds blur into a continuous stream. My heart races. My legs shake. Rage and sorrow battle for control. Another opportunity I let slip away. Another failure.

I reach the parking lot. A cab waits. I pour myself into the back. "Round House."

The driver says, "Sorry, man. It's closed."

"I don't care. Just take me there."

The morning comes slowly and awkwardly. I replay the interaction with Astrid over and over. Why didn't I just stay home? I knew I shouldn't have gone out. Now things are even more messed up.

With time to kill before meeting my parents, I take my guitar and join Caldwell on his blanket in the park.

I strum a much-improved G.

He nods approvingly. "You been practicing."

"Not much else to do these days."

He plays a steady rhythm in G. "What's your plan at the end of the summer?"

"I was going to stay here, but not sure if I can now. Maybe Key West."

"You should stay here. Gets mighty quiet."

"That's what I'm afraid of."

Caldwell strums a C. "Next chord to learn is C. Low E string not used. Fifth string, third fret; fourth string, second fret; third string is open; second string, first fret; and first string, open."

I stretch my fingers into position. "Haven't got the G down yet."

Caldwell strums a G for two beats, then a C. "That's what practice is for."

I strum the C. It sounds sickly. I adjust my fingers and repeat. The sound improves.

He says, "Now try the G-C combo with the strum pattern."

I strum in a slow rhythm on the G.

Caldwell keeps the time. "One, two, three, four. One, two, three, now, C, two, three, four."

I am slow on the change, not making the C until the four. I stop. "A little behind on that one."

"Don't worry about it. Just keep going. It'll come. The changes are difficult. When something sounds good, you don't want to let it go. But it will always be there when you're ready to go back to it."

We spend the next hour with Caldwell counting and me trying to keep up. Time spent with Caldwell is the only thing that feels real anymore—or maybe I'm just hiding behind a new mask.

While entertaining my parents throughout the weekend, I recognize in them the same affinity toward the island I experienced upon my arrival. It puts all of us at ease. For me, it reinforces that my comfort here is more than the party. For them, it opens the possibility that I might know what I'm doing. I just have to finish what I started.

Although the day breezes by—lunch at Frosty's, visit to the top of the monument, golf cart tour of the island, two-bottle stop at the winery, dinner at the Boardwalk—as we move to the porch after dinner, I know I can't avoid it any longer. I say, "I can't believe you leave tomorrow already. Time flies here. It'll be fall in a blink."

My mom says, "At the end of the season, you're still welcome to live with us while you figure out your next move."

"You know I love you," I say, setting up the inevitable "but" that we all know is coming. "But my future is not in St. Louis."

My comment disintegrates the restraint she's exhibited and the progress we've made for the past thirty-six hours. "Your future is checking IDs and sweeping floors in this Disneyland for alcoholics?"

"At least the immediate future. I don't have all the answers, but I feel like I'm finally on the right path."

Ever the diplomat, my dad says, "You understand why we're worried, don't you?"

"Of course. This whole change has been tough on all of us. I spent the past ten years building a life that I'm not sure I want anymore. I just don't know what the next step is."

My mom holds back the tears my words trigger. She's still not able to see beyond herself. My decision to leave and now my decision to stay here both amount to a rejection of the life she built. I know my dad understands and would encourage me under other circumstances, but he still has another day and a half until he's safely home. One wrong move and he'll become the enemy in her eyes. Looking at them, all I can hope is that they've finally heard me.

CHAPTER THIRTEEN

TIME PASSES SWIFTLY WHEN A PERSON DOESN'T THINK ABOUT ANYTHING. Or maybe it's that when a person looks back, he doesn't recall anything significant to mark the passing time, so he remembers it as one complete piece of his life.

After the weekend with my parents, the next few weeks run together, as much of my time here does when I reflect on it. Why wouldn't it, though? Monday through Sunday the island fills with visitors who have a single objective: to get fucked up. The islanders' also remain unchanged: Herd 'em in, take their money, herd 'em out. The unexamined life may not be worth living, but it sure makes time pass quickly.

My continued sobriety and increased time practicing with Caldwell don't seem to affect the others. They really don't slow down or speed up. They simply maintain the same frantic pace they've set throughout the season. It has become the norm, and they aren't about to break the routine.

Fortunately the guitar shields me from their activities. It is an acceptable excuse. They never pressure me to join them. They offer; I decline; they go without me. More than anything it reduces the probability that I will see Astrid and distracts me from replaying the story over and over, devising new scenes in the drama.

There were two more interactions since our run-in at the Skyway, both at the monument and neither ending well. I played off the meetings as coincidences, but inside I knew that I went there every night hoping to see her. The hooks she had in me made quitting the cocaine seem easy.

Every time I thought of stopping by the Boat House or going where I expected her to be, I simply picked up the guitar and channeled the frustration and hurt. Now I understand why heartache fuels artistic growth. I had to do something, anything to get rid of the sting. Unfortunately, nothing could completely eradicate the pain. I was forced to live with it.

With August here, many of the college students will start to leave in a few weeks, only to return for the Labor Day weekend to receive their bonuses, which won't be much—one dollar for every hour worked throughout the season—but enough to get them to stay through that last busy weekend.

This evening, another annual tradition on the island commences: the Bartender Olympics. The event varies significantly from others on the island in that it's staged for the workers instead of the tourists. Tonight, for once, will not be about the almighty dollar. In fact, minimal money will be exchanged. As a way to give back to the workers, the bar owners comp all drinks for team members.

The twelve scheduled contests vary, ranging from a bar knowledge test to drink presentation. Judges award points according to each team's finish in an event. At the end they declare an overall winner, and that team has bragging rights for the year. The

Round House is the two-time defending champion, and Haley is not ready to give up the trophy yet.

Our security staff is responsible for the Keg Roll Relay, in which each team member rolls an empty keg down a thirty-yard lane to a waiting team member who then rolls it back. The last person travels two lengths and finishes on the same side where he started. The only rules are that you can't pick up the keg and you have to stay in your lane. The winning team receives twenty points and a full keg, donated by Bob.

I'm also entered in the "What It Means to Serve" contest. Although technically I'm not in drink or food service, I was chosen because my previous life as a teacher and my new guitar hobby labeled me as the most qualified to write and perform a song about service in front of a crowd.

The course of planned events runs parallel to the modern Olympics: opening ceremony to light the torch, singing of the national anthem (for which Mad Dog will be coming to the island), then commencement of the games. But the similarities stop there. Tonight, I've been told, is no display of athleticism, but rather an homage to alcoholism. Each event centers on, or at least involves, drinking, which is the main reason why there is no closing ceremony. By the end of the evening, everyone is so blasted that it's impossible to have an organized event.

This morning at the boat ramp I practice my song over and over to ensure that it will flow when the time comes. Word by word, line by line, verse by verse I broadcast my message out over the water, hoping to feel something come back like when I first arrived.

Behind me I hear a bike roll down the ramp and into the gravel. "Ready to get your butt kicked tonight?"

My hands tighten. I recognize the voice. Blood rushes to my face. I don't know what to do.

She says, "At least they give points for second place."

Just play along. Don't get heavy. I turn around and force a smile. "Funny, I was just thinking of telling you the same."

Astrid steps off the bike and rests it in the grass. She wears a baseball cap backward with a few blonde strands hanging down on each side of her face. Does she ever not look amazing? The sleeves of her T-shirt are bunched around her shoulders and her shorts are rolled up so that they angle upward from her inner thigh to her hip. She walks toward me. "I don't need to beat you; you'll beat yourself, or Cinch will. He'll have you so messed up, you won't even know your name."

I say, "Let me guess, you're wearing a sundress tonight? You're going to play the sex card. Walk up there all shy and cute, looking the way you do, and nobody will even care what comes out of your mouth. We'll see what they really judge on."

"Come on, give me some credit." She pushes her lips out in a pout. "Do you think I'd really want to win that way?"

"No, but you're not going to walk up with a bag over your head, either."

She tilts her head and offers a shy smile. "Care to make a side wager? How about winner's choice? Winner gets what the winner wants."

I hesitate. Now I'm confused. She won't talk to me for weeks and now she wants to make a bet? Just doesn't make any sense. Wait. Don't think. Keep it light. I smile back at her. "I'm listening."

She sits on the rock next to me. "We're entitled to some fun, aren't we?"

I look out over the water. The message I hoped to receive is now coming back. Each wave splashing against the rocks drives the message deeper inside me. I turn toward her. The softness has returned to her face. I'm afraid to speak. Words will end this moment and bring on the next. I want to stay right here.

She slaps my leg. "Of course if you're afraid, I understand."

I shake her hand to cement the deal. "Even if one of us finishes fifth and the other sixth, fifth place is considered a win, right?"

Her sportive smirk indicates that I can't lose. Maybe winning isn't everything. One just needs to hedge the bet and minimize the risk.

The final notes of the "Star Spangled Banner" ring in different keys as other voices excitedly drown out Mad Dog's for the start of the games.

The torch constructed in the park consists of four empty kegs welded together and anchored in the ground with an old TV satellite dish mounted on top. A propane tank supplies fuel for the flame through a hose that runs along the base and attaches to a fixture in the center of the dish. Mad Dog turns on the propane and lifts the flame toward the center, eliciting cheers from the crowd as it lights and then burns on its own.

When it's time for the Keg Roll, our team marches down the alley from the red barn in reverse order, with Griffin holding an empty keg above his head. With a shirt on, Griffin doesn't appear muscular, but now as he struts down the alley bare-chested and glistening with sweat, several people gesture to one another regarding his physique. Robin is no slouch, either, but our team goes drastically downhill from there. My excessive indulgence and lack of exercise have taken their toll, and Cinch gave up trying to stay in shape years ago.

Seeing that Lane 2 is the only vacant slot, Griffin walks to the starting line and sets the keg down.

Cinch says, "Don't worry if you're a little behind. It's more important to stay in your lane. The team that finishes first usually ends up getting second or third place because of penalties. Be fast, but be under control."

Griffin and I follow our shadows to the other end, as the sun at our backs is beginning to dip behind the trees in the park.

Bob serves as the referee. He raises the starting gun. "On your mark, get set, go."

The blast sends the contestants scurrying down the lanes. I can't tell who gets the early lead, but it's easy to see the difficulty each team has moving in a straight line. The Beer Barrel contestant is the first to break out of his lane.

Griffin says, "We're in third place, but only ten feet separate him from the leader. Just keep it close."

Cinch crosses the line and brings the keg to a complete stop. After the judge's signal, I keep my head down, focusing only on the ten feet in front of me to avoid the sun, which bobs up and down behind the tree line as I run.

I take my eyes off the keg to check my position, and the keg skips away to the right. I scramble after it, catching it before it crosses the lane line, but not before all the other teams pass me. I hear Robin cheering. I must be close. I push forward, crossing the line and stopping the keg.

Cinch walks down from the other end. "Good job, Shep. Nice save."

"Yeah, right. We're in last place now." I raise my hands above my head to catch my breath.

He says, "Don't worry, we don't have any penalties. That's what'll kill you. Look, Robin already moved up two spots and Frosty's just picked up a penalty. Let's go to the finish line. Griffin will pull it out. He lives for shit like this. Plus he knows I'll kick his ass if he lets the team down."

Robin hands off to Griffin as we break through the crowd to wait in our lane for his return. In the first ten yards Griffin moves into third place. His hips are low, his back arched at a forty-five-degree angle, his head level.

I say, "He's a machine."

Cinch smiles proudly. "He should be. I've had him practicing for weeks."

By the time Griffin gets to the end to turn around, he's even with the Boat House team, which is in second place and only five yards behind Frosty's.

Robin joins from the other end. "Holy shit! Can you believe that? This is in the bag."

The three of us, along with the spectators, watch in awe as Griffin effortlessly chews up the remaining distance, finishing five yards ahead of Frosty's team, not even needing the penalty to beat them. But the penalty does cost Frosty's second place, dropping them behind the Boat House. Fourth place goes to the Crescent Tavern and fifth to the Beer Barrel.

"Now where exactly is our keg?" Griffin says, emerging through the crowd barely winded.

Cinch says, "Don't forget a trash can and some ice so we can tap it later. It'll need to sit for a while after being carried up the steps."

Our focus immediately shifts from the competition to setting up for our post-competition party, which is pretty consistent with the way our whole summer has been. Everything is always about the party.

Unfortunately, our first-place finish vaults us into the lead for only one event. Our skit flops, dropping us into second. Only three events remain: the 16-ounce Beer Chug, the Bartender Speech/Poem, and the Drink Presentation, in which each team creates a signature cocktail and presents it to the judges.

I say, "I'm going upstairs to get ready for my event. Come get me when it's time."

"We should be back in first by then," Cinch says. "We got the

Beer Chug locked up. Our guy wins every year. He just opens his throat and pours it back."

I recite the song as I walk out the side door of the Round House onto the patio.

"You talking to yourself again?"

In the darkness only the red glow of his cigarette is visible, but I know the gravelly voice. I launch my words at the scarlet flare. "Caldwell, why you hiding out here?"

"You know this is the crazy time of year. I try to stay out of the way. Only a few more weeks left, though."

"Are you going to be here for a little bit? I'd love for you to hear this since you helped me with the music. It's just a stupid song about service, but I'm still nervous."

"Do you know it? Then why be nervous? Get up there, be open, and let it rip. Truth flows when you allow it to."

—

In the barn, confident that I know the words, I stand in front of the mirror to watch my body language. Cinch comes up after my second time through. He says, "The first person just walked on stage, but you've got seven other people in front of you."

"Tell me which rendition is more effective."

He sits down at the table with the lock box. "Do you care if I prepare a few packages while you do it?"

"Do what you gotta do." I go through both versions. "So which do you like better?"

"The first one," he says, although he hadn't been watching. "How about a little boost to get you ready?"

"No way. I'll be too edgy."

"A little won't hurt."

"I can't. Bad shit always seems to follow."

"Nonsense." Cinch scoops some on a spoon and prances over. "Here comes the airplane. Just a little sniff of jet fuel."

I stare at the end of the spoon. "Not now. Maybe later."

"Come on. Be a good boy and take your medicine."

"Fine. But this is it. No more." I take a blast in each nostril.

Cinch licks the spoon in triumph. "Now was that so bad?"

The inside of my nose burns. My throat swells. The roof of my mouth and my gums numb. I shake my head and shoulders and wiggle my fingers. A wave of anxiety surges through me. "Fuck. Knew that was stupid." I put down the guitar and pace around.

Cinch says, "Here's what you do. Walk on stage with a bucket of beer. Hold it to the crowd and then take a long drink. It'll get them going and calm you down. When you're done with the song, dump the pitcher over your head. They'll eat it up."

I head toward the door. "Let's get this over with."

Cinch walks to the couch and picks up the guitar. "Uh, don't you want to take this?"

"Shit. I'm such a space cadet." I take the guitar from him. "This is going to suck."

Cinch gathers the packages he prepared. He says, "At this point in the season, it would be wrong not to be under the influence when you go up there."

⸻

I wait behind the Round House. Astrid's voice flows over the PA. I can't listen to her. Walking back toward the parking lot, I move my tongue around my mouth. But the only moisture in my body streams from my forehead. I repeat the first few words. "Let us be merry, let us be merry." I walk into the back room and wait behind the curtain.

"And now our final contestant, from the Round House. All

the way from the Show Me state, please give a nice welcome to Brad Shepherd."

Astrid winks at me from the other side of the bar as Cinch hands me a bucket of beer. A gulp from the bucket prompts cheers from the crowd. I continue to drink, not to encourage their enthusiasm, but because my body soaks up the liquid as I pour it in. Jeers emanate when I stop with half remaining.

The lights in my face shield me from the piercing gaze of the spectators. I appreciate the blindness. Hundreds of eyes are staring at me, but I can't see them.

I clear my throat, ready to begin, but can't remember the first word. My smile fades. The lights, which only seconds ago provided cover, now expose me. Again I feel the sweat burst through my forehead. I strum the G-C-D-D pattern, hoping the words will come. After the fourth time through, the first line crystallizes. I sing, "Let us be merry with song and drink, to the point we may not think. Full of laughter and friends abound, here's to forgotten minds but souls found." I can hear the shakiness in my voice and the stiffness in my strumming. "Acts of courage and full of nerve, due to the spirits that we serve. To create a shot of particular flavor, or pour a drink for one to savor." I feel my pace quicken, wanting to get to the end. I need to slow down. "Whether it's a stein, a glass or ordinary cup, with beers and cocktails, we'll fill you up. Not in money from tips we receive, but in people is what we truly believe." Almost there. Just need to hold it together. "Free from the everyday stress and strife, to serve another is a great joy in life. So gather near and tip your cup, I will always do my best to fill you up." I hold the guitar up to the crowd and pick up the bucket and pour it over my head, putting the bucket on like a hat, just as I have seen the drunks do so many times this summer. The crowd eats it up. I feel more relief that the experience is over than from the liquid on my sweaty skin.

"Great job, Shep," someone says as I rush out the back door.

I push over a stack of empty kegs in frustration. Cinch comes out the back door. I sit down on one of the kegs. "Fucked up. That really sucked. I stunk up the joint."

Cinch says, "What do you mean? That was fine."

"I wasn't exactly hoping for fine. I spoke too fast. See, I knew I shouldn't have partied."

"Fuck it. Who cares? Let's enjoy the rest of the night."

"You go ahead. I'm going around front."

I loop back around and up the alley to the Park Hotel patio. Caldwell is in the same spot on the porch where I left him. I say, "Did you witness that disaster?"

"The bucket of beer was a nice touch."

I stare at his silhouette, searching for his eyes. "Don't bullshit me. I choked. I went too fast."

"You did seem nervous. Maybe you should switch to decaf."

"I know. You're at your best when you're sober and well rested. You told me that before."

"There's more to it than that. Somebody like Birch or Mad Dog can get up there all messed up, and most people won't even notice because they've been on stage hundreds of times. That was your first."

"Probably my last after that suckfest."

"You can't expect to do something well the first time. You probably shouldn't expect to do it well after ten or twenty times." The rocking chair creaks in time with his words. "When I first started playing guitar, I was seventeen. I was convinced that my fingers weren't meant to bend that way. And when I could finally make a few chords, it was my right hand that couldn't hold a pick and strum at the same time. It was so difficult for me to pick up the guitar because every time I did, I had to face how much I sucked. Eventually I realized that it really didn't matter how good I was. All that mattered was that I played. The more often I practiced, the quicker I'd learn. It took me two years before I would even try to play in front of other people. And then, even after becoming a pretty decent guitar player and making a living playing in bands, I went through the same process when I learned to play the mandolin."

Life always seems so simple for Caldwell. I say, "You've got natural talent, though."

"There's no doubt that some people have a gift for things. It might take you 108 tries at something when it takes another person only eight. You want to be good at things, but that's not why you do them. If it is, you'll never be happy because as soon as you get something down, you'll move to something else. Find something you love doing and do it because you enjoy it. The skill will naturally follow."

I want to believe him, but things just never seem to work out for me. I say, "I didn't do myself any favors by being banged up."

"What would you tell one of your students who was disappointed with a test result?"

Cinch opens the side door to the Round House. "Hey, they're about to announce the winners to your event."

Caldwell says, "Be the teacher to yourself you strived to be for others."

—

Astrid is standing with Cinch a few feet inside the side door. "You sure you don't want to wait outside to hide your tears when you lose?"

I smile and turn my focus to the judge announcing the outcome on stage. "In third place, receiving twelve points, is the Boardwalk. Second place and sixteen points go to the Round House." I smile at Astrid, knowing what is coming next. "And taking the first-place prize of twenty points, and moving into the lead with one event to go, the Boat House."

Cinch gives Astrid a congratulatory hug. He probably would've given her a consoling one if she'd lost; he never misses an opportunity to wrap his arms around her. I walk over to be gracious, feeling the full sting of the loss more because my finish caused our team to surrender first place. I say, "Winner gets what the winner wants."

Astrid says, "I'll settle for a hug right now, but I plan to collect tonight. So keep yourself open."

"Don't fraternize with the enemy," Cinch says. "We still have one event left. There'll be plenty of time for that after we win."

The last event is the Drink Presentation. Each team creates a unique shot or cocktail for the judges to assess on overall taste and presentation. It's probably not the most ideal event with which to finish, since drinking throughout the competition has hindered each team's presentation skills. But in years past, when the event was held earlier in the evening, Haley said the judges were so drunk by the end that some didn't stick around for the rest of the competition.

The order of presentations is the reverse order of the standings. Our drink, a shot named Perry's Cannonball, pays tribute to Perry's naval victory at Put-in-Bay. It's peppermint schnapps and vodka chilled and strained into a shot glass with a quarter shot of Jagermeister, which coagulates in the bottom to resemble a cannonball.

The key for our team is the presentation. One of our bartenders is a true professional. He's tended for fifteen years in a variety of locations around the country and even in the Caribbean for three winters. He can do all the tricks—flip bottles in the air, catch them behind his back, whatever.

The clincher with our performance will be how he pours twelve shots simultaneously. He'll stack thirteen small rocks glasses inside one another and pour only into the top glass. After the glass fills, the liquid will flow into the one underneath it, and so on until he fills all the glasses. He'll line up twelve empty glasses on the bar, remove the top glass, pick up the stack of glasses, and tip the entire stack so that the liquid in each of the glasses runs into the ones on the bar. Then, after a couple flips and spins with two bottles of Jager, he'll drop in the cannonball. The whole time the song "You Dropped a Bomb on Me" by the Gap Band will be playing.

Our team is presenting a simple shot because after a few drinks, the judges won't be able to taste anything anyway. But they always remember the presentation.

It probably works to our advantage that we're in second place because we go before the Boat House team. All the pressure will be on them to hold the lead, especially if we nail our presentation.

Cinch and I watch each team through the curtain. Most focus more on the drink than the presentation, and each time, the judges drink less and less, eventually only sipping the cocktails offered them.

As the music starts, our bartender's flashy moves seize the judges' attention. He fills the glasses without spilling a drop and tips the stack so that each glass is filled evenly. As he flips the Jager and drops a splash into each glass, I know we'll be tough to beat. He finishes by sliding a glass in front of each judge, leaving one for him and each team member.

"You guys better have something good to top that," I say to Astrid, who is standing on the other side of the bar.

"Care to make another side wager?"

"Whatever happened to competing for the sake of competition?" I ask.

The sportive smirk returns to her face. "You're right; you're already into me for one favor. You don't want to make commitments you can't live up to."

The Boat House team had obviously learned from years past as well. Not only do they have Hawaiian music, but a fog machine blows a white stream of smoke from the middle of the stage, and tiki torches outline the bar. The female bartenders wear grass skirts and drape leis around the judges' necks. The bartender doing the mixing is dressed as a witch doctor, but he refers to himself as a mix doctor. Their drink is called the Island Volcano.

Puffs of smoke from the fog machine collect and dance around the torches. The mix doctor pours vodka, black raspberry liqueur, rum, and banana liqueur into a large hollowed-out coconut. He puts the top on, shakes it, then strains it into six martini glasses garnished with pineapple wedges.

Two of the girls in grass skirts finish the drink by pouring shots of 151 rum on top. The mix doctor lights a smaller torch and ignites the alcohol floating on top of each of the drinks. After he lights the last drink, he tips his head back, lets the girls fill his mouth with 151, raises the flame to his lips, and spits the alcohol into the air, shooting a six-foot flame.

Cinch and I slink into the back room. There's no way we beat that performance. Haley knows it, too. "Looks like we have to settle for second place this year," she says.

Now I really feel like shit. I say, "Sorry I let the team down."

Haley glares at me. "Just because you finished second you think you let the team down? This is for fun, remember? Come on, let's do a shot, and then we'll go down to the Boat House and let them rub it in." As usual, one shot turns into three. She says, "In a way I'm glad we lost because hosting the party afterward is a pain in the ass. Not to mention that the amount of alcohol consumed is staggering. I'm going to enjoy being a guest tonight."

At the Boat House, people whisk Haley away to do shots. Cinch suggests we get Astrid and go to the monument because he has something to tell us. We locate her by the bar with the rest of the Boat House crew and absorb the jeers as they remind us about who won and who lost.

Astrid leans over. "Feeling up to settling our bet?"

"Cinch and I want to leave now," I say, "Come with us to the monument, and then you and I can have the rest of the night to ourselves."

"Okay, but Cinch isn't part of the bet."

It takes another twenty minutes and three more drinks before we make it to the door. People are at the emotional stage of their buzz, which means we're escaping at the perfect time. Fifteen minutes more and we wouldn't be able to get away.

The three of us climb up to our usual pod in the southwest corner of the monument plaza. Cinch opens a bottle of Pink Catawba. "I got a call from my dad today. A school district on the mainland wants me to come in for an interview."

I say, "And you're going?"

"This summer can't last forever."

I take the wine from him. "I'm not ready for it to end yet."

"Sure you are. Think about the past few weeks. You've already grown tired of partying and going out. It's only a matter of time before the Round House and red barn are on that list."

"Come to OSU with me and get an apartment," Astrid says. "Take some classes, substitute, find a job, whatever."

Cinch says, "I'm done with campus life."

"My plan is Key West," I say. "But that could easily change. That's why I love it here. I don't have to think about tomorrow— only today."

Astrid says, "That's unrealistic. You have to have some picture of the future."

"Why?" I ask her. "My future isn't connected to any decision I make. Things are always just out of reach. You know why? Because I've been stupid enough to think I can control my future and make it happen. I thought coming here would change that, but now that the end of the season is almost here, I'm in the same situation again. Why not just go with it?"

Astrid says, "Maybe you're just trying too hard. I've had a blast this summer, and I know more about myself now than I did at the beginning of the season. That's enough for me."

"That's what makes it tough to leave," I say. "You do learn about yourself here. In the real world, other forces determine your life."

"I need distractions," Cinch says, seeming not to recognize that he is a major one. "The only things for me here are friends and partying, and the friends leave at the end of the season."

Astrid takes my hand. Her touch sends a jolt through me. "Brad, maybe you should just stay here. If you can't think of a reason to leave, then don't. You might be home."

Cinch drains the rest of the bottle of wine and drops it into the bottom of the stone urn, where it clinks against another bottle someone else has left here. He laughs, looking down at it. "We're not the first to come here, and—"

"We won't be the last," I finish. "What do you think the people who drank that bottle were talking about?"

Cinch says, "Who cares? Let's go home. I'm tired of thinking."

We climb down and walk along the seawall. Astrid pauses when we get to the intersection. "You still up for hanging out?"

"Don't be ridiculous," I say. "A bet is a bet."

The smell of beer mixed with marijuana conveys that we've just missed Griffin and the others. I count thirteen cups, all filled with varying degrees of beer.

Astrid draws from the keg. "There's a note on the table: *2:45 a.m. Went to the cove.*"

Cinch says, "Fuck it. No reason for me to stay here . . . unless the three of us aren't done for the evening."

"Nice try, Cinch, but Brad has his hands full with me. I'm not sure he could handle both of us."

Cinch does a healthy blast right from his bag. "I was talking about partying, but maybe I should stay to help."

I motion toward the door. "Maybe I should go to the cove while you two finish abusing me."

"Relax. Astrid's not my type," Cinch says. "I like the cerebral ones."

Astrid tilts her head to the side. "That's so disappointing because I love fat, balding men."

"Are you really sure you should go?" I say. "It's been a long day. Maybe bed is the best place for you."

Cinch downs his beer. "Who cares? I'll have plenty of time to sleep when I'm dead."

———

I light a candle on my dresser and sit on the bed. "We can just go to sleep if you want."

Astrid kicks off her shoes, sending them in opposite directions like scurrying mice. Her dress falls to the floor. She drifts across the room toward me. I can't believe this is finally happening. The candlelight blankets her curves, a hypnotic flickering light against her angelic frame.

She pushes me back on the bed. "I don't want you to say or think about anything. Just relax."

"But I lost—"

"Shhhhh. Winner gets what the winner wants. I want you to lie there and be quiet."

I rub her chest and back, creating a mental snapshot. How I've longed for this moment. Her skin feels as creamy as I imagined. The same curves I watched swallow the candlelight, I now trace with my fingers. She eases down on top of me, placing both hands on my chest and extending her arms. She rocks back and forth, slowly increasing the length and the force of each stroke until our bodies tense, and she collapses on my chest in silence.

—

Astrid shakes me. "Hey, I think somebody's here."

"It's probably just Cinch."

"No, I think something's wrong."

We both listen. Someone rushes into Cinch's room, calling his name. It's Stein.

I put my shorts on and open the door. "What's up? What happened?"

"Cinch is missing," Stein says in a panic. "A bunch of us went to the cove to jump. Afterward we built a fire on the beach. Cinch came late all fucked up and wanted to jump. I told him not to, but he wouldn't listen. He kept talking about doing a flip. I don't know if he did the flip or not, but there was a huge splash and then nothing. It was so fucking quiet. At first we thought he was screwing around. You know how he is, always playing jokes. After a few minutes we went into the water. We looked everywhere but couldn't find him. We hoped he'd just come back here, laughing about how he fooled us. He did, right? He's probably fucking around, right?"

CHAPTER FOURTEEN

THE SUN CLIMBS ABOVE THE HORIZON ON THE EAST SIDE OF THE ISLAND. It'll still be another thirty minutes before light reaches the west.

Griffin is wading through the water twenty-five feet from shore when we arrive. The fire the others had built on the beach smolders, giving off puffs of smoke that rise up to the cliff. I stand on the edge as a spotter.

For the next hour we search the coast for a quarter mile in each direction. The sun, now fully visible above the tree line, warms the morning air but does nothing for the cold, aching realization hanging over us. I motion them in. "He's not here. He has to be playing with us."

Griffin says, "Let's go check the barn. If he's not there—" He hesitates, inhaling a deep breath. "If he's not there, we should go to the police."

Stein and I follow Griffin up the steps of the red barn. I've climbed these steps countless times this summer, often at this very hour after a long night, but never this slowly. I hear Griffin ask Astrid if Cinch has come back. I know her answer by his response. "Fuck! That fucking asshole."

Stein urges me forward. Inside, Griffin paces frantically. Astrid is sitting on the couch, cocooned in a blanket. No one speaks; we all just watch Griffin. Minutes of silence build like drops on the end of an icicle. Each one combines with the ones before, collecting . . . building . . . increasing the discomfort and anticipation as we wait for this bubble of awkwardness to burst. We can't just sit here. We need to do something.

"Griffin, try to relax," I say. "Nothing is definite right now."

"Easy for you to say. My brother's dead, and you're telling me to relax."

"That's not fair. He's a brother to all of us. Getting yourself upset isn't doing any good." The words don't feel any better coming out of my mouth than they probably sound, but surprisingly Griffin listens and sits down next to Astrid. She puts her arm around him. He drops his head and buries his face in his hands.

I turn to Stein. "Did Cinch have any drugs on him?"

He shakes his head. "I don't think so. He gave me what he had before he jumped."

"Gather up all the stuff in this place and take it down to a rental locker by the dock," I say, taking charge.

Stein says, "Just stash it at my place."

"No, I don't want it associated with anyone. But you know the chief of police, right? We'll all go to the station together after you get back."

While we wait for Stein, I shower and convince Griffin to

do the same. Astrid asks, "What are the chances he's kidding around?"

"He's done it before," I say, "but he wouldn't be gone this—" The sound of someone on the steps fractures my words. We all turn to the door. Griffin emerges from the bathroom but reverses course when he sees Stein enter.

A silence descends during our walk to the police station. The torch in the park stands as a memorial to the simplicity that existed only twelve hours ago.

Although today appears to be a typical August day—boaters working off their hangovers, preparing their boats for a day of sun and fun; the fishermen returning from their morning excursions and gathering in Frosty's for a Bloody Mary and some breakfast; the store owners, prepping their storefronts to attract eager tourists; and island workers, scurrying to work to avoid being late due to another hard night of partying—we know that once we enter the police station, nothing about today will be typical.

Skip is drinking a cup of coffee in the hallway of the police station when we enter. "Oh shit, look at this crew. This ought to be good."

Stein says, "Is the chief here?"

Skip frowns, catching something in Stein's tone. "Yeah, he's in his office. Something wrong?"

Griffin says, "Cinch is missing."

"He probably hooked up or passed out somewhere. Last night was crazy."

Griffin motions for Skip to proceed. "There's more to it than that."

Skip knocks then opens the door. "Chief? Some people are here to see you."

The room smells of cedar and pipe tobacco. Chief O'Connor is sitting behind his desk facing the windows overlooking the park. Clouds of smoke rise above his head. Still not turning around, he says, "What can I do for you boys this morning?"

Several golf carts passing in front of the station draw my attention to the windows and the framed view of downtown. He must've watched us walk down the street. How many other mornings has he seen us walking the other way after an extended party session?

Stein says, "We were at the cove last night, and Cinch went up to jump. We heard him hit the water, but he never surfaced. At first we thought he was fooling around, but we've looked everywhere and no sign of him. I know we're not supposed to be there, but we've done it hundreds of times and nothing's happened before."

Chief O'Connor removes a clipboard from his desk drawer and directs Skip to get two more chairs. "All right. Technically we're not supposed to do anything for missing persons until forty-eight hours have passed, but since other people were present, we'll start the process now. If Cinch turns up, we'll throw this form away."

While Stein relays the details, Chief O'Connor writes, never lifting his eyes or pen from the form until Stein stops talking. As the chief scans the form for any missing information, Griffin asks what the next step is. The chief explains that he'll alert the Coast Guard to begin searching but that we shouldn't expect any news soon. Since the wind was out of the northeast last night, the water level is high. If Cinch did go under, he could be anywhere.

After we leave the station, Stein goes to work, and Griffin and I spend the morning in the red barn formulating scenarios to explain Cinch's disappearance. Eventually getting punchy from being cooped up and only theorizing about where he could be,

we put some action to our words and check some places we think
he could be holed up. We even try a few long shots by talking to
girls at the Beer Barrel and the Crescent that he might've hooked
up with, but by three o'clock we've exhausted our options, so we
check in with Astrid at the Boat House.

News about Cinch has spread, and a steady stream of people
flows in to offer support. On the surface no one has given up
yet, but as day turns to night, the tension shows in everyone, and
everyone attempts to deal with it the same way they deal with
everything: alcohol.

After a person I don't even know stops over to offer their
condolences, I suggest we leave. Griffin says, "If one more person
comes over and offers to buy me a drink, tells me not to give up,
or relays some story about Cinch, I'll puke. I need to get off this
island. I need to see our parents."

After the long day, I slide into bed with Astrid. I'm still replaying
the events in my head. "We should've—"

"Shhhh, don't. It won't do any good. There's nothing we can
do now."

I curl up behind her and bury my face in the back of her neck.
I'm not sure when she falls asleep, but I can't.

On most mornings I fight reality by hitting the snooze to buy
a few more moments of peace. Today I preempt the alarm by
twenty-three minutes. No reason to let the alarm wake Astrid
and Griffin. I kiss the spot on the back of her neck where I took
shelter during the night.

The living room smells of stale beer. I open the door, but the
humid air oozing in offers no relief. The depleted keg floats in
the water at a derisive slant. I place it on the porch to return it

to Bob. Since we didn't deliver Tuesday, today will be busy. But it doesn't matter. What else is there to do?

Bob, like everyone, has heard about Cinch. He urges me to take the morning off, but I convince him I need to work. The weight of the kegs will distract me from thinking about Cinch.

Most of the morning passes in silence. Bob is probably searching for the right thing to say, some cliché that will sum up the whole situation and lessen my pain, as he has so many times during the summer when I seemed troubled. But this time there's nothing he can say or do. There's nothing anyone can say or do. Time is the only thing that will heal this, and even that will only lessen the grief. There's nowhere left to run; nowhere left to hide. I'm surrounded by death, just as I was in the classroom months ago. Everywhere I look are reminders of how things were and will never be again.

* * *

The last people exit the ferry from the mainland. Griffin and I remain in the car, staring straight ahead. He says, "Thanks for the ride. You got my parents' number if you hear anything."

"You should tell them right away."

"That's easier said than done," he says. "They think I'm coming home to tell them my vacation is over."

My "I'm on vacation" mantra from earlier in the summer rings hollow at this point. I truly wish this were a vacation, that all of us were leaving together and returning to real lives on the mainland.

Griffin walks down the hill to the shelter house where the foot passengers wait to board. I want to stop him, but I know it will only postpone things. I recall the marvel with which I watched my first ferry arrival only in May. Novelty and excitement overflowed when I started this new life. Now I'm drowning in a worse reality than the one I was trying to escape.

—

Wednesday's search concludes with no news. Now two full days of searching have passed without finding anything. The policy, Chief O'Connor has explained, is to search for three days. If nothing is found, a decision will be made about whether to continue or not. One of the problems regarding the search for Cinch is that since he was wearing only shorts when he jumped, there's not much to find except his body. If he did hit his head, he would've swallowed a lot of water and probably sunk to the bottom. If one of the divers doesn't find him, he probably won't turn up until he washes ashore.

Although the day is uneventful, I'm exhausted when I get off work at eight. My mouth is parched, my jaw tight. Even my nose, which has been running continuously for the past two days, is dry.

Uncomfortable in the living room, I go to the bedroom. I need to stay busy. I gather all the clothes scattered on the floor and pile them in the corner. I collect the mounting pile of mail and pay stubs on the dresser and move it to the bed to sift through it all. Mixed in with the pile is a full green baggie. I shake my head. How many other packages have we misplaced this summer?

I stare at the contents and think of all it represents. Fuck it. Why not? The rest of the stuff is safely locked away. What else is there to do? Astrid and Stein are working and Griffin is gone. I'll dispose of this, have a few drinks, then come home and get a good night's sleep. If I feel bad later, I'll make a different decision next time.

My hands trembling, I dump the contents onto the mirror. My nose begins to run as the familiar smell rises. Saliva pools in my mouth, I remove a twenty from my pocket and repeat the steps I know so well: smashing, crushing, dividing the small rocks into four lines of fine powder. The person in the mirror stares back at me. My eyes flip back and forth between the cocaine and my reflection. I think about how many times Cinch, Griffin, and I were in this same position. What does it ever get anyone? What are we all searching for? What is everyone running from?

The four lines captivate my attention. I should just dump it on the floor. What does it matter? What does any of it matter? It's not like anything will change. It won't erase the past; it won't determine my future.

Ssshhhump.

Ssshhhump.

The tension dissipates in my jaw. I rotate my head, sending a shiver down my back, causing my shoulders to shake. My eyes are no longer tired and itchy; my chest and shoulders are no longer tight; my hands no longer ache.

I'll leave the other two for later. Probably should stay close so I don't have a long walk for my return visit. What would I base my decisions on if I didn't party? I only hang around people who do drugs, and I only go to bars that are close to home or that have private stalls. I never quit this stuff. I was just taking a break.

I don't even know what to believe anymore. Lying to mask my true motives has become so involuntary that I can no longer tell the difference between truth and falsehood. When lies come so easily, who am I really deceiving?

I stare back at the two white, powdery, parallel lines. I blow them across the mirror. I inhale and blow harder. The dust sprinkles to the floor. I rub the powder into the carpet with my feet. I'm done with this stuff. I don't ever want to see it again. I hold up the mirror. The pathetic face stares back at me. I smash the mirror on the dresser and fling it against the wall.

I've got to get out of here.

The band playing in the Round House provides cover so I don't have to talk to people—just sit and drink. Haley makes sure I don't even have to order, and a shot is always in front of me. Soon I won't feel or remember anything.

The light by the middle cash register flashes, indicating a phone call. Haley goes into the back to answer it. When she returns, she slides a note across the bar. I sip my drink, attempting to delay any real consequences with casual gestures. I can't receive bad news this way.

I go in the back to return the call. Griffin answers on the first ring. "Any news?" he asks.

"No. They called off the search for today and will begin again in the morning. How'd things go with your parents?"

"They wish I would've called them right away."

"What good would that've done?" I ask. "We still don't know any more than we did a few days ago."

"If there's still no news, we're coming over Friday morning so my parents can talk to Chief O'Connor and we can pack up Cinch's stuff."

"Do you really think it's come to that?"

"Where else could he be?"

Griffin saying that makes me face the inevitable: Cinch is gone forever. Somewhere deep inside of me I was holding on to the slim hope that Cinch could still be alive. That somehow he had snuck off the island and was waiting at his parents' house when Griffin arrived, and it all was a sick joke. Hearing the resignation in Griffin's voice destroys any fleeting traces of optimism.

There's no way I can go back to the bar after the call. I can't be around anyone. The only thing to do here to be alone is to walk.

The sun has disappeared behind the trees, and a brisk wind charges off the lake toward shore. Boats speckle the docks. I turn left onto Bay View Avenue and walk out of town. At Peach Point I continue onto West Shore and head south, still without a destination. Two parked golf carts at the boat ramp impel me onward. I follow West Shore until it bends to the left, giving way to Trenton Avenue. I'm at the cove.

The water beckons as it did the first night we came here, but I don't feel free or energized tonight when I step onto the cliff. My legs weaken at the sight of the watery coffin. I step back from the edge. The leap that once represented trust and belonging is now an abyss of pain and loss, and most of all of foolishness.

A gust of wind shakes the trees behind me. Through the darkness the faint outline of the fire ring on the beach sneers back at me. The waves crash below, mocking me. I drop to my knees. A burst of warmth explodes in my stomach and then rushes up through my throat into my mouth.

A gush of liquid splatters onto the edge of the cliff. It runs back over my hands and sticks to my knees.

"Why did we have to be so stupid?" I whisper.

I stare at the water below, wiping my hands on my shorts. My tone changes to pleading. "Why did we have to keep pushing? Please give him back. You made your point. You don't need him any more. Let his family have him."

I sit in silence, alternating my gaze between the sky and the water, expecting an answer or some sign that my message has been received. Instead the only reply is the scornful repetition of the waves against the rocks. Not even the stars offer hope; they just stare back at me, silent and cold.

CHAPTER FIFTEEN

THE VISIT TO THE COVE PURGED JUST ENOUGH OF THE EMOTIONAL WAVE I HAD BEEN HOLDING BACK THE PAST FEW DAYS TO ALLOW SIX HOURS OF UNINTER-RUPTED REST. But the same haunting emptiness still chases me out of the red barn early. At least I got some sleep. I have to burn off this anxiety. I do three laps around the island on my bike before I meet Bob at the winery to help deliver beer.

He says, "The wind finally switched directions last night. It was due north when I went to bed, out of the west when I got up, and by the time I got on the boat, it had dropped down out of the southwest. Fishermen should be happy. Fish scatter when the water level shoots up."

I climb up into the cab, grateful for the small talk. Anything to get me out of my own head. I keep it going. "How's the load today?"

"Pretty average, nothing to bust a nut over." He glances in the mirror. "We've got company."

Chief O'Connor exits his car and approaches the cab. He says, "Griffin told me to come find you if there was any news. Do you want to go down to the station for this?"

My body stiffens. I can't move. I have been pleading for resolution, but now that it is here, I'm not sure I can face it. I take a long, staggered breath. "Sir, you better tell me right here."

He opens his notebook. "About 6:45 this morning, two fishermen in a rowboat north of the cove were drifting close to shore. One of the fishermen spotted something bobbing in the water, trapped in the back of the cave. They had seen the rescue team and the divers around the island, so they called 9-1-1. Coast Guard responded to the call. At 7:04 a.m., the Coast Guard confirmed a male in his mid-twenties had apparently drowned and was trapped in the cave. They worked quickly to remove him from the water, and at 7:12, they lifted him onto the boat. The subject meets all descriptions of Cinch, and his injuries and the apparent cause of death match the report filed." He lifts his eyes to mine. "Are you able to come and identify the body?"

His question hangs in the frozen moment.

"Brad, I know this is a difficult time, but we need somebody to identify the body."

"Don't even ask," Bob says to me. "Just go."

Chief O'Connor leads me to his car. Looking at him through the wire mesh reminds me of my first time in one of these cars only months ago. After that night, I worried I might end up in a police car for the wrong reason, one that would put me behind bars. Now that almost seems like a preferable outcome.

There's no morgue in Put-in-Bay, not even a hospital—only a small paramedic outpost that consists of an examination room and a garage for the ambulance. The chief leads me into the garage, where the divers are breaking down their equipment. A gurney covered with a beige blanket stands conspicuously behind the ambulance. All eyes turn to me.

"Are you sure you're up for this?" Chief O'Connor asks.

I motion to proceed.

He peels back the blanket. The face is pale and bloated. Small chunks of flesh are missing from his neck and shoulders. The right side of his forehead is badly bruised and swollen.

I close my eyes. "It's him. That's Cinch."

The chief replaces the blanket over his face.

I try to block out the image and remember him as he was: full of life, unconquerable. He doesn't look peaceful at all.

I follow the chief back to the cruiser. "What are those marks on him? Can they fix him up?"

"It could be from scraping against the rocks or from fish feeding on him. The funeral parlor will restore him as best they can."

The chief drops me off at the red barn. I walk directly to the phone. Two rings. A male voice, but not Griffin, answers. It's Cinch's father. I don't want to have this conversation, but what can I do? There's no way out without lying directly, and he doesn't deserve that. He doesn't deserve any of this.

I say, "Is Griffin there?"

"No, he's not. Is this Brad? Anything new?"

"Yes, sir, I'm afraid there is. Apparently when Cinch dove in the water he hit his head and drowned. They found his body this morning. I just got back from the rescue station."

The line is silent.

"Sir? Are you there?"

"I—we'll be over as soon as we can."

"I don't think that's necessary. Chief O'Connor said they'll send him to the mainland wherever you want."

"Brad, I need to see my son. I'd appreciate if you'd tell the chief to hold everything until we get there."

———

Three hours later I repeat the same procedure I hoped never to have to do again. It isn't any easier looking under the blanket the second time.

I need not chronicle the events of the next four days except for the basic facts for one simple reason: I don't want anyone to have to live through the experience unless forced to do so. The visitation was Sunday and Monday, and the funeral was Tuesday. Every dark emotion—pain, anger, shock, guilt, and for me, even jealousy—collected and stuck to the walls and floors of the funeral home like thick sludge.

Just as a wedding doesn't prepare a person for the days after, neither does a funeral. Ceremonies are only the midpoint between when the waiting and anxiety stop and the rest of your life begins.

Wednesday morning is the day after another event I won't be able to escape. Every other day will merely be another "day after," filled with the same deep-seated pain and guilt as the previous one. My decision not to fight for my job is now only another step that led to this outcome. I thought that coming here was both an end and a new beginning, but I found a way to keep spiraling down.

When I first came to the island, I was leaving a life that collapsed around me. After the funeral I feel as if I am in a vacuum, one in which all the important things in my life are siphoned out.

Griffin cleans out his room the same day he packs Cinch's things. Each morning I open the doors to their rooms and hope to see them passed out, their heads hanging off the bed, snoring. And then each night I close the doors, hoping to shut out the nightmares that have filled the place in my heart each of them used to hold.

Another weekend, another band, another mob of drunks. I float through the days, numb to my surroundings.

On Sunday, Haley helps me clear tables on the porch. "You know we're still going down to Key West right after the holiday to secure a place to live for the winter." Her behavior follows the same pattern everyone else's has lately. After a tragic event, no one speaks about it, but their tone of voice and actions draw attention to the experience like a buoy with a bell in turbulent water. She says, "White Spider night is Monday, then we plan to catch a flight out of Cleveland on Tuesday afternoon, stay with some friends in Miami that night, and drive to Key West Wednesday and stay until Sunday."

"What about missing the weekend here?"

"It'll be slow after Labor Day. We've already got the days off and the ticket is cheap, so think it over and let me know by Friday."

Think about it? Since returning from the funeral, getting out of here is all I've been thinking about. Lately I'm not sure if I'll make it through most days, let alone the fall and winter. I say, "Count me in. I need a change."

Haley hugs me. "Going back there will be the best thing for all of us. It's where we met, remember?"

"How could I forget?" I say. "That's the whole reason I'm here."

Tears swell in her eyes. She buries her face in my chest.

I say, "I'm sorry—"

"I know what you meant." She kisses my cheek. "We all need a break from here."

We start clearing tables again. I redirect the conversation. "What's White Spider night all about?"

"Years ago, long before the Jet Express—when the only ferry was the Miller ferry—the boats stopped running and all the businesses closed after Labor Day. All the islanders would gather at the Lime Kiln dock and bid farewell to the last boat. Since the season was over and the bars would close for the winter, the establishment owners poured all the white liquors together to get rid of them, making a drink called a White Spider. Most of the island entertainers perform at the dock, and then everyone comes to the Round House."

"Sounds like a nice evening," I say.

"Not anymore. Now it's just another excuse to party for tourists, so it takes something away from the ceremony. I used to know every single person in the bar at the end of the night. Last year I was a little salty and didn't have that much fun because it was like any other night in the Round House. I've been here too many years to wrestle with tourists for space in this bar."

As with other holidays, people trickle in Wednesday evening for the Labor Day weekend ahead. By Thursday night the docks are full, and every room on the island is booked until Monday. I open the bar at eleven o'clock a.m. and close it at one in the morning. The fourteen-hour shifts are easy because I have nothing else to do. I go to bed right after work and am up for several hours before I have to leave in the morning. Remaining sober, getting to bed early, making it to work on time, and managing an unruly group all comprise a familiar life for me. It is the same one I wanted to escape. I am right back to where I started.

For visitors, the weekend is probably no different than any other holiday. We clear people out after Mad Dog's show and re-open an hour later to fill the house for Whiplash.

Tourists still come to the Round House and ask for Cinch and Griffin or inquire about the party favors they have become accustomed to. I simply tell them everybody and everything is gone and don't go into any other detail. People don't really care anyway.

On Monday I watch the clock like a third grader on the last day of school. Each Mad Dog joke and song puts me closer to being released from it all. There's no chance he'll play late today because he has to perform at the ferry dock for White Spider.

The festivities begin at seven o'clock with each performer playing some of their island songs. At twenty minutes past, the vehicles and the people will board, and at seven thirty the ferry will depart. It takes away from the event to know that the boats actually stay in service until Halloween, but I still want to see the crowd and listen to the music.

After my shift I catch a ride with Haley. Like most events on the island, things are running late. The PA isn't working, and Birch's soundman is arguing with one of the other performers about how to fix it. We exit the car. I motion toward the stage. "Behind schedule as usual."

She shakes her head. "They better figure it out in a hurry because whether they're done or not, the boat leaves at seven thirty. It doesn't wait for anybody or anything."

A loud popping noise sounds, followed by high-pitched screeching. Appearing triumphant, Birch's soundman glares at the other performer who had doubted his prowess and adjusts the knobs on a small monitor.

Three hundred people have gathered at the dock, most of them complete strangers to me. Haley and I join Astrid and some other island workers on a blanket in the grass. Astrid hands me a bottle of Pink Catawba. I sip and pass it back.

Birch takes the stage and breaks into "Friends of the Bay." The words rip through me. "*Hello, Friends of the Bay. Thank you for coming today. Hello, water so blue. I'll always remember you.*"

I am surrounded but feel alone. I lean toward Astrid. "I have to go. I can't stay here." I hesitate, remembering leaving her before and how that made her feel. "Do you want to come?"

She takes my hand. Her eyes scan my face. She says, "No, unless you want me to. You seem like you need some time alone."

I kiss her good-bye and dart through the crowd, trying to outrun the sound of Birch's voice. I clear the last group of people as he breaks into the chorus again.

The tears I've been holding for weeks stream down my face. I turn right onto Langram, and with each step the words and music fade. I repeatedly wipe my face, hoping that if I clear away the tears, I'll prevent future ones from flowing.

The horn from the approaching ferry sounds. Soon the road will fill with the same people I'm trying to avoid. There's not enough time to get downtown.

A road ahead leads back to the water. I'll just go down by the shore and wait for the traffic to clear.

The lane dead-ends into a cul-de-sac with three houses, their fronts facing the water. A wooded lot on the right stretches to the lake. I cut through one of the yards and follow the tree line to the shore. The lot gives way to a small rocky beach that extends twenty-five feet before disappearing into the water.

Down the shoreline, the last car drives onto the ferry. From here it looks like any other ferry trip and reminds me again of the awe I felt watching the ferry for the first time. I thought it was coming to rescue me from my pain. It only delivered me to more.

I retrace my steps to Langram and embark on the two-mile walk to town in darkness and more important, in solitude.

Headlights from an approaching truck brighten the road around me. I wait for it to pass, but instead, slowly, the throttle decreases.

Caldwell's voice flows from the cab of the stopped pickup. "Why you walking?"

I peer into the dark cab. "Didn't feel like being around people."

"I'll let you go then."

"No, I'm glad it's you. What are you up to?"

He flips on the interior light. "I was cleaning up the mess down at the dock. Fucking people—just leave shit everywhere, expect somebody else to clean up after them." He shakes his head. "Where you headed?"

"Nowhere, anywhere. I mean, I don't care. Wherever you're going is fine."

"I got a six-pack in the back. I'm going to Crown Hill Cemetery to drink a few if you want to join me."

"As long as it's not the Round House," I say.

The headlights of the old truck fan across the entire road. I
sink into the seat, listening to the rise and fall of the RPMs as
Caldwell shifts. He says, "It's got to be tough being here after
everything that's happened."

"The hardest part is that I didn't just lose one friend because
of the accident; I lost them all. How do you stand it? People are
always leaving."

"Remember, the boat goes both ways," he says. "People are
always coming, too."

I say, "Coming to get fucked up."

He angles the truck off the road and through the entrance
to Crown Hill Cemetery. The headlights illuminate the rows
of tombstones and memorials. Mayflies swarm from the distur-
bance. He pulls over and kills the engine. The night swallows the
sound. We hesitate, adjusting to the quiet. The buzzing of cicadas
fills the air.

We exit the truck. Caldwell gets a small cooler from the back
and we meet in front. He hands me a beer. "I come here every year
after the last ferry leaves. All alone but completely surrounded."

"Best company on the island," I say.

Caldwell removes two more beers and puts them in the side
pockets of his baggy work pants. We walk down a row of graves.
Most are overgrown and decaying. The smell of a skunk drifts
through the air. Fallen mayflies crunch under our feet.

"I know it's difficult burying one of your friends. You never
expect it's going to be you in that situation." He lights a cigarette.
"Little over thirty years ago I was playing in a band with my best
friend. We lived gig to gig, trying to see who could get the most
pussy. Thought we had the world by the balls."

"Sounds like a blast." Just like my first few weeks here.

"One night in Gulf Shores we were tripping on acid and drinking tequila with two girls at their campsite. My friend wanted to leave to get a few hours of driving under our belts before the next gig in Florida."

Caldwell's voice is deliberate. His eyes remain fixed straight ahead. He pauses only to raise a beer with his right hand or a cigarette with his left. I don't think he's told this story many times.

"What happened?" I ask.

"Don't know. I passed out shortly after we left. When I woke up, I was in a hospital and my friend was dead."

We pass by a Romanesque mausoleum surrounded by a grove of trees. There's a rustling in the weeds. A rabbit darts from the darkness. My eyes follow the black form skipping across the graves.

"Even today I don't know why I wasn't killed along with him. It's not like I've done any great deeds in my life or made a difference."

I say, "You seem at peace now."

"Took me a lot of years. Now I just accept that we're born each day and we die each night. In between we live our lives. People come and people leave, and in between we live our lives. Everything has a beginning and everything has an end, and in between we live our lives. I just try to follow through to the end and close the loop. Leaving might have been the best thing for others after what happened, but you have to figure out what's best for you."

"Nothing's exactly turning out like I thought it would."

We stop in front of a tombstone. The name reads John Brown Jr.; Caldwell pours beer on the grave. "It may not be the life you imagined, but it's your life. You came here for a reason. Is it time for you to go and begin again?"

I understand his question, but as usual I know he doesn't expect an answer. I can give one because I'm leaving tomorrow for the trip to Key West. But is that the right answer for me? Maybe I've run enough.

Caldwell drains his beer and squeezes the empty can. "Sorry about dumping that on you. Watching you go through all this has brought back memories."

"That's okay. Did you know I'm leaving tomorrow to go to Key West to find a place for the winter?"

"No shit?" he says, laughing. "Don't worry, though. You'll do the right thing."

"A lot of people would take that bet." I slug the rest of my beer.

He puts his hand on my shoulder. "Don't be too hard on yourself. You just have to learn how to recognize your truth—the answer that's right for you."

I say, "Pretty selfish approach, isn't it?"

Caldwell pokes his finger in my chest. "Quit trying to save the world and just save yourself."

CHAPTER SIXTEEN

A FAINT TAPPING FROM CINCH'S ROOM WAKES ME. Although gentle, the consistent rapping prevents me from sleeping. I get up to investigate.

In the vacant room, a white ceiling tile lies on the floor. The other tiles will fall soon as well—rattling, waiting for a burst of wind to send them tumbling.

I reposition the tiles, securing them with duct tape, just as I did the ones in my room when I first arrived. The wind shakes the entire building with each gust.

A loud crash sounds from outside. Kegs slide across the cement, banging into one another at random intervals. First a blast of wind, then the sound of metal rolling on concrete: *Thung!*

Outside, although the sky is clear, the air is damp. Usually at this time the silence is consuming, but tonight the sounds call out. The clasp on the flagpole in the park strikes repeatedly against the aluminum pole. The back screen door of the Round

House slams with each gust. The wind rushes through the trees, mixing with the leaves, as if trying to quiet everything: *Shhhhhhh*.

To silence the kegs I stand them in the grass. Unsure whether I'll be able to sleep anyway, I check out the other noises in the park. I go to the flagpole and place my hand on the line, pressing the clasp against the pole, quieting the din. Other sounds caused by the swirling gale ring out. The chain swings on the playground collide with one another as they dance wildly. The water from the fountain strays from its natural course, splattering on the concrete. And still, even more convincingly than before, the leaves call for silence: *Shhhhhhh*.

I release the flagpole line, allowing it to mix with the dissonance again. I become more and more aware of the noises, eager to choose a sound and trace it to its source. I go from place to place, staying only long enough to satisfy my curiosity. Why haven't I noticed these sounds before? Why did I only notice the silence in between, whereas tonight I hear the noise?

I approach the monument from the front, watching the light on the top turn on and off as I climb each step. Even the strongest wind can't sway my stone companion. I place both hands on the granite. "What should I do?" Sitting down with my back against the column, I ask again. "What the fuck should I do?"

Only the wind rushing through the trees responds, now shaking the branches as well as the leaves, sending a chill through me. I fold my arms across my chest, rubbing each arm with the opposite hand.

I get up and walk to the plaza wall. A *smack* sounds on the water, but I'm still unable to see through the black curtain in front of me.

I climb over the plaza wall and descend the hill to the cement seawall. The moonlight blankets the rolling water. I sit down on the barrier and allow my feet to hover above the water, occasionally extending my legs to avoid an incoming wave.

Water covers the wall and soaks through my shorts. Thoughts of former students, Caldwell, Astrid, Haley, and Cinch simmer. A few I'll never see again. Others I'm not so sure, which frightens me even more. Has all of this been for nothing?

I walk down the seawall and onto Langram, retracing a familiar path. Where have I gone wrong? Each of my decisions now appears to have been a subtle nudge, small enough that I didn't notice where I was heading but significant enough to culminate in the lie that I've been living. I have made so many changes, but is anything really different? I am still on the outside looking in. Still wanting what I can't have, regretting what I didn't do.

I turn right on Thompson Road toward the winery. Am I really an insignificant player in a sick, twisted game, or do I just have bad luck? Either way, I'm tired of it all: tired of running, tired of searching, tired of expecting.

I pass through the winery parking lot onto Catawba Avenue. The loneliness of the deserted road closes in around me. I veer off the road into the vineyards. The grapes won't be picked for a month, but the sweet fragrance is still salient. I wander down the alley formed by the vines, shuffling my feet in the rocky soil.

The void I tried to fill by coming to the island has merely swollen.

Coming to the island didn't change anything.

Grass replaces the dirt that was under my feet, and trees supplant the vines that were on my right and left. I weave through the bushes and trees and stumble upon a path with deep grooves from bike tires. Where am I? Does it really matter? I have nowhere to go and no place I'm supposed to be. Am I lost or completely free? A week ago, I might've said free, but now I know I'm lost, just as I've always been.

I emerge from the woods into a familiar area. I'm at the cove.

I can't run anymore. If I do, I just carry everything with me.

Feelings from earlier return as I step into the moonlight on

the edge of the cliff. Sickness again swells inside me. I straighten
my body in defiance, bringing my feet close, closer than I've yet
dared to step. "Fuck you! You want me? You can have me. I'm not
playing this game anymore. I'm sick of you following me, hunting me like an animal. You can't beat me because I'm giving up.
It's over."

A gust of wind bursts through the trees and pushes me to
the brink. For a moment I think about fighting, trying to correct
my balance. Then I stare down at the macabre surface and let
myself fall.

Splash.

Surrounded by water, I exhale to force myself to the bottom.
As my feet touch, I swallow a mouthful of water.

Stay calm. Let your body sink.

I ingest another mouthful and open my eyes, straining to look
through the blanket of water I have pulled over my face.

Digging my fingers into the stones around me, I resist the
urge to fight for the surface. Why shouldn't it end this way? I'm
no different than any of these rocks, each slowly worn down by
life until it's barely distinguishable from the others.

I swallow another gulp. My body convulses. How long will
this go on? I peer at the surface only several feet away but have
no desire to reach it.

My limbs relax. A thin glow of light hovers above the surface.
I no longer feel the rocks underneath me. I focus on the light. I'm
floating. I'm free.

Finally, peace.

The glow burns in smaller flashes through my closed eyes. I
squeeze my eyelids tighter, but the radiance engulfs me. A surge
of heat rockets through my body.

The stones I felt kinship with just moments ago now offer
nothing. The warmth surrounds me. My body rises. I grope for
something to hold on to.

A flood of fear fires through me. Wait. Not yet.

Faces of students flash in my mind. Each one, a universe of possibilities. I shake my head to dispel the images. They return. I have tried so hard to forget them, convinced myself I don't care. But they won't go away. They won't leave me alone. Filled with hope, they plead for me to stay.

I open my eyes. The glow blinds me. My arms drop; my fingers graze the lake floor. I can't give up. I reach down and latch onto a rock. I squeeze the end and pull myself down. As my right hand firmly wraps around it, my left hand touches the bottom.

The heat reduces to a warming sensation. The light is visible only above me. The firmer my hold, the more the light fades, again appearing as a thin coating covering the surface. My legs drop. I plant my feet on the bottom and maneuver myself upright. Still disoriented, I focus my attention on the thin layer of moonlight painted on the surface.

It wasn't the administration I was fighting in St. Louis; it was responsibility. I couldn't do enough—I couldn't save Barry—so I shut down. I quit. I thought that by teaching I was living for other people, putting my life on hold. I was so wrong. Each person I helped revealed another piece of me. I can't give up.

I exhale what little air I have and propel myself upward. The force of my thrust pries my eyelids open.

The best parts of me are reflections of others.

My hand vanishes through the surface and then my wrist and forearm until finally my face breaks the threshold.

Air blasts into my lungs. I slip back underneath the surface and swallow another mouthful of water. Struggling back above the waterline, I locate the shore seventy yards away. I roll over on my back and kick.

Only water in front of me and stars above me, but at least I'm alive. Maybe I had to become who I'm not to understand who I truly am. I've been searching so desperately to find my identity, try-ing to fabricate the person I wanted to be. All I had to do was let go.

I have been here all along.

I spin around and allow my feet to sink and finally connect with the bottom. The probing glare from the stars has softened, and some encouragement returns. I made it. I can no longer hide from myself. I'm finished putting on masks and rearranging the world around me. I'm home. My cord has been reattached, and I accept the responsibility.

I finally belong.

I trudge the remaining thirty yards to shore.

On the beach the waves wrap around my ankles and willfully let go. I'm free. Free from more than just the pain and suffer-ing of past events. Perhaps I haven't been running from anything after all, but rather have been running *toward* this moment when I finally have a conversation with myself and honestly examine where I've been, where I am, and where I want to be, this moment when I take responsibility for my past and present and say: I am me. The time is now. Let's begin.

I take two more steps to clear the waves and collapse on the beach.

━━

"Brad? Brad, are you here?" Astrid's voice rains down from the cliff.

I squint to block out the sun.

She follows the path to the beach. "What are you doing? Are you okay?"

"Yeah, I'm fine." I close my eyes and tilt my head back. "Just fine."

Haley and Birch trail behind. Astrid extends a hand to help me up. "They came to my place looking for you and said they had already been to the barn and that your car and bike were there, so I got worried. Did you know it's after ten? You have a long day ahead."

I stand. Water squishes from my boots.

Birch says, "Decide to go for a swim and forget to take your boots off?"

"Something like that. I went for a walk and ended up here."

Haley says, "Let's go, jackass. We can still catch the eleven o'clock boat."

I gaze out across the lake. "I'm not going anywhere."

No one responds because they don't have to. Haley's incensed "What?" answers for them.

I say, "I thought a lot about it last night—and this business isn't for me. I'm not a bartender or a bouncer. I'm a teacher. It doesn't mean I have to do it forever, but teaching is what I need to be doing right now. That's where it began, and that's where it continues."

Haley says, "Unbelievable. How selfish can you be? Of course you need those kids after the summer you've had. But do they really need you? Is a drug-addicted, alcoholic teacher really the best thing for them?"

"Come on, Haley," Birch says. "You're upset. Don't say something you'll regret."

"No, if we're going to be honest, let's be honest. I'm sorry about Cinch. I really am. But what did you guys expect? You're partying all summer, jamming that shit up your nose. Did you really expect good things to happen? Sure, you feel bad now, but it'll pass, and you'll go right back to doing the same stupid shit. Quit kidding yourself, quit fucking lying to yourself. You want to stay here so you can keep partying and not lose your drug connection."

As I listen to her, I think: She's not thinking about what's best for me. She's thinking about what's best for her. Maybe she has been all along, ever since the moment when I lay on her lap and she told me to come to this island. It was always about what she wanted. I just fit nicely into her plan.

"Maybe you should just go," Astrid says. "This isn't going to solve anything."

"You're right," Haley says. "I'm tired of wasting my time on this loser."

If I were playing a game, the best move would be indifference. Let her go and live with the bitterness. But after last night, it isn't a game anymore. It's my life. Besides, I'm not completely sure she's wrong. Do I just want to hide, using the kids to purge myself of guilt?

"Wait." I block the path to the cliff. "I don't claim to have been a saint since I came here."

Her scowl pierces me. "There's an understatement."

"I don't expect you to understand or even believe me. I'm doing what I think is best for me. I don't care whether it's logical, rational, or appropriate because I know it's the right move for me."

"Are you finished?" Haley says. "Good. Have a nice life."

Birch waits for Haley to leave. "Don't worry about her. She'll cool down in a few weeks. Are you serious about the teaching? Are you really ready to go back into the classroom?"

"I'm ready. If not here, then I'll go to the mainland and substitute. I want to go back; I need to go back. My vacation is over."

Once I decided to go after the open teaching position the school district had been unable to fill, I knew I had to trade the red barn for more suitable living accommodations. It's amazing how many options opened up, and how fast, once word traveled that I was a certified teacher and wanted to stay on the island and work at the school.

On the first day of school, I reach over and turn off the alarm, hoping not to wake Astrid.

She rolls on top of me. "Nervous? I think I'm more excited than you are. I'll be honest, I was hoping to tempt you to go back to OSU with me for the fall quarter, but this is the place for you. I could see it that morning at the cove. Your fear and uncertainty are gone. You belong here—on the island—and you belong in the classroom."

I place my hand on her face, gently rubbing her cheek. My eyes focus on her chin and follow the angle to her cheekbone, then across the bridge of her nose and back down to her chin, admiring the symmetrical frame the three points form. I raise my eyes from her chin to her pursed lips, attempting to memorize every curve and indentation. Her nose is neither flat nor pointed but begins in a rounded tip that melts into her cheeks. Her eyes narrow and draw me in as our stares connect. Her pupils catch what little light is in the room and sparkle, further feeding the growing hope inside me that a new life is beginning.

"You've been a great friend to me over the summer." I slide my hand along her neck and rest it on her shoulder. "I knew from the first time I saw these shoulders I would fall in love with you. Just like everything else in my life, I had to run from it, but I'm tired of fighting, and I'm finished running. Each—"

She puts her hand over my mouth. "You talk too much. For once will you just shut up and kiss me?" I lean over, but she pulls away. "Besides, you're still going to be living here, on an island in the middle of Lake Erie. I'll know where to find you . . . if I want to." She pushes me on my back and finishes the kiss.

As I walk to school, memories of Cinch and Astrid and our summer together take my mind off the anxiety that bounces between my head and stomach. I don't know if I understand life any better, but I accept it. The choices will never stop. Whether the outcome is good or bad, each one opens the path a little more. We never truly arrive. There is no there. Only here. The most important thing is to keep going.

I've never liked good-byes, but with Astrid it'll be different. There's neither sadness nor regret because we know we'll see each other again. For now it's time for each of us to begin again in different directions.

I'll be teaching. In the mornings, four periods of math ranging from pre-algebra to pre-calculus; in the afternoon, monitoring study halls and tutoring. The salary is paltry, but I would've accepted even less. After what I've been through, I'm not about to put a price tag on my life. For the first time I know exactly where I want to be; I know where I belong.

The five ninth-grade students who make up my first period class file in. I write on the blackboard to stay busy. After the principal concludes the morning announcements, I place the chalk in the tray and turn to face them. "Good morning, class. My name is Mr. Shepherd. I'll be your math teacher this year."

ABOUT THE AUTHOR

DOUG COOPER has traveled to over twenty countries on five continents, exploring the contradictions between what we believe and how we act in the pursuit of truth, beauty, and love. He now lives in Las Vegas. Connect with him on Facebook or Twitter, or at ByCooper.com.

READER'S GUIDE

1. The book's island setting of Put-In-Bay, Ohio is a major ele-
    ment of the book. How does the island's connection with
    American history help to reveal the underlying meaning of
    the book? How might the island's qualities (such as isola-
    tion, the presence of water, and finite resources) influence
    the characters?

2. What does Brad's statement upon seeing the Oliver Perry
    monument, "How I wish I could encounter my true enemy,"
    ultimately mean?

3. The book's plot starts when one of Brad's students, Barry,
    asphyxiates while in the classroom. Do you think Brad had
    any responsibility in this death? Why or why not? Do you
    think Brad perceives himself as having responsibility in
    Barry's death? How might his sense of responsibility—or
    lack of a sense of responsibility—be influencing his actions
    throughout the book?

4. When Brad leaves his life as a teacher for life on the island,
    he becomes a kind of student to various other characters:
    Cinch, Caldwell, Astrid, etc. What do these characters have
    to teach him? At the end, Brad becomes a teacher again:
    what's the significance of this?

5. What values do each of the book's major "teacher" characters—Caldwell, Astrid, Haley, and Cinch—represent? Do any of their lessons contradict one another? Is Cinch really a friend to Brad?

6. Brad's experimentation with drug use drives much of the book's plot. Discuss the ways in which drug culture is presented in the book, from the initial "sharing with friends" encounters to more extreme moments such as Brad's supply run to Cleveland.

7. During the summer, Brad has numerous sexual liaisons with different people on the island: Astrid, Dawn, Meadow, Randy. What does each of these liaisons contribute to Brad's gradual change throughout the book? What leads Brad to enter into these encounters? Additionally, Brad doesn't tell Astrid about all of these encounters by the end of the book: do you think this is understandable, or a mistake?

8. How does the theme of drug experimentation relate to the theme of sexual experimentation in the novel? What role does experimentation play in a person's growth and development? Are there other forms of experimentation in the novel? How does Brad's experimentation allow him to reach his final epiphany?

9. A typical coming of age story deals with a character in his or her late teen years or early college years, yet Brad doesn't truly "come of age" until his late twenties. Why is this? Is a belated coming of age story relevant in modern times? Are individuals maturing more slowly, and if so, why? What factors in Brad's life and character might have delayed an earlier coming of age?

10. At the end of the book, do you feel that the transformation in Brad is permanent or temporary? Do you think that there will be any lasting negative effects on Brad as a result of his experiences?

11. What do you think the title of the book means? In the context of the narrative, what elements of the book might be considered "outside," and what elements might be "in"? What are some examples of the outside-in versus inside-out theme in the book?

AUTHOR Q & A

What experiences led you to write **Outside In?**

Thoreau said, "The mass of men lead lives of quiet desperation."
During the five years when I was a junior high teacher and spent
my summers at Put-in-Bay, I recognized that the desperation was
not so quiet any longer. Although the settings were very different,
students and adults were more outwardly and inwardly destructive in expressing their unhappiness and looking for anything to
escape and numb the pain. It all came together—the contrast, the
similarities, the beauty and history of Put-in-Bay, the uniqueness
of island life. It just seemed like a story that needs to be told.

*You've written in many genres, including screenplays, poetry,
and short fiction. What drew you to the novel as a form for this
story?*

The beauty, history, and island characteristics of PIB and the self-
doubt and uncertainty associated with a journey of self-discovery
just seemed ideal for a novel told in first-person present tense. It
gave me the best medium to weave past and present, interior and
exterior dialogue, and individual and universal experiences into
a single narrative. There's nothing like a good novel to transport
you to a different time and place and allow you to see life through
someone else's eyes.

You've previously worked as a teacher. How did those experiences influence your characterization of Brad?

A teacher makes for a great character because everyone has been a student at some time, so we all have personal experiences to draw from that help us immediately identify with a teacher. Directly experiencing the increased stress put on the school system to do so much more than merely provide academic instruction was also a major influence on Brad's character, as was experiencing the unfortunately magnified destructive and violent behavior of students—both inwardly and outwardly destructive behavior.

Why did you choose Put-In-Bay, Ohio for the novel's setting?

The beauty, history, and island characteristics provide an idyllic atmosphere for a novel. In addition, setting the novel in the Midwest in the middle of Lake Erie fit well with the theme that dreams don't lie on the horizon; they lie within. It also contrasts the classic theme of Manifest Destiny by starting the journey of the lead character in St. Louis, the "Gateway to the West," but rather than continuing west, Brad turns deeper into the heart of America.

Drug and sexual experimentation are critical themes in the novel. Why did you choose to take these on as subjects? Do you have strong opinions about these and American attitudes toward them?

In the context of Joseph Campbell's archetype of the hero's journey, I would consider this type of experimentation as part of The Road of Trials, a series of ordeals a person undergoes to begin his or her transformation. I wanted to write a modern myth that shows a group of characters confronted with the difficult choices of contemporary times.

Excess and instant gratification characterize our modern existence, and people respond by self-medicating to alleviate the resulting chaos and confusion. The problem is that we are attempting to solve the problem of excess with more excess. This is not a uniquely American problem; it's just more prevalent and publicized here.

The supporting characters, with all of their individual foibles and sometimes stunningly bad advice, are a major delight in this book. How did you come up with these characters? In particular, have you ever known anyone like Cinch?

The four major characters surrounding Brad—Haley, Astrid, Cinch, and Caldwell—represent points on a compass that pull Brad in opposing directions: respectively, despair, hope, irreverence, and respect. They are all an amalgamation of various characteristics I have observed in people. But out of all of them, I would have to say that Cinch is probably the most inspired by one individual.

Many of the characters have philosophical advice for Brad that he chooses either to accept or reject. Do you have a personal interest in philosophy? How did that interest develop, and what roles do you see your personal philosophies as playing in the book?

I've always been interested in why people do what they do in an individual sense and also in a broader cultural sense. As a child, I was always drawn to adults, and I was one of those annoying kids who had a seemingly endless string of questions. This curiosity led me to the seemingly disparate paths of math education and a master's degree at Saint Louis University in American Studies, which was interdisciplinary and incorporated a lot of philosophy. The characters' views in the story are not my own, but collectively they tell a little bit about my views.

Have you ever actually played the Name Game the characters play in the book?

Because of the first person present tense point of view and because of the fact I was a teacher and spent some summers at PIB, some people who read *Outside In* assume that the story is autobiographical, which is not true. But I will say that some of the experiences are borrowed from real events. The Name Game is one of them. Don't ask me to comment on the more incriminating ones [laughs].

How do you see your work fitting into the tradition of American literature? Are there particular writers whom you feel yourself to be strongly influenced by?

I would classify my writing as literary fiction, and more specifically in the subgenre of transgressive fiction. But overall I aspire to write modern myths that offer readers the opportunity to experience contemporary dilemmas and to learn vicariously from characters, rather than having to learn everything about those dilemmas directly with all of the associated risk and danger. I envisioned *Outside In* to be a cross between *Fear and Loathing in Las Vegas* and *Catcher in the Rye*, so I would have to recognize the influence of Hunter Thompson and J. D. Salinger. I wanted to tell a story of becoming like *Catcher*, but my story would be set ten years later, after someone had crossed the threshold into adulthood but still didn't know who he was. I think this is very common today because of the abundance of choices, uncertainty, and a rapid rate of social change. I also wanted to incorporate the gonzo journalistic style of Thompson to capture the excess and instant gratification side of modern existence.

Given the sometimes grave subject matter of the novel, there are a lot of really funny scenes: the bar competition, the encounter with Meadow, and many more. What made you choose to blend this more humorous material with the serious underlying subject matter?

In my view, storytelling is like playing music. You have to use a variety of instruments, vary the tempo, and play different notes and beats to establish a good rhythm and envelop the readers in the flow so that they forget they are reading and lose themselves in the text. Humor is one way to do this and to balance the darker emotions: serious, sad, tragic, etc. No one wants to read a story that is all doom and gloom, just like no one wants to listen to a song that is the same note and beat repeated over and over. Also, we should never take ourselves too seriously. Regardless of the journey, a lot of funny stuff is going to happen along the way. That's just life.

In a way, this story ends on a cliffhanger: Brad largely returns to his "normal life" at the conclusion, with the lessons he's learned from the island. Have you ever considered continuing Brad's story in a future novel?

One of the early titles of the novel was *Conversations with Myself*. At the time, I thought about following up with *Conversations with My Wife* and *Conversations with My Kids* to continue Brad's development toward becoming a husband and eventually a father. For now, I am happy to leave Brad where he is and move on to my next project, *The Investment Club*, a novel about five broken people who meet at a blackjack table in Vegas and who discover that the greatest return is what you get from contributing to one another. But if Brad resonates with people and they want to see more of him, I would consider continuing his journey.